Bayou Cocktail

a novel

Rennie Howard

Rennie Howard

outskirtspress

DENVER, COLORADO

Bayou Cocktail
A Novel
All Rights Reserved.
Copyright © 2013 Rennie Howard
v2.0

Cover Photo © 2013 JupiterImages Corporation. All rights reserved - used with permission.

Outskirts Press, Inc.
http://www.outskirtspress.com

Paperback ISBN: 978-1-4787-1376-0
Hardback ISBN: 978-1-4787-1369-2

Outskirts Press and the "OP" logo are trademarks belonging to Outskirts Press, Inc.

PRINTED IN THE UNITED STATES OF AMERICA

ACKNOWLEDGMENTS

I am grateful to many folks who helped make this story possible. First, my wife, Becky, gave me hours of uninterrupted time when she would much rather have been doing something else. My kids, Tad Howard and Scottie Brown were the first to read the manuscript and offered much valuable advice, all of which I took. Several friends, including Linda Berryman, Joyce Tiller, Justin Borland, David Brown, Tony Taylor, Bill Warrick, Emily McCardle, and Ann Julian read the story and offered encouragement and help. A big thanks to Dr. Marian at First Editing. And to the folks at Outskirts Press I owe special thanks for accepting the book for publication and for their kind and professional attention to detail and for leading a novice through the publication process. It's been fun.

Rennie Howard

CHAPTER ONE

MONDAY, JUNE 5

D r. Charlie Leveau stared into the open belly of the twenty-
five-year-old, 300-pound dealer, shot three times in
the abdomen after a deal gone bad. Both hands worked expertly and fast, removing large clots and searching frantically
for the source of the hemorrhage. The patient's blood pressure bottomed out, and he was seconds from a cardiac arrest
when Charlie clamped the large artery and vein leading to the
spleen, stopping most of the blood loss.

With the major part of the bleeding controlled, he glanced
at the clock on the wall. Damn, he thought, he hadn't had time
to call Jan and then he'd forgotten.

"Has my wife called?" he asked the circulating nurse, who
had her nose in the computer screen.

"Yes, Dr. Leveau, she called about half an hour ago and
wondered where you were. I told her you were in the operating room with a gunshot wound and might be a while."

"Why didn't you tell me she called?"

"At the time you were occupied, and I didn't think I should
interrupt. Then I forgot."

"Call her back and tell her I'm trying my best to get there."

"Where?"

"Just tell her I'm trying and will be there as soon as I can."

Tonight was the Junior League's big charity ball to benefit the hospice that Jan had been working on for over a year. It was a huge black-tie affair, with all the chefs in Riverton contributing different courses for the elegant dinner and a big band for dancing afterward. Jan was chairwoman. She and her friends had spent countless hours planning, meeting weekly for the last six months and nightly for the past two weeks. She made sure three months ago that Charlie would not be on call. He had scheduled office hours to end earlier than usual today to be home in plenty of time to do a good job knotting his bowtie.

He was driving home when his pager beeped, the display showing a stat page from the emergency room. His partner was already in the OR with another emergency. The victim of a gunshot wound had just rolled in shocky, pale, and in excruciating pain. "Dr. Leveau," the ER doc had said, "we need you here. This man can't wait for Dr. Newman. He'll be dead in another hour. He needs to go to the OR stat to have any chance at all. We've run in a lot of fluid and have called for type-specific blood. There's no time for a CT scan." Charlie did a quick U-turn and tried to call Jan at home, dreading to hear what she might say, but didn't get an answer. In minutes he was dressed in scrubs, washing his hands at the sink and looking through the window into the operating room where the nurse was pouring Betadine over the patient's massive body. No time for a formal prep. He made the incision and didn't give the charity ball or Jan another thought.

With the spleen out and the bleeding under control, he explored the rest of the abdominal cavity and followed the bullet paths. There were several small bowel holes and a colon injury that would require a colostomy. Pulling part of the colon up through eight inches of fat would be a problem. He quietly calculated the time that would be required, looked again at the clock on the wall and thought he might be late, but still had a chance to make some of the party. Then, following the last bullet track he discovered a pancreatic injury that would take at least two hours to repair. At his request, the nurse tried one more time to call Jan but didn't get an answer.

By the time he completed the operation and accompanied the patient safely to the ICU, it was after midnight and the party was over. The patient would probably live and never understand how close he had come to dying. He also would never contribute a dime to his care and after recovery would return to his drug business. With blood covering the front of his scrub clothes and soaked through to his skin, he wondered if the man had AIDS or some other blood-borne disease. Too late to worry about that, he thought as he showered and dressed for the ride home.

A gnawing pain racked his stomach as he anticipated the coming encounter with Jan. She had so counted on his being there for her big moment, and as usual, he was absent without leave. Jan had been patient. Times were great when the kids were small, before his practice had gradually taken over his life. She was a great mother and often had to function as both parents, attending all the school and sports events while Charlie worked. She had endured many times like tonight with growing annoyance and was nearing the end of her tolerance. Charlie was proud of his practice and the reputation he enjoyed. He had provided well for Jan and his two grown children. His son Chuck was a surgery resident in Dallas, and his daughter Page, married to a soldier deployed to Afghanistan, was five months' pregnant. But going home now after a long day, dead tired, to face a tongue lashing made him nauseated. Guilt that he had not been at the party to support Jan was mixed with resentment, knowing how unappreciated he was. He would sincerely apologize for missing the function, tolerate her rage quietly, and wait a few days for it to blow over so they could return to their usual state of tired indifference.

He parked his vintage 1959 Mercedes, recently restored, behind Jan's Cadillac Escalade, entered the house through the side door, walked up the stairs and down the long hall to the master bedroom. Three suitcases were open on the bed. He heard Jan in the large walk-in closet. She came out with an armful of hang-up clothes. She did not look at him, just walked over and laid the clothes on the bed.

"Hon, I'm really sorry." It sounded pathetically inadequate even to Charlie. "I tried to get to the party." This was met with a frigid stare, then her backside as she walked back into the closet. He walked over to the door and was knocked out of the way as she came back out with another load of clothes. "This kid got shot three times, and Mike was already operating. He was gonna bleed to death. I didn't have a choice." A curled-up lip was added to the frigid stare, still no sound. On her third trip out of the closet carrying a shopping bag full of shoes, she tripped and stubbed her toe on the dresser. Charlie reached to catch her. Trying to avoid his touch, she fell flat on the carpeted floor. Still sitting, she picked up a shoe that had fallen out of the bag and threw it at Charlie's head. He ducked just in time as it sailed over his head and through the window, shattering glass over the floor and the ground below.

"I'm leaving you, Charlie. I've had enough. How could

you? No, don't answer that. I don't want to hear any excuses. I just want out. You had to know how important this was to me," she sobbed.

"Come on, Jan, be reasonable"

"Reasonable! Reasonable? You want reasonable?" she screamed as she picked up another shoe and drew back her arm. "I'll show you reasonable." Shaking the shoe at him, she continued. "I have gone to parties by myself for over twenty years. I know you make a lot of money, but what good is it if I don't have a husband? How many times have we talked about this, Charlie, and how many times have I said I won't do it anymore? You've needed another surgeon in Riverton for years, but you have refused to recruit one."

She got up and continued to pack the suitcases with the clothes from her chest of drawers. Charlie thought it a good sign that she didn't throw the other shoe. "You made it easy tonight, Charlie. Thank you at least for that. It is over. I am going to live with my sister, and before the week is over, you will be served with divorce papers. I'm tired. I'm unhappy. I'm unfulfilled at best. I want something different for the rest of my life. I am angry about tonight, but this isn't just about tonight. This is about a lifetime of waiting, and hoping, and making excuses, and pretending we're married while you're in love with a profession. No, Charlie, this is real. I'm out of here, and I won't be back."

She carried two suitcases out the door and down the stairs. He heard her car door slam and the motor start. One suitcase and some shoes were still on the bed, but she was so ready to leave that she left them. The motor of the Escalade raced, and tires squealed. A crunching sound signaled the Cadillac forcing the old Mercedes out of the way. She raced away from the house, leaving rubber marks halfway down the block.

Charlie dialed her cell. "You left some stuff."

"Give whatever is left to Goodwill. I'm not coming back, and don't call this number again." All Charlie heard next was silence and a slight ringing in his ear. Then the phone rang. "There is a letter on the kitchen counter from a lawyer. I signed for it this afternoon. You are being sued for malpractice." Again the click, then silence.

Charlie went down to the kitchen to pour a drink. *What in the hell just happened?* As he was pouring a shot of bourbon, the opened letter caught his eye. In official legalese it said a patient named Denise Mouton, vaguely familiar to him, was suing him for something to do with misplacement of a central venous catheter. Before he was through the first paragraph, the phone rang again. He walked over to answer, thinking Jan had forgotten something else.

"Charlie." It was Delphine. "You gotta come home. Your dad done had an accident. Fell and hit his head. They took him to the hospital. Jake came by here and told me. I don't know how bad it is, so please get here fast as you can. I been leaving messages since late this afternoon."

Charlie sat down. If he passed out he wouldn't have far to fall, and the grand piano across the room was swaying back and forth.

"Charlie, you there?"

"Yes, Delphine. Sorry. When did this happen?" He massaged his forehead and the bridge of his nose, his eyes closed.

"Sometime this afternoon, I reckon. Billy Jack found him inside the camp house. There was blood all over the floor. Doc was out. Lucky the ambulance got there in a hurry." Delphine had worked for the Leveaus for over forty years and was part of the family. Charlie had never seen her without her big hoop earrings and a scarf on her head. Delphine was aging now but there was no doubt she had once been a Creole beauty. She virtually lived at the house, looking after Doc Leveau since Charlie's mom died several years ago, and pretty much ruled the roost. She claimed to be "keepin' him in line."

"I'll leave here as soon as I make some calls."

"Charlie Leveau, you come right now. I don't care what you think you got to do. May not be much time." Her voice choked. "I'll see you when you get here." The line went dead.

Charlie called the ER at Bayou Belle Community Hospital, said who he was, and asked about the ER doctor.

"Doc Cummings is on call," the nurse said. "He's in x-ray right now. I'll have him call you when he comes back."

"Thanks." Charlie gave her his cell number. He packed the suitcase Jan left behind with enough clothes to last a few days. Then he called Mike to sign over his patients. He tried Jan's cell to tell her about his dad, but she didn't answer and he did not leave a message. Just then Dr. Cummings called back. He and Charlie had grown up together in Bayou Belle. Jim had returned home to practice, but Charlie chose a bigger town and more lucrative opportunity.

"Charlie." Jim's familiar voice came on the line. "Tried to call earlier, but you were in the OR and they wouldn't put me through."

"Sorry, Jim. I missed a lot today. What happened to Dad?"

"He hit his head awfully hard," said Jim. "He has a skull fracture and a subdural hematoma. Lost a lot of blood through a big scalp laceration."

"Is he responding at all?" Charlie was afraid of the answer.

"His vital signs are stable and his pupils react, but he's unconscious and so far responds only to painful stimuli. We have a call in to the neurosurgery unit at LSU. They'll take him when a bed comes available. Charlie, you should come home soon as you can."

"I'm flying out tonight and should be there around four or five o'clock in the morning." He snatched the certified letter up, crumpled it, and threw it across the room. *Screw them all,* he thought. *Nobody except my dad understands what I do and now he, the most decent person in the world, is in critical condition. I'll go take care of him and screw the rest.* The front of the Mercedes was bashed in, but the wheels were free and one headlight worked. If the police didn't stop him, it should at least get him to the airport.

Riverton had an uncontrolled airport for small private planes. After a quick preflight check, Charlie took off at one o'clock and set his course for the three-hour flight home. When he reached cruising altitude, he relaxed against the back headrest. The familiar guilt for not joining his dad's practice in Bayou Belle overcame him again. Doc Leveau was a grand old man, the only surgeon in Bayou Belle for the past forty-five years. A couple of others had come and stayed a year or so but moved on to bigger places. No surgeon would ever become wealthy in Bayou Belle, but Doc had done well. He was comfortable and happy. Never turned away a patient who couldn't pay and never knew who paid and who didn't. He always wore a coat and tie to work before changing to scrubs. The coat might be threadbare; the tie might not match his shirt. Style didn't concern him; patients did.

The last time he talked to his dad, Charlie had been busy and in a hurry to get off the phone. He pushed the throttle to make the plane fly faster, but it was already all the way in. "Please God, just keep him alive until I can get there," Charlie prayed out loud.

CHAPTER TWO

Earlier that day Dr. Aloysius Leveau had finished his surgical rounds and was leaving the hospital to go fishing. He needed time to relax and time to think. Since Ken's accident, events in Bayou Belle had spun out of control. A new hospital CEO, Ruben Martin, was hired by Hubert Polk, the board chairman, without interviewing anyone else. Martin took control quickly, replacing Doc Leveau and two other longstanding hospital board members. Then he recruited a new surgeon without consulting anyone on the medical staff. Of most concern to Doc was that on Martin's advice, the newly constituted hospital board was negotiating the sale of Bayou Belle Hospital to Great Northern, a national health care corporation currently buying up small community hospitals across the country. Martin had never asked for Doc's advice and sneered at any Doc offered. So this afternoon, Doc was going to his camp on the bayou to have a glass of bourbon, put a line in the water, and consider his options. He and Ken Adams, the first and only CEO Bayou Belle had ever known, gave birth to the hospital, raised it with care, and took pride in what it meant to the town. When Ken died, Doc lost a close friend and fishing buddy. Maybe it was time to retire.

On the way to his car, an old Jeep Wagoneer, he remembered that his fishing gear was still in the anteroom of Ken's old office. Doc had left it there before their last planned fishing trip, having been called to the emergency room as they were getting ready to leave. Ken had gone on by himself. Later that day their johnboat was found empty. Ken's body was recovered the next day. At the time Doc thought it odd that Ken hadn't been wearing a life preserver because he couldn't swim and would never go near water without one.

The anteroom was small, used mostly for coats and storage. An outside entrance allowed the CEO to enter his office without going through the public waiting room. Doc unlocked the door, surprised that his key still worked. The fly rod and tackle box were in the corner. Ruben's voice could be clearly heard through the door. "You listen to me. I brought you here for the work you do on Sunday night, not for the surgery you perform at this hospital. I already got Ken Adams killed to get this job, and if you don't do exactly as I say, I'll have you fed to the same alligators." Stunned by what he heard, Doc got a small Dictaphone out of his coat pocket and pressed the record button. Moving closer to the door, he tripped over an old mop. It clattered loudly as it hit the floor, and Doc dropped the recorder. Ruben opened the door as Doc was picking it up.

"Hi," said Doc, unsuccessfully attempting nonchalance and putting the recorder back in his pocket.

"How long have you been here?" demanded Ruben, panic in his voice.

"I just came in to get my fishing gear. When I opened the door, it knocked the mop over. Sorry to disturb." Doc hoped Ruben hadn't noticed the recorder, which was still running in his pocket.

"The door was locked." Ruben accused him.

"I have a key."

"What's that in your pocket?"

"My Dictaphone." Doc added, "It fell out of my pocket when I tripped," pleased with his reply. He could tell the suave CEO thought him to be old fashioned, using such antiquated technology.

Ruben eyed him suspiciously. "Don't ever let me catch you in this office again unless I send for you. Now, give me that key and get out." Ruben pointed a long, skinny finger at the door.

Doc turned to go, then turned back. Looking at Ruben with undisguised hatred, he said, "Don't ever talk to me that way again or I'll break that long, ugly nose in so many places you'll have to be cross-eyed to look down it." With that he walked out the door toward his car, leaving Ruben staring at his back with clenched teeth.

Ruben returned to his office, picked up the phone, and made a call.

Doc drove toward the camp, trying to digest what just happened. If Ruben suspected the conversation had been over-heard and a portion recorded, Doc could be in real danger and he knew it. Glancing in his rearview mirror, he saw nobody following. Hearing what he said about Ken, he knew Ruben was capable of anything. His hands were shaking, his stomach uneasy, and cold sweat formed on his brow. His call to Jake went to voice mail. "Come by the house this evening or call back when you get this message. I have something important I need to tell you."

Doc's camp house was a few miles out of town. The lane leading to the camp was long, curvy, and bordered on both sides by moss-draped live oaks that formed a canopy. He and Charlie planted them when they built the camp. At the time,

Charlie was in elementary school, but he had been helpful. The camp house itself was a simple structure, with a large combination living room and kitchen. The back door led to a deck that jutted out over the water and served also as a pier. Charlie was in high school before they added a bedroom and bathroom on the side to encourage Charlie's mother to spend time with them there. She adamantly refused to use the privy. She later added some feminine touches to the inside décor but not so much that it was not still a camp. When there, she spent most of her time in the flower garden near a fishpond shaped like the state of Louisiana. The koi were long gone, but frogs and turtles enjoyed it. Doc often sat by the garden, which he attempted to maintain to honor Charlie's mom, who had died years before from breast cancer.

Doc drove up to the front of the house, got out, and slammed the door, causing a bullfrog to jump into the fishpond, momentarily startling Doc. A few limbs were down in the yard from the thunderstorm the night before. "Get hold of yourself," he said audibly to himself. He tried Jake's number again, but there was still no answer. He didn't leave another message. Once inside, Doc locked the door, took the Dictaphone out of his coat pocket, and put it in the fly rod box, throwing his coat over a chair. No longer in the mood to fish, he poured a glass of Blanton's, went out on the deck, and sat in the rocker. He waved at Billy Jack Boudreaux, a fisherman whose home was across the bayou and who was one of a group of morning coffee drinkers at Julius' Café. Billy Jack would be insulted if he knew Doc was drinking Blanton's and not the moonshine that he produced in quantity in the woods beside his house. Doc drank it only when Billy Jack was with him. He was sure that pouring it in the bayou killed fish.

A blue Ford pulled into Doc's long driveway. Vinnie parked behind some trees around a bend out of sight of the camp and walked through the woods. Told by Ruben to make it look like an accident, he couldn't do his usual head shot. At the edge of the woods, he crouched in the thick brush. He couldn't see anyone in the house. An old Jeep was parked near the front door. Running low, he hid behind the Jeep, then crept up to a window and peered in. The old man was sitting in a rocker on the back deck. Vinnie found an unlocked window on the side of the camp house. He eased it open and climbed into the bedroom. Finding Doc's coat draped across a chair, he rifled through the pockets but found no recorder. He hid, waiting for the old man to come back in. After fifteen minutes, Vinnie was growing impatient when the old man finally got up to come in. Vinnie hid behind the bedroom door.

Doc was going to get his shotgun, more likely now to need it than his fly rod. Passing close to Vinnie, he walked to the front window, looked out, and checked to be sure he had locked the front door. Walking toward the closet to retrieve his shotgun, his back was turned to Vinnie. Vinnie was close behind with his gun raised to strike when a floorboard creaked. Doc turned around quickly, in time to look at Vinnie and see the gun coming down on his head. It happened too quickly for Doc to dodge the blow, but he moved enough to avoid the full force of the impact. All went black and he hit the floor with a thud, blood pouring from a large scalp laceration. The blow was hard enough to kill, but Vinnie checked to make sure. He couldn't hit Doc again, so he got a pillow off the sofa. Bending over he placed it over Doc's face and was pressing down when a boat pulled up to the dock. With no more time he ran out the front door through the woods and back to his car.

Billy Jack had come over to visit, bringing a bottle of moonshine for Doc. He tied the boat to the dock and hollered out as he went in the back door. "Doc, it's Billy Jack. I got a sample of my new batch, single-barrel stuff." Just then he heard a moan. Not seeing anyone, he rushed over and found Doc unconscious, lying in a pool of blood. Grabbing a towel from the bathroom, he held pressure to Doc's head, but he needed help. His cell phone was back at his house, and Doc had never installed a landline at the camp. He ran out on the deck and yelled, but nobody was close enough to hear. Doc's cell was in his pants pocket. Kicking himself for the extra time he had taken, Billy Jack called 911. The ambulance arrived in eight minutes, which seemed to Billy Jack like eight hours. He held Doc's head and watched to be sure he continued to breathe until the firemen arrived. The EMTs placed Doc on a board, dressed his head wound, took his vital signs, radioed the hospital, and put him in the ambulance. They left with the siren blaring. Billy Jack was standing on the front porch watching it leave when Jake drove up.

Jake was listening to Doc's message when he heard the emergency call on the scanner. Instead of following the ambulance, he would get Billy Jack's story about what happened before he had time to embellish it. He may have exaggerated his role, but the details were accurate. No, he hadn't seen anyone else.

"I figure he tripped and fell like us old folks do, but maybe he had a heart attack or a stroke." Billy Jack followed Jake back into the camp and showed where he had found him. The blood made that obvious.

"Did you use the pillow to hold pressure?" asked Jake.

"No, I used a towel from the bathroom. The pillow was already there." He hadn't even noticed it until asked.

Jake looked around, took some pictures with his cell, and offered Billy Jack a ride home. He was in no condition to go back in his boat. "Billy Jack, you probably saved Doc's life."

Billy Jack thrust out his chest, his thumbs hooked in his wide red suspenders and his tattered straw hat pushed back on his head. A tear showing both joy that he had helped and concern for his good friend formed in the corner of his eye. When they got to his house, he didn't invite Jake in because he was afraid the sheriff would see the still. Jake smiled as he drove away to the hospital. He had known for years what the old fisherman was making, but as long as he wasn't selling it, he didn't care. Maybe he was selling some. He still didn't care. He tasted some once and judged it to be pretty good. Sworn to enforce the law, he believed his job was also to include protecting the local culture.

When Jake got to the hospital, Doc was alive but unconscious and on his way for a CT scan. Jake drove to Doc's house to tell Delphine.

"You comin' by to check on your mamma in the middle of the day? You must be hungry." Delphine met Jake at the front door and could tell by the look on his face that this wasn't a social call. She sat down on the sofa and put her hand to her mouth. "Oh Lord, don't tell me something done happened to Jeremiah. Jest don't tell me. It'll kill me dead."

"No Mamma, it's not Jeremiah, it's Doc."

Her eyes got big. "What's done happened to Doc?" she

asked, afraid to hear the answer.

"He must have fallen out at the camp and hit his head. He's in the emergency room, alive but in mighty bad shape." He reached over and took her hand. "You need to call Charlie. He'll want to come home as soon as possible. Doc may not wake up."

CHAPTER THREE

SIX MONTHS EARLIER

Hubert Polk ordered a Sazerac cocktail at the Bon Ton, anticipating a sumptuous New Orleans dinner. The invitation to the hospital association's annual meeting, all expenses paid by Great Northern, surprised him. Great Northern was buying small independent hospitals all over the country but owned none in Louisiana. Hubert was a small-town lawyer who served as chairman of the board of the Bayou Belle Community Hospital. His law practice was successful by small-town standards, but was not the big law firm partnership to which he aspired. Hubert was morbidly obese, slovenly in appearance, and the butt of many jokes. He pictured himself a powerful figure and would one day prove it to the community.

He was seated in the middle of the small restaurant considering the menu, deciding between the trout amandine or the blackened redfish, when a tall, thin, well-dressed man sat down at his table. Hubert was startled by the man's approach. He had narrow eyes, thin lips, and a long nose that he looked down like he was sighting a gun. Speaking with a New Orleans accent, he said, "Mr. Polk, my name is Ruben Martin. I understand Bayou Belle is looking for a new CEO for its hospital," jumping right to his purpose for being there.

"Yes," replied Hubert suspiciously, "but how did you hear

about that? We just began our search and haven't even advertised the position yet. We lost our CEO unexpectedly barely a month ago."

"I make it my business to know. I have a lucrative proposal for you," he said, still looking down his nose across the table at Hubert.

The lucrative part got Hubert's attention, but he said, "Mr. Martin, I am in no position to make any offer. The hospital board will have to make that decision."

"Please call me Ruben and, yes, I am completely aware of that, but I thought it would be good to meet with you first. You will see why."

Hubert thought for a moment. "Then I presume you sent the invitation and are footing the bill for this meeting. Are you here on behalf of Great Northern?"

"Unofficially I am," Martin replied. "I am currently the CEO of a hospital in Oklahoma that was just bought by the group and, as a result, I now work for them. Let's order and I will present my proposal. I hear the Bon Ton is one of the best kept secrets in New Orleans."

"It's always been a favorite of mine. But how did you know where to find me?" asked Hubert.

"I'm also staying at the Royal Sonesta. The concierge told me you made reservations here."

"Okay," said Hubert, "so what is this proposal?"

"Let's order first and it's on Great Northern. I haven't eaten since arriving in New Orleans, and I'd rather talk business on a full stomach." Hubert ordered turtle soup, shrimp remoulade, and the ten-ounce center-cut filet with mushrooms and cabernet wine sauce. Ruben opted for the crawfish bisque and crabmeat imperial. Before the food came, Ruben began his proposal. "Great Northern is very interested in having a presence in Louisiana. Bayou Belle Hospital is just the size we are looking for."

"But Bayou Belle is not for sale," Hubert broke in. "We've never even considered that possibility. Our financials are excellent." Not giving Ruben a chance to interrupt, he continued. "The community has a lot of pride in the hospital and their medical staff. Just two years ago we did a major renovation, adding new operating rooms, updating the emergency room, and installing a state-of-the-art intensive care unit." He paused, then added, "I thank you for the invitation here, but I'm afraid you're wasting your time." Looking at Ruben, Hubert thought of Cassius in Shakespeare's Julius Caesar. He looked ambitious, with a lean and hungry look. However, he had paid for Hubert's trip and would be paying for his center-cut filet. He should be polite enough to hear what the man had to say.

"So, Hubert—may I call you Hubert? Here's the deal." Ruben acted as though he hadn't heard what Hubert said. "If you hire me to be your new CEO at a smaller salary than you paid your last one, we'll begin the process of convincing the community and the board that they would benefit from a new hospital built entirely at Great Northern's expense. Great Northern will buy the old hospital from the community by funding a large trust, then appointing a health commission composed of community VIPs to manage the trust and distribute funds as they think best to local health concerns. If you can make this happen, you will be made special counsel to the hospital on a large retainer that Great Northern can afford to pay, and you will be given a paid position on the national board of Great Northern." Ruben had Hubert's full attention. "Part of my job is to infiltrate small hospitals and manipulate takeovers. The community will be all for it when they hear the benefits. You, Hubert, will be a much wealthier man."

After another Sazerac, Hubert could clearly see the wisdom in the proposal. He would be rich. His wife would for once be proud of him. His kids could go to the private college of their choice instead of the local state college. *Yes*, he thought, *this could work.* The people of the town would have a new respect for him.

Ruben could see that he was making the deal and almost didn't offer the coup de grace, but he reconsidered. It wasn't his money, and he needed Hubert to be in his debt. "I'm also prepared to offer you a $100,000 bonus for signing me. It will be placed in an account in your name at Hibernia Bank, and nobody but you and I will ever know about it."

Hubert frowned. That sounded too much like a bribe.

"Think of it as a reverse finder's fee," Ruben quickly added, seeing the look on Hubert's face. "We won't make that part of the deal if you don't feel right about it."

Hubert's eyes blurred as he stared up at the rotating ceiling fan. A red convertible Porsche came to mind. He would be inspired to lose weight so he could fit into it. "No, that sounds good," he heard himself say. When they shook hands on the deal, Ruben's was cold, moist, and soft. Hubert thought it felt like he was shaking hands with a snake. Perhaps he was.

The maître d' came over to greet the two men and to make sure they had enjoyed their meal. He liked talking to his customers and had met many interesting people through the years. Many came back to enjoy the Bon Ton time and time again. He discovered that Ruben was from Oklahoma and Hubert from Bayou Belle. "Bread pudding with whiskey sauce is a delicious dessert," he recommended.

Both men followed his advice. Ruben ate a few bites before excusing himself. Hubert stayed for a cup of cappuccino. When he thought no one was looking, Hubert ate the portion of bread pudding that Ruben left behind. He hated waste.

The next morning they had breakfast at the hotel and made plans to present Ruben to the board at its next meeting in two weeks. Hubert was to tell them he had met him in New Orleans, had looked into his background, and found him to be ideal for the job. He had the right kind of experience and would accept less money than they had paid Ken Adams. Old Doc Leveau might cause some trouble, but Hubert thought he could control the majority. Hubert had planned to have lunch at Mother's and take a walk in the Quarter. Instead, he treated himself to lunch at Brennan's, then went to Saks and bought two new suits with accessories. As an afterthought he bought his wife a new pearl necklace. On such a tremendous emotional high, he hardly remembered the drive back to Bayou Belle. Calling the Oklahoma hospital to check up on Ruben Martin crossed his mind, but he dismissed it. He didn't want to discover anything negative. He preferred to believe it as he had been told. After all, if Ruben was good enough for a company like Great Northern, how could he not be good enough for Bayou Belle.

CHAPTER FOUR

TUESDAY, JUNE 6

The airplane motor sounded a steady drone. The instrument panel lights were dim and the Texas countryside was dark. Charlie navigated by instrument only. The business of flying the plane kept him awake, but soon the monotony was hypnotizing. He nodded off for a moment, then jolted awake, momentarily panicked and heart racing. He was still on course and maintaining altitude and afterward, with help from an open window letting in cold air, stayed alert.

Soon the GPS said he was over Louisiana. In the dark he could only imagine the marshland and lush green forests. The air felt heavier and he was sure he could smell the bayou. He was home. He felt about Louisiana like Scarlett felt about Tara. He loved Texas and was grateful for his life there, but his heart would always be in Louisiana. He flew over Bayou Belle, waggled the wings as if someone could see it, called in his approach to the airfield, and made a perfect landing. He parked the plane, tied it down, and made his way to the small airfield office.

Jake was there to pick him up. "Hey, Charlie, good to see you, man. Sorry 'bout your dad."

"Morning, Jake, thanks for picking me up. How's he doing?"

"Jim says he's holding his own for now, but everybody's

anxious about a bed opening up for him soon at LSU." Before
he let go of Charlie's hand, Jake looked him up and down. "You
don't look so good yourself. You okay?"

"Yeah, I bet I don't. Been a long day and night. Went to
sleep and almost crashed the damn plane somewhere in Texas."
Charlie put his bag in the backseat of the police cruiser and got
in the passenger side.

Jake was the twice-elected sheriff of Bayou Belle. He and
Charlie had grown up together, fishing and playing ball. He
would often come to Charlie's house with his mother. His dad
was an abusive drunk, and Delphine was sometimes afraid to
leave Jake at home. So he and Charlie were a lot like brothers.

They drove through Bayou Belle on the way to the hospital. It was a quaint, peaceful South Louisiana town, built along
the bayou that gave it its name. A white antebellum courthouse
with large Doric columns around all four sides occupied the
square in the middle of downtown. Almost all the stores were
locally owned family businesses. The center of activity was
Julius' Café, located across the street from the courthouse,
where coffee, politics, sports, and friendly bickering were the
daily fare. Old Mr. Watson, the night watchman, asleep in his
pickup, didn't stir when Jake drove by. Charlie chuckled to
himself, remembering the night he and Jake set off a cherry
bomb under his truck, almost giving the man, much younger
then, a heart attack. They rode with the windows down and
the sweet smell of honeysuckle in the air.

Jake pulled up to the emergency entrance and let Charlie
out.

"Thanks, Jake. Come by the house later."

Jake saluted and drove off.

Charlie held the door for a woman walking a teenager into the ER. The boy was walking bent over, holding his right side and putting his right foot down very gingerly. *Appendicitis*, thought Charlie. He reached for a wheelchair and had the boy sit down.

"Thanks, Charlie," said the woman.

Charlie looked back at her more closely. She was wearing baggy sweat pants and an LSU sweatshirt that was several sizes too large. She wore no makeup and looked like she hadn't slept. Her thick black hair was partially held in a clip, but a few locks had escaped the clip and fell across her forehead, partially hiding two of the most beautiful black eyes he had ever seen. He stepped closer and stared speechless for a long moment, then said, "Ellie? Ellie Boudreaux?"

She laughed and smiled so sweetly the tiredness left her face.

"I haven't seen you in years. Except for those eyes, I might not have known you at all."

She laughed again and said, "I guess the last time you saw me, I was batboy for the legion team."

"Or climbing under the bleachers looking for ice cream money," Charlie teased, then added, more seriously, "Delphine tells me it was your dad who found mine and took care of him until help arrived. I'll never be able to thank him enough for saving his life."

"Yeah, he called to tell me about it," said Ellie. Then, giving Charlie the once-over, she said, "You look like you played a double header, then went out drinking all night."

"I bet I do," said Charlie. Then pointing at the boy he asked, "Is this...?"

"My son, Beau." She put her hand on Beau's shoulder. "He's

been sick for a couple of days and now he's worse. He's been vomiting and now it hurts him to move. Thought it was the flu, but I'm afraid it might be appendicitis."

"Watching him walk, I think you might be right." Charlie pushed the wheelchair to the registration desk, then turned back to Ellie. "Tell you what, I'm going up to check on my dad, then I'll come back down."

Charlie found his dad surrounded by IV poles and monitoring equipment. A large dressing adorned Doc's head, and the endotracheal tube coming out of his mouth was connected to a ventilator. He had been standing there holding his dad's hand for just a minute when Jim Cummings and Dr. Solomon, the hospitalist, came in. Jim shook Charlie's hand and introduced him to Dr. Solomon. "Glad you got here," said Jim. "We just heard from LSU. They have a bed and the Nightingale helicopter is en route to pick him up."

Dr. Solomon checked Doc's pupils and commented that they were reacting, then said, "Dr. Janetta, the chief of neurosurgery at LSU, agreed to accept Doc in transfer. We were going to repeat the CT here this morning, but it can be done there. I suspect he is still slowly bleeding internally, but he's been stable through the night."

The distinctive sound of an approaching helicopter grew louder as it neared the hospital helipad, then idled after landing. Seconds later the EMTs burst through the door and prepared Doc Leveau for transfer. In ten minutes, with Doc secured to the stretcher, they hurried back to the chopper. Charlie murmured a silent prayer and watched from the window as the helicopter rose slowly in the air, pointed its nose in the direction of New Orleans, and sped away for the half-hour flight. Jim led Charlie to the coffeepot. The coffee had been brewed around midnight and was very strong. Charlie, thinking this was what he had needed on the plane, downed one cup quickly and poured another.

"Charlie, I was thinking," said Jim. "Your dad has several post-op patients still in the hospital. After you get some rest, would you mind rounding on them?"

"Glad to," said Charlie. "But I'll need hospital privileges to do anything but a social call."

"We'll talk to Ruben Martin about that when he comes in."

"I've heard Dad speak of him and not in very good terms. You think he'll be a problem?"

"Probably," said Jim. "He usually is."

Charlie walked back to the ER with Jim. They found Ellie sitting alone in a cubicle with her head in her hands. Beau was in CT.

"You okay?" asked Charlie.

She looked up. "Just worried sick. Don't know what I'd do if something happened to Beau. He's all I've got." She was wringing her hands, feeling guilty about taking so long to get him to the hospital.

"He should be fine, Ellie. He's a strong, healthy boy." Charlie tried to reassure her. "Probably just needs his appendix out and in a couple of days he'll be back to normal."

"I wish I felt that way," Ellie said as she stood up and started to pace. "Who will do the operation with Dr. Leveau gone?" Pointing a finger at Charlie, she said, "And before you even suggest it, Dr. Kaiser will not come near my son."

"I hear you," said Charlie, "but I don't know who Dr. Kaiser is." Then he asked somewhat shyly, "How 'bout if I do it?"

She stopped pacing and looked up at Charlie. "Can you operate better than you can hit a baseball?" Before he could answer she continued. "If you could, I'd feel so much better." She already looked relieved, like a weight had been lifted.

Charlie was concerned that he had offered something he might not be allowed to deliver, and dreaded the thought of having to tell her later that he couldn't do it after all. "Jim and I are going to the front office this morning and try to get me temporary privileges so I can help with Dad's patients." Then like he just remembered something he had heard, he said, "And by the way, I thought I hit pretty good."

"You were good, Charlie." She brushed some hair out of her eyes. "Should have used a lighter bat. You were always trying to hit for distance when your strength was bunts and base hits. I kept trying to give you the smaller bat, but you always took the heavier one." She was smiling again, her mind temporarily off her sick son.

The stretcher with Beau rolled back in. Jim came in and told Ellie that, according to the CT, Beau had acute appendicitis. Charlie thought he could have told them that without an expensive CT, but that's the way it was done nowadays. Too many lawyers. His mind wandered back to the crumpled letter on the kitchen floor in Riverton.

"I'll page Dr. Kaiser," said Jim.

"No, don't," said Charlie, his mind coming back to the present before Ellie had a chance to respond. "If I get privileges I'll do it myself."

When Ruben got to his office, Jim and Charlie went to see him. Charlie looked and felt completely worn out. Ruben probably thought Jim was bringing in some derelict off the street.

"Ruben," Jim said as they walked past the secretary and went unannounced into his office. "I'd like you to meet Dr. Charlie Leveau."

Ruben was momentarily speechless. He hadn't even checked to see if Doc Leveau had a family. "Good morning, Dr. Leveau," he managed to say. "Sorry about your dad. Is he making progress?"

"He should be in New Orleans by now and in the OR before long, so it's hard to say yet." Charlie thought he detected a fleeting look of disappointment before Ruben recovered.

Jim interrupted, "Kaiser is now the only surgeon, Ruben, and lots of people haven't warmed up to him. Charlie here will be in town off and on while his dad is sick, and he could really help us out." Jim studied Ruben. "What do you say?"

Ruben rubbed his chin and looked doubtful but couldn't think of a reason quickly enough to say no. "If he'll fill out some basic forms, we should have him set to go by tomorrow." Delaying it would give him time to come up with a reason not to allow it. The last thing he needed was another Leveau in Bayou Belle.

"Tomorrow will be too late," Charlie blurted, getting a quick glance from Jim. But he went on. "I need to do an appendectomy for an old friend today." Charlie tried to be friendly, but he had taken an instant dislike to Ruben. "My file can be faxed here from Riverton, Texas, in just a few minutes. You'll see that there are no black marks. Jim here can vouch for me, and you do need another surgeon. How about it?"

Ruben pondered for a minute, then relented. "Okay. You have privileges until this appendectomy gets out of the hospital. Anything further will need to go through proper channels."

Ruben picked up his telephone and said, "Now if you'll excuse me, I have some calls to make."

"Fair enough. Nice to meet you," lied Charlie. He and Jim returned to the ER. "He's a sour SOB. And I get the distinct impression he would prefer my not being here at all."

"He enjoys power," said Jim. "To tell you the truth, I'm a little surprised he gave you permission."

Arrangements were made with the operating room. Charlie went over with the nurses the instruments and sutures he would need. He talked to the anesthesiologist, who then went to the ER and interviewed Ellie and Beau. Soon they were on the way to the operating room. Ellie stayed close by in the OR waiting room. Charlie reassured her that they would take good care of Beau and that he would be out to talk to her as soon as the operation was over, probably about forty-five minutes.

The operation went well. The appendix had not ruptured. Charlie thanked the surgical team for their help. One of them asked, "Don't you want to come home to practice, Dr. Leveau?" Another of the older nurses remembered him from before he went to college and commented, "It won't be right for there to be a Bayou Belle hospital without a Dr. Leveau." Then, realizing what she said, she apologized.

Charlie just smiled and said, "Thank you. We all hope he comes back soon." He then dictated his operative note, wrote post-op orders, and went to find Ellie. He found her in the waiting room watching the door. She jumped up and ran over to Charlie when he came in.

"How is he?"

"Great. He did great. The appendix wasn't ruptured. He'll be sore for a few days but should be back to normal in a week or two."

"Thank you. Oh Charlie, thank you so much." She wrapped her arms around his waist and hugged him tightly. "You can't know how worried I was." She loosened her grip and looked up. "When can I see him?"

"He is in recovery now, but he'll be transferred to his room in a little while. The nurses will come get you then, and I'll be by to check on him later." He reached over and brushed some hair out of her eyes. "Meanwhile, I plan to shave, shower, and get to New Orleans to check on Dad." Charlie prayed his dad's operation was going as well as Beau's had.

Still in scrubs, Charlie went to see Jim.

"I called Betty and told her you were in town. She said to come to supper tonight if you don't already have plans. How 'bout it?"

"Sure it's okay, short notice and all?"

"Betty will be mad for a week if you don't come. So do it for me. I get off at seven and we eat at eight."

"Great, then I'll be there. Thanks."

Charlie then went to let Ruben know that all had indeed gone well. His secretary said he was gone, but she promised to relay the message. Just then, his cell phone rang.

"Dr. Leveau, this is Dr. Janetta at LSU." Charlie sat quickly in the nearest chair in the lobby, dreading the news. "Your dad's surgery went very well. He will be in the ICU for several days. I can't say at this point how much damage was done, but it's possible that he'll make a full recovery. I don't expect him to come around for a day or two, but you are welcome to visit anytime. I'll keep you posted if there are any changes."

Charlie thanked him, knowing from personal experience how much easier it was to give good news to a family. He felt great relief and renewed hope.

Beau was still sleepy but waking up and smiled when Charlie walked in.

"How you feeling, Beau?"

"Much better, thanks. It's sore but the pain is different." Grimacing, he tried to turn.

Ellie, standing on the other side of the bed, had fresh tears in her eyes, and her voice choked when she looked up at Charlie and thanked him again. He gave the nurse and Ellie his cell number and instructed them to call him with any problems or questions.

Charlie called the town's only taxi for a ride home. Jake had delivered his suitcase, which Charlie had left by mistake in the patrol car. Getting out of the taxi, Charlie stood for a moment and looked at the house that had been his home for the first eighteen years of his life. It was one and a half stories with two dormers. A wide, covered front porch extended the length of the house, which was white with dark green shutters alongside the four front windows that reached all the way to the floor and could function also as doors. The main front door had a gas lantern that burned year round and gave the house a warm, welcoming ambiance. Two large clay pots that had always contained beautiful begonias when his mother was alive were still there minus the flowers. He walked up the brick cobblestone path. Delphine met him at the front door. "So glad you're home, Charlie. How is Doc doin'?" she asked as she hugged his neck.

"The call from New Orleans was good news. Dad is doing well. His operation was successful, and there is a chance for a full recovery."

"How 'bout a ham sandwich and a bowl of gumbo? I have some ready."

"That sounds wonderful. I'm starved, haven't eaten a thing since lunch yesterday." Charlie hadn't thought about food but suddenly realized just how hungry he was. At one point as he was eating, he nodded off, and only the jerk of his neck woke him in time to keep his nose out of the gumbo. He finished the lunch with Delphine watching, then said, "I need a long shower and a hot nap." He was so sleepy he laughed at himself for getting the sentence mixed up, but he did remember to tell Delphine, "Jim and Betty Cummings asked me to supper at eight."

"I have something fixed but it'll keep. When you go, take the sweet potato pie with you for dessert."

"Thanks, Delphine. After I clean up I need an hour to sleep. Would you wake me up at noon? I want to drive to New Orleans and see Dad this afternoon."

It suddenly dawned on Charlie that he hadn't even talked to Page. She was probably frantic. He called her cell.

"Dad? Where are you? Mom called and said she'd gone to stay with Aunt Ruth. Then I go by the house and you are nowhere to be found. Your cell didn't answer. Mr. Waltrip called from the airport and said your car was there all smashed up, and your plane was gone. I'm so glad to hear your voice, but

I'm mad as hell. I was about to go into premature labor."

"Sorry, hon, just slow down a minute." Charlie was truly sorry he had worried her that way. "I should have called to let you know, but I'm in Bayou Belle seeing about Granddad. He had a bad fall yesterday and is in the hospital. He got transferred to LSU this morning and has already had surgery." He proceeded to give her some of the details, then remembered the crumpled letter. "Page, I need you to do me a favor."

"Sure, Dad." Her voice was still cracking with sobs. "I'm just so glad to hear your voice. I was imagining all kinds of things, none of them good."

"I'm really sorry, sweetheart, but I'm okay. Just pray for Granddad. Hon, if you go in the house, there's a wadded-up letter from a law firm notifying me of a malpractice suit. I need you to take it to the office and have my secretary fax it to my malpractice carrier. If possible, I'd like for you to do it today before they go home."

"I'll go right now. And what about your car? Do you want me to arrange to get it fixed?"

"That's down the list right now. When you have time, have it towed to the place that restored it. But like I said, that's a very low priority."

"Gee, Dad, never thought I'd hear you say that car was a low priority."

Amazing how priorities can change in a short time, thought Charlie.

When he hung up he looked around the familiar room. It was just as it was the day he left home. The sports trophies were in the same place. The cigar box with the baseball card collection was on the shelf where it had always been beside the baseball autographed by Stan Musial and a purple and gold felt football autographed by all the members of the 1958 national champion LSU Tigers given to him by his dad. The old radio was still tuned to WWL out of New Orleans. It had always carried the Cardinal games during the summer and the Tiger football games in the fall. A picture of Mickey Mantle from *Sport Magazine* was pinned up beside the sports page headline from the state championship game his and Jake's senior year. Times were simpler then. What he would give to have those times back.

He never made it to the shower. He lay back and was asleep across the bed almost before his head hit. He had managed to remove his shoes while talking to Page, but he slept in everything else.

At noon as requested, Delphine woke Charlie up. For a second, Charlie had no idea where he was or why Delphine was talking to him. He shook his head and it began to clear. "Thanks, Delphine. I think I may have slept through tomorrow night." He shed his clothes and stumbled into the bathroom.

After a long, hot shower and shave, Charlie stood in front of the mirror, contemplating his form. Though not in the athletic shape he had once been, he was still in good physical condition. His light brown hair was graying at the temples and beginning to thin on top. He stood right at six feet tall and weighed 190 pounds. Turning sideways he noted his belly to be reasonably flat. Green eyes and thick eyebrows framed a nose that had been broken at least three times, once by a baseball, once in football practice, and he couldn't remember the other time. A jagged scar on his right cheek marked where his face hit the curb when he wrecked his bicycle. Burn scars on his chest were from a Scout campfire when Chucky Benoit decided it would start faster with gasoline. He guessed he should just be happy to be alive. Chucky wasn't. All in all, he didn't look so bad. He had looked good enough to win the prettiest girl at LSU even if now he might lose her.

He borrowed Delphine's car to drive to New Orleans, afraid that his dad's old Wagoneer wouldn't make it. He took a thermos of strong coffee and bought sunflower seeds to help stay awake for the drive. Delphine tried briefly to talk him out of going, but Charlie was like his dad, determined and not likely to take advice.

He found his dad in the neurosurgery intensive care unit and was given a comfortable chair to sit in beside the hospital bed. Doc's color was ashen, but Charlie could tell from the monitors that he was stable, but still unconscious as expected. Reassured again, Charlie slept almost three hours in the chair. The ICU nurses were laughing among themselves about needing to take his vital signs. He awoke with a start when another patient's alarm sounded, and couldn't believe the clock. His dad looked the same as when he arrived. If he left now he would barely make it to Jim and Betty's in time for dinner. Giving his dad's hand a squeeze and a kiss on the forehead through the dressing, he thanked the nurses, made sure they had his cell number, and made his way to the car.

CHAPTER FIVE

TUESDAY NIGHT, JUNE 6

Jim and Betty lived in a 1920s house they had been working to restore. Betty greeted Charlie at the door, accepted the sweet potato pie, and gave him a big welcoming hug.

"Come on in, Charlie, it's been way too long. You look good." Charlie knew it was a lie, but he appreciated it anyway. "Jimmie is just getting out of the shower and will be down in a minute. He got tied up at the hospital as he was about to leave. I have turtle soup cooking and some redfish to blacken. What would you like to drink?"

"I haven't had a Sazerac in a long time. If you have the makings, I'll fix us both one."

"Sounds good. Just like old times." She pointed to the bar and headed toward the kitchen. "You do that while I check the soup, and you might as well make three. Jim will want one too."

Jim came down looking refreshed, with his hair still a little damp, and joined them in the family room. They drank their cocktails and ate heartily while catching up on news of family and friends. After a while the subject turned to the situation at Bayou Belle Hospital.

"So tell me, Jim," said Charlie, "what the hell is going on at the hospital?"

"A lot has changed since Ruben came," Jim replied. "It isn't a fun place to work anymore."

"Tell me." Charlie took his last bite of redfish. "Dad tried to, but I didn't ever have time to listen."

Betty began to clear the dishes and went to the kitchen to get the pie and put the coffee on.

Jim settled back in his chair. "It began, I guess, when Ken Adams was killed in the boating accident. His boat apparently capsized while he was fishing. Before the dust had settled, Hubert Polk found Ruben Martin in New Orleans at a hospital meeting and was so impressed, he offered him a job and then persuaded the board to write the contract. This was done over your dad's and Tom Bradshaw's objections." This sounded familiar to Charlie. "Then Martin brings in a new surgeon without asking your dad or the medical staff, and after being here for just a few weeks began making moves to sell the hospital to Great Northern. He reconstituted the board so it would vote with him, then spoke all over town at various clubs. Folks seem to be going along with it. Those of us practicing medicine dread the thought of losing our autonomy to a national concern. As a matter of fact, the medical staff voted to stay independent, with only one dissenting vote, Kaiser, the new surgeon recruited by Ruben."

"Very interesting," said Charlie. "Tell me what you know about Kaiser. He doesn't seem to have made a positive first impression."

"Kaiser came with great reviews from his colleagues and his professors." Jim took a sip of his coffee. "We were excited to be getting such a distinguished and talented new surgeon on the staff, especially since your dad isn't getting any younger." He paused, looked down, then back up. "Sorry, Charlie."

Charlie made a dismissive gesture and said, "Hey, I've wanted him to slow down for years."

"Anyway, Kaiser has been a major disappointment. I can't figure him out." Betty came in from the kitchen and refilled their coffee. Jim passed the cream and sugar and continued. "He can't make decisions. He fouls up so much in the OR that some nurses refuse to work with him. His reputation in town is poison, and he hasn't been here but three months." Jim looked down at the floor, then back up at Charlie. "I mean, we'd all much rather transfer patients to Lafayette, Baton Rouge, or even New Orleans than consult him."

"What's his background?" asked Charlie. "Where did Martin find him?"

"That is also a very compelling story, and Martin's excuse for why it's taking him a while to adjust. Kaiser was raised in a Catholic orphanage somewhere in Kansas. He was an Eagle Scout, president of his senior class, and, according to letters from the priests, a model citizen. When he completed his residency, he felt he owed them so much that he organized a missionary trip to Africa. He took along a couple of nurses, a surgical assistant, and a nurse anesthetist. They set up a field hospital deep in the jungle and were to be there a year, but tragedy struck after nine months." Charlie listened without interrupting. "It turned cold one night, so they built a fire outside their tent. During the night Kaiser got up to take a leak and the full bladder saved his life. A gust of wind came up, blowing the fire into the tent, which apparently went up like an explosion. He told us at his interview that the screams still haunt him. He sustained second- and third-degree burns on his arms and some on his legs trying to rescue his friends. He got two out, but they died shortly from their burns. Kaiser was naturally devastated. He stayed in Africa until his physical wounds healed, then wandered the continent. Ruben Martin knew him from when he was in medical school in Chicago. He heard about the accident and recruited him to Bayou Belle, thinking that a small town and low-key practice would help him and help us. Sadly, it hasn't turned out that way. The accident must have really affected his ability to think and operate. It hasn't been long and we hope he'll regain his former abilities, but from what I've seen, that's a long shot." Jim finished the coffee and shook his head as he placed the cup back on the saucer.

"That kind of thing could screw anybody up," agreed Charlie. "The guy has been through a lot." Recalling the scene in the ER, he said, "I know Ellie Boudreaux wanted no part of him." He seemed to enjoy the memory. "I barely recognized her. It's been so long."

"Yes," said Jim, "and she's also been through a lot."

"How's that?"

"She went to USL and married a football player named Clay Boudreaux, no relation of course. They lived in Mississippi, where he coached high school football. She taught school. Beau came along very soon after they were married, maybe too soon. Clay was demonstrating a drill at practice one day and tore the ligaments in his knee. He got it fixed at the local hospital. A couple days later he was walking in the hall with Ellie and Beau when he threw a large pulmonary embolism and was dead before he hit the floor. At the end of the school year, Ellie and Beau moved back here to be closer to family. That was about five years ago. She got a teaching job, and Beau makes friends easily. He and Jake's son Jeremiah pal around together."

Betty broke in here. "And because of the way she looks, there've been no shortage of men trying to beat down her door." She laughed. "But I don't think she's given any of them the time of day."

The coffee and pie were consumed, and it was getting late. Charlie stood up to leave. "So good to see y'all. I'll be here for a few days. Hopefully we can get together again, maybe barbecue something out at the camp." They agreed. Charlie thanked Betty for a great meal and made his way to the car.

Thinking about what Jim had said, he went by the hospital to check on Beau. Given his dad's history, he wanted to be sure Beau was on clot prevention treatment. He went into Beau's room without knocking. Beau was asleep, but Ellie was sitting in the bedside chair looking at him. She looked up, alarmed. "Is something wrong, Dr. Leveau?"

"No, no, no. I had dinner at Jim's house and came by on the way home to check and see how he's doing. I thought you'd be home in bed by now." He listened to Beau's chest and checked his dressing without waking him up. "And what's this Dr. Leveau business? I'm Charlie, for crying out loud."

"You were Charlie when you were living here playing ball with my brother. Now you're a big-time Texas surgeon."

"I'm home now and I much prefer Charlie. Say, you remember the time Emile and I stole some moonshine from your dad." He laughed. "You caught us and told on us." Scratching his chin, looking at her, he said, "Maybe you should call me Dr. Leveau. I never got you back for that." They both laughed.

"Charlie it is," said Ellie. "How's your patient?"

"Looks good. We'll get him up walking in the morning."

"Are you sure we should get him up?" Ellie looked worried.

Charlie understood. "Jim told me about what happened to your husband, so I can understand your apprehension, but the best way to prevent a clot is to be up moving around. We also have him on mild blood thinners." He gave her his most convincing, reassuring smile and she seemed to relax.

Home by midnight, he lay in bed going over the day. If he were a single man, he too would be beating a path to Ellie's doorstep.

Charlie slept soundly until seven the next morning, two hours past his usual wake-up time. If Delphine hadn't been cooking bacon, he might have slept until ten.

Going downstairs and into the kitchen, still rubbing his eyes, he yawned. "Good morning, Delphine. How's a guy get any sleep with smells like this coming from the kitchen?"

"Time you got up anyway," she said. "Jake came by earlier hopin' to see you. Said he had something to talk to you about." Delphine opened some homemade mayhaw jelly to go with the biscuits.

"Thanks. Do you know what Jake wanted?"

"No, but he said he'd find you later."

CHAPTER SIX

WEDNESDAY, JUNE 7

The Wagoneer started on the third try, rattling as it idled. The odometer read 351,545. Charlie suspected his dad planned to get another hundred thousand out of it. He drove to the hospital, parking in the physician lot. The odometer still read 351,545. Maybe Doc had already gotten another hundred thousand.

Walking down the hall toward Beau's room, he passed a janitor busily mopping the hall floor.

"Hi Doc," the janitor said. "How's your dad?"

"So far so good," said Charlie. "Thanks for asking. How long have you known him?"

"Not for too long, I just been here about five months. But he was a nice man. Always spoke kindly."

"Thanks for saying that," said Charlie. "What's your name?"

"Donnie. Like I say, I been here just a few months, but I can see what is going on."

"Well, Donnie, it's good to meet you. See you around." Charlie smiled and walked on down the hall to Beau's room, wondering what Donnie meant by that.

Ellie was still there but asleep in the chair. Beau was awake.

"How you feeling, Beau?"

"A lot better, Dr. Leveau. Thanks." Beau had light hair, blue eyes, and a muscular build. Charlie suspected that he looked like his father.

"Have you had breakfast yet?"

"No, but I'm hungry."

Ellie stirred, and when she saw Charlie, she sat up straight, stretched, and yawned. "Excuse me," she said, "I must have dropped off. Have you been here long?"

"Just a minute. Glad you got some rest."

A clear liquid breakfast came and Beau sneered, but finished most of it. "Okay," said Charlie, "it's time to take a walk." Beau looked at his mother and she nodded. Before they reached the door, Beau was walking on his own holding on to the IV stand.

Nearing the end of the hall where it adjoined the lobby, Hubert Polk came out of Ruben Martin's office. Hubert saw Charlie and came over to express his concerns about Doc Leveau and asked if there were any reports back from LSU. Charlie told him everything he knew and asked Hubert if he could come by his office to discuss a legal matter.

"Certainly," said Hubert. "I had a case that was cancelled. Come around about one if that fits your schedule."

"My schedule is pretty open. I'll be there at one."

Donnie came by with a broom and a cart. Hubert looked at him for a long moment, wondering why he looked familiar.

Back in Beau's room, Ellie asked, "Charlie, I know you said he could go home soon, but I'd feel a lot better if he were here another day or so. Would that be too much to ask?"

Charlie would lose his clinical privileges as soon as Beau was discharged, so he said, "I think that's a good idea. He does have a low-grade fever, and his bowels haven't moved. That may take another day or so to happen, and when it does, you'll feel better about taking him home." Also, he didn't mind having a reason to keep Ellie around another day. "Let's get him on some regular food for lunch. I'll be back this afternoon to check on him after I run a few errands." Then he reminded her to call if she needed anything.

On the way to Julius' Charlie's cell rang, showing a number from Texas. "Hello?" He didn't recognize the number.

"Is this Dr. Charlie Leveau?" asked a female voice.

"Yes, it is."

"This is Linda George. I'm the defense attorney assigned to your case. Is this a good time to talk?"

"Sure," said Charlie. "I've had so much going on, I had almost forgotten."

"Never heard that one before," replied Ms. George. "Before you forget again, when can we meet to discuss the case?"

"I'm in Bayou Belle, Louisiana, right now seeing about my dad. I don't know exactly when I'll be back home." He wished this would just go away so he'd never have to deal with it, but it now seemed like a minor irritation compared to the way he felt when he first read the letter.

"I have to be in New Orleans tomorrow regarding another case and would have time at lunch to meet with you for an hour or so. How far away is Bayou Belle?"

"It's a couple hours away, but I was going there tomorrow anyway to check on my dad at the LSU Medical Center. I'd love to meet and start to get this behind me." Charlie thought, *What a lucky coincidence. About time for one of those.*

"I'll be staying at the Royal Orleans. Could we meet for lunch somewhere close by?"

"How about Brennan's at noon? I'll wait for you outside. Look for the one with the worried, persecuted look on his face."

"And I'll be the distinguished lawyer type with a huge briefcase. See you then."

"Thank you. Look forward to meeting you in person." Charlie parked in front of Julius'.

Mr. Julius was the second-generation owner of the café, which had been doing business in Bayou Belle since the early 1920s. A group of older men were holding court in the back of the restaurant. They called him over.

"Charlie, you know these folks," said Mr. Julius.

"Sure do, but haven't seen them in a long time." Charlie shook hands with everyone and said how good it was to see them, just wishing it was under different circumstances. They were all longtime friends of Doc Leveau. He spent a little of each day with them, drinking coffee and solving the world's problems. Mr. Julius, Billie Jack Boudreaux, Ellie's father, Pete Charlet, funeral home director (or undertaker as his friends liked to call him), and Tom Bradshaw, retired judge and former member of the hospital board made up the group.

"What do you hear from Doc?" Mr. Julius asked.

"He came through surgery well, but it will be a couple of days before we know how much damage was done or how fully he'll recover."

Mr. Julius, to lighten the mood, asked, "I wonder if he was drinking too much of Billy Jack's moonshine."

Billy Jack took great offense to that. "Just because you can't serve it here, don't be disparaging the best whiskey this side of Kentucky." He went on to describe how much blood was on the floor. The quantity got bigger with each telling. "It's a wonder he has any left. What he needs now is some of that moonshine to build his blood back up."

"Serve it here? Are you crazy?" asked Mr. Julius, feigning insult. "I wouldn't have to worry about the IRS as much as the health department. I spilled a little of the last batch you brought on my bathroom floor and burned a hole clean through to the basement." Mr. Julius was on a roll. "It's a wonder there aren't more deaths around here. That's why Doc and Pete hang around with you. They both get lots of business on your account. Pete here ought to give you a free burial after all the business you've sent him. Hell, Billy Jack, as much of that crap as you drink, it's a wonder you aren't pickled. Serve it here? It must have gone to your brain. The fact that Doc is still alive after your first aid is a proof of God."

Billy Jack, acting like his feelings were deeply hurt, replied. "If I die, it won't be because of the whiskey. It'll be because I've been eating here for years. And just so you know, Charlet," he said, pointing a finger at the undertaker, "I have decided to be cremated. I'm not giving you my body to play with, and I'm not buying an expensive casket to put in the ground never to be seen again."

Tom Bradshaw took a sip of coffee and said, "Billy Jack, don't you think that if you do get cremated, it'll be hard for the Lord to make a heavenly body for you out of ashes?"

Billy Jack looked over in the mirror at his ruddy complexion, big red nose, and potbelly. Rubbing his chin with one hand, the other on his belly, he said, "Maybe the Lord could do a better job next time."

"Hope so," said Tom. "There's going to be lots of children

in heaven, and it'd be a real shame to go around scaring them."

Pete Charlet was lost in thought and had paid little attention to the bantering. "You know," he finally said, "I spent too much time learning how to make people look good in a coffin to go burning them. Anybody can do that. I'll retire first." He was shaking his head, looking perplexed. "But you know, strangely enough, Ruben Martin came by my office soon after he got to town and asked if I had a crematorium." He looked over at Charlie and said, "It'd be just my luck to get Billy Jack for my first cremation. With all that bootleg whiskey in his system, it might light up the town, and I'd never get my money back."

It was lunch time so Charlie ordered a cheeseburger and fries, then asked, "Speaking of Ruben Martin, what do you all think about selling the hospital?"

The men looked at each other. "At first folks thought it was silly," said Mr. Julius. "But now they're hearing about the money the town will get to use for other things, and the talk now is mostly positive."

Tom Bradshaw said, "I know Doc was strongly opposed to the idea. He really couldn't see the point and hated the idea of giving up local control when the hospital has always done very well. There's a town hall meeting coming up soon, Charlie. You ought to come. Doc said your hospital in Texas was recently taken over. You could give us a different perspective."

"I might do that," said Charlie, "if I'm still in town."

Charlie enjoyed his cheeseburger and listened as the conversation turned to the local sports scene and the chances of the local American Legion baseball team, remembering the days when he, Jim, and Jake had been a big part of the team.

Billy Jack recalled that team and remarked about Ellie being the batboy while considering herself the assistant coach. Charlie told the group he would keep them updated on his dad's progress, excused himself, and walked to Hubert's. On the way there he mulled over the conversation and wondered why Ruben Martin would be interested in a crematorium.

Hubert's office was upstairs over a jewelry shop. Charlie walked up and entered the door that said "Hubert Polk, Attorney at Law." Hubert was a few years older, a few inches taller, and two feet bigger around than Charlie. He had on what looked to be a new suit, which used enough material to make two or three for Charlie.

"How can I help you, Charlie?" Hubert was standing behind his desk but came around to shake hands, offered Charlie a chair, then sat down beside him.

"If Dad doesn't make it through this, I may need your help with his estate. I don't think he has a will." Charlie didn't know if he did or not, but it gave him a good excuse to come see Hubert.

"I do that sort of thing and will be glad to help, but let's hope that won't be necessary for a while."

"For sure," said Charlie. "But I will call you if the need arises." Then, as adroitly as he could manage, Charlie asked, "Say, Hubert, what's going on at the hospital?"

"What do you mean, what's going on," asked Hubert, walking back behind his desk. "I hope what is going on is good medical care as it always has been."

"No, I mean this talk I've been hearing about selling it to a corporation. Bayou Belle has always done well. Why would anyone want to sell it?" Charlie noted a change in Hubert's demeanor. He seemed to back up and looked uncomfortable. "The hospital where I work in Texas was recently bought by a national firm, and it hasn't worked out well at all. Nobody is happy but the hospital administrators. Who is supposed to benefit from this proposed sale?"

"Charlie, as chairman of the board, I know a lot of things that I am not at liberty to discuss. There is an upcoming town meeting, where it will all be explained."

"So you can't tell me anything about it?" asked Charlie.

"No, the board members have agreed not to discuss it until the town meeting, when everyone will be able to ask questions and everyone can hear the same answers."

"It just seems strange since not so long ago a lot of people in this town gave a great deal of money to have the hospital renovated," said Charlie.

"There is a lot you don't know, Charlie." Hubert stood up, indicating that the conversation was over. "Come to the meeting if you're still in town." He walked toward the door and held it open for Charlie. "Let me know if I can help with your dad."

"I will, Hubert, and thanks for meeting with me." They shook hands, nodded to each other, and Charlie went back down the stairs.

Hubert walked over to the window and watched Charlie walk down the street, then picked up the phone and called Ruben. "Charlie Leveau was just here asking questions. I sure do hope you know what you're doing. This whole thing is making me very uneasy." Scared to death was how Hubert really felt, but he didn't want to say that to Ruben.

"Calm down, Hubert," said Ruben. "There is no way anyone

can suspect what is happening if you don't say anything. Now stop bothering me. Just remember the money and stay calm."

Hubert was thinking about the money. That's precisely why he was so nervous. That reverse finder's fee felt more and more like a bribe.

Ruben hung up the phone confident that Hubert was scared because of the bribe. He also knew he'd be absolutely catatonic if he knew everything else. Meanwhile, he had to get Charlie Leveau out of town. If he were as savvy as his old man, that could mean big trouble.

CHAPTER SEVEN

WEDNESDAY, JUNE 7

Charlie drove back to the hospital. He found Beau asleep and Ellie in the hall talking on her cell. She smiled and held up a finger, signaling him to wait a second for her to complete her call.

"If someone can cover for me today, I'd really appreciate it," she said. "I'll be back tomorrow to meet my classes." She looked at Charlie and shook her head. "Great. Thank her for me please. I'll return the favor anytime. Bye bye." She had obviously gone home, cleaned up, and gotten some rest. Wearing well-fitted blue jeans and a starched white shirt tucked in at the waist, she looked like a dream. She had put on makeup, which Charlie didn't think she needed, and her dark hair fell to her shoulders. A pearl necklace and large hoop earrings dressed it all up. Large sunglasses were perched on her head. "Sorry, Charlie. I teach summer school history and need some help with classes while Beau is sick."

"Looks like he's asleep. Is he doing all right?"

"Seems to be. He dropped off a few minutes ago after we took a long walk. I came out here so I wouldn't wake him up."

"They have fresh coffee in the cafeteria. Would you like to get some?" He pointed the way.

"Sounds good." She took his arm as they walked down

the hall.

They had the cafeteria to themselves and chose a table close to an outside window.

"I just saw your dad at Julius'," said Charlie. "He's still quite the character."

"Oh yeah." Ellie laughed. "He doesn't let facts get in the way of a good story."

"In this case, according to Jake, he was telling it like it was. And even if he embellishes the details a little, the fact is he did save Dad's life." He couldn't seem to look away from those eyes. "Beau seems to be a great kid. You must be proud."

"He is," said Ellie, "and I am so proud, but he misses his dad. I try my best to be both parents, but I tend to be overprotective."

"From what I can see, you've done a great job. Does he see much of his granddad?"

"That's been the best part of being back here. Dad takes him fishing and doesn't miss any of his games." Then she mused, "My concern is that he will want to skip college and open a distillery. What about your family, Charlie? Do you have kids?"

"Two grown kids. My son is a surgery resident in Dallas, and my daughter Page is married and lives in Riverton. She's pregnant with our first grandchild."

"Did your wife come with you?"

"Jan is visiting her sister in Houston. She went the day that I heard about Dad before I got the news." Charlie left it at that. He was telling her about his practice in Riverton when Dr. Solomon came in to the cafeteria, saw Charlie, and came over.

"Hi Ellie," he said. "I saw y'all in the hall. Looks like Beau is doing well."

"Yes, thanks. He's coming along." Ellie looked up at him and shifted uncomfortably in her chair.

Charlie sensed that he might be one of those single men beating a path to her door. Dr. Solomon looked away from Ellie and at Charlie. "Charlie, I have a patient with a bowel obstruction that is getting worse, and Kaiser refuses to operate. Would you talk to him? I don't understand his thinking."

"I'd be glad to talk to him," said Charlie, "but I doubt it'll do much good. It doesn't sound like he's open to suggestions."

"Maybe he'll be more open if the suggestions come from another surgeon. I'd sure appreciate it if you'd give it a try. The lady is getting worse, and I'm afraid before long it'll be too late. I may just send her to Lafayette or Baton Rouge."

"Sure," said Charlie, "I'll talk to him and see what happens. But if you're that concerned, I'd go ahead and arrange a transfer."

"That would probably be best. Thanks." Then he looked at Ellie again, nodded, said "Ellie," and left.

Ellie watched him walk away, then turned to Charlie. "Be careful getting involved with Kaiser. I know two people who went to him and had bad results. He cut some duct doing a gallbladder operation, and the patient had to be transferred to Baton Rouge. Another one was worse. He did a colon operation and the patient got an infection; his wound opened up and his bowels were all in the bed beside him. Your dad tried to put him back together, but the patient died. Kaiser blamed it on the nurse who was helping him do the colon operation, and Ruben Martin fired her."

Charlie was listening, trying not to stare when Jake walked up.

"Hi Ellie." He took off his police cap. "Beau okay?" Jake was polite, but he had something else on his mind.

"He's fine, and according to Dr. Leveau here, he will be going home soon."

"Good," said Jake, then turned his attention to Charlie. "Charlie, when you have some time, there is something I want to show you."

"Sure," Charlie replied, thinking Jake's timing could have been better.

"It's time I got back to check on Beau anyway. Thanks for the coffee, Charlie."

Charlie and Jake both watched as she left the cafeteria. He was reminded of the line in the old country song, "I hate to see you go, but love to watch you walk away."

"Who would have ever thought that the batboy could grow up to look like that?"

Jake nodded in agreement.

When Ellie was gone, Jake asked Charlie, "Do you know if your dad had any dealings with Vidrine Trucking Company?"

"Not that I know of, but he certainly could have. Why do you ask?" Charlie cocked his head and looked at Jake, a puzzled expression on his face.

"Charlie, I have reason to believe your dad may have been assaulted. I don't think he just fell. There's no proof, but I'm almost sure someone tried to kill him. Billy Jack Boudreaux may not just have stopped the bleeding; he may have arrived just in time to run the assailant off before he finished the job."

Charlie was completely taken aback. "Seriously? I have never known my dad to have an enemy." He was confused. "Who would have done something like that, and what makes you think so?" Charlie indicated doubt.

Jake looked around to be sure nobody else could hear.

"I went out and had a look around the camp earlier today. There was no furniture near where your dad fell that could have caused the laceration. None of the furniture in the room had any blood on corners. There's no indication that he had a heart attack or stroke. His blood alcohol level was negligible. I walked around outside the camp house. There were footprints under a bedroom window that were highly visible because of the rain the night before. The window was still partially open."

"He could have left it open the last time he was there. He does tend to be absentminded." Charlie still looked doubtful.

"I found this on the ground under the window by the footprints." Jake handed Charlie a Vidrine Trucking Company business card. It was mud smudged but not wet. It had not been in the rain two nights before.

"Turn it over. Look at the back." Jake waited while Charlie studied the card.

On the back of the card was a crudely drawn map showing the way from Vidrine Trucking Company to the camp. "What do you think this means?" asked Charlie, a bewildered look on his face.

"I'm not sure yet," said Jake. "But I wouldn't be surprised if we find out that someone at Vidrine wants Doc dead. I've heard something fishy is going on out there, but there've never been any formal complaints, and I haven't heard any specifics, so I haven't had a reason to investigate. I think it's time I had a look.

"Can you get a search warrant?" asked Charlie.

"Not hardly. So far we have no hard evidence of a crime.

Your dad may actually have fallen and we might be barking up a wrong tree."

"Do you believe that?"

"No, I don't."

"Neither do I." Charlie studied the card. "If someone did this to my dad, I want to know who and why." He looked at Jake. "If we find out who, you'll have to be fast to beat me to him. What do you suggest we do?"

"While it's still daylight, what do you say we take your plane up and have a look from the air. I haven't been on the property in a long time and need to get the lay of the land, see if I can tell how it's guarded."

"Sure," said Charlie, "won't hurt to look."

After Charlie did a thorough preflight check, they took off, Jake in the copilot seat with his camera.

"Charlie, let's get high enough and stay out over the bayou as much as we can so we don't look suspicious."

"Seems a little paranoid to me, but you're the sheriff. You think they might have surface-to-air missiles?"

Jake gave Charlie a withering look. "Humor me," was all he said.

They got up to two thousand feet and approached the site from the highway. Many trucks were being loaded and offloaded, contents stored in warehouses. A lot of people were working. Nothing looked unusual. Toward the back of the property was an old home that had been used as a hospital during the War Between the States. Outbuildings around it included a kitchen, a storehouse, and a wine cellar. A new airstrip ran along the back of the property, ending near the old home. It was long enough for jets to land and take off as several did every Sunday night. Charlie and Jake had seen the house from the bayou while fishing, and the Boy Scouts had camped near it. The historic preservationists tried to have it declared a historic monument before Vidrine bought the whole property. Nothing was different except the airstrip.

Satisfied they had seen all they could from the air, they headed back to the airport. Jake was quiet all the way back. Charlie glanced at him. "What are you thinking?"

"Just thinking," he said, "give me a minute."

Driving back to town, Jake finally spoke up. "Charlie, let's go have a look at that old house. There's something just not right, but I can't put my finger on it. It might help explain the heavy air traffic."

"I don't know," said Charlie. "When do you want to do it?"

"Tonight." Jake looked at Charlie. "We could approach it from the bayou. No fence there. We used to fish that water near the house. All we do is look in those old buildings and leave. I didn't see any dogs."

Charlie wasn't convinced. "You sure about this, Jake? Seems risky without a warrant. I got plenty of trouble as it is."

"If you don't want to go, I'll get one of my deputies to help, but I'd rather they didn't know about it." Jake hesitated a moment, then added, "Wouldn't be setting a very good example. I guess I could go by myself."

Charlie thought it over some more. "It'd be worth it if we find a clue about what happened to my dad. What do I have to lose but my life? Hell, the kids are grown, the wife is gone. Why not? Sure, I'll go."

"Not the ringing vote of confidence I would have preferred, but I'll take a yes, however it comes."

"Can we eat first?" asked Charlie. "I'd rather die on a full stomach."

Delphine fixed meat loaf with butter beans and mashed potatoes. Charlie was thinking that if this were his last meal, at least it was a good one. Dessert was apple pie. Charlie and Jake had two pieces each. "You boys are mighty quiet. What's going on?"

"Going fishing. Hear they're biting good at night." Charlie almost choked on the mashed potatoes as he said it. "We'll have a big fish fry tomorrow."

Delphine raised an eyebrow and looked back and forth between the two men. Neither Charlie nor Jake would look back at her. "I know you aren't going fishing and I hope you aren't putting another cherry bomb under Mr. Watson's truck. He really will have a heart attack this time at his age. He needs a good six hours sleep while he's working." She stood there but they still didn't say anything. "You gonna tell me or just let me worry?"

"We'll be okay, Momma," said Jake. "We just can't tell you right now."

"Shuh," said Delphine as she shook her head and took dishes back to the sink. "Jake, you know if anything happens to you it will kill me, and no tellin' what it would do to Mary and Jeremiah. You two are up to no good. Fishing," she muttered, taking off her apron. "You shouldn't lie to me that way." Jake rolled his eyes and hugged his mom as they left.

CHAPTER EIGHT

WEDNESDAY NIGHT, JUNE 7

Dressed in black they drove in silence toward the camp. Charlie was looking out the window, then turned toward Jake and asked, "You sure about this? You know I'm not trained for this sort of thing. What do you expect to find?"

"Not sure," said Jake. "Maybe nothing, but something is going on, and there's a good chance it's connected to Doc's accident. Just seems like the next step. You with me?"

"Of course, but I do wish I'd paid more attention in basic training."

"This wasn't covered anyway, Charlie. Just stay close and be alert. We should be in and out quickly, and nobody'll ever know we were there."

Jake planned to go most of the way to Vidrine's by water, then walk through the swamp where the cypress trees could provide cover. The walk would be about thirty yards to land and then another thirty or so yards to the old house.

The moon was full with partial cloud cover, the bayou smooth and black except for the yellow trail left by the moon that seemed to point to where they were. Except for crickets and the occasional bullfrog, the night was eerily quiet. They rowed silently, trying not to make noise with the oars. Charlie was thinking he'd rather be operating all night than doing this.

The closer they got to the Vidrine property, the more anxious and shaky he became. Suddenly a large fish jumped out of the water right beside Charlie, re-entering the water with a loud splash, causing Charlie to rise six inches off his seat.

"Shit," Charlie murmured loudly enough to be heard in the next parish.

"Shh," whispered Jake, but his shoulders were shaking, trying so hard not to laugh out loud that he almost capsized the boat.

Jake almost had control when Charlie said "Shit!" again, causing a new fit of quiet but uncontrollable laughter. They sat there a few moments longer, the tension broken, then continued toward the cypress grove just this side of the old house. Clouds moved over the moon. The two fished there so much as kids, they knew instinctively where to go.

After tying the boat to a cypress tree, they eased themselves over the side. Water came to their waist; the bottom was mushy. Visibility was poor but sufficient.

"Seen any alligators around here lately?" Charlie whispered, looking around for eyes that might be looking back.

"There are a few, but it's cottonmouths I'm worried about." Jake was marching steadily on with Charlie close behind.

"Great," said Charlie. "Just great. Tell me again why we're doing this."

"One more time. We're trying to find out who tried to kill your dad and why."

"Right," said Charlie. "That's worth a snake bite, I guess, but could we walk a little faster?"

They reached dry land, stopped, and looked around. As noted from the air, there were no guards. When a cloud covered the moon, they made their way to the first outbuilding, the former kitchen. The door wasn't locked. In one corner of the large room was an industrial oven. The room was otherwise empty.

The big house was a short distance away. They ran to the back door. Jake picked the lock without difficulty and they went in. At first nothing seemed out of order, but in one room were large gas tanks of oxygen and nitrous oxide. Another room was equipped with medical supplies. What appeared to be an OR table, lights, and an anesthesia machine were in the dining room.

"Looks like Dr. Frankenstein's lab," commented Charlie. That's when they heard the dogs. They looked at each other. *Time to go.* They ran out the back door and headed toward the water. Jake ran for the cypress grove where they had come in. Charlie chose a shorter route directly to the water but with no concealing trees. The barking was getting louder and closer. His legs would not go any faster. The water was close, but maybe not close enough. Gunshot blasts sounded like bombs. A bullet whizzed by Charlie's right ear. A large Doberman was at his heel two steps from the bayou's edge. He dived like an Olympic swimmer, went under water, and swam several strokes toward deeper water. He heard other gunshots. After thirty seconds, his lungs bursting, his body hungering for a gasp of air, he was coming to the surface to take a breath when light shone on the water above him and he heard the dogs barking and splashing. Then there were more gunshots. The dogs thrashed about for what seemed like forever. One stepped on his leg, then retreated. The next time the light glare left the surface and all was again black, Charlie came up for air. He had no choice. The guards and dogs were going toward the cypress grove.

"I think I got him," he heard one guard say. "Where's the other?"

"He's out there under water. He can't stay under much longer. Let's make sure of this one now, then we can get the other. He can't hide long in open water. If we don't get him, the gators will."

Charlie eased the nine millimeter out of his shoulder holster and punched off the safety. He'd brought it unbeknownst to Jake. In the dark he eased toward the grove and toward Jake with just his head out of the water. The flashlight began to come his way again. He ducked under the water and waited until all was black, then continued toward the grove.

Suddenly the first guard yelled, "There he is," and fired three shots in rapid succession. Groans came from the grove. Charlie saw Jake behind a cypress tree, leaning against it and holding his left shoulder. Jake did not see Charlie. The guards were walking out toward Jake to finish him. Jake, considering his options, ran for the boat. The guards were in the water now closing in. There was no way Jake could make it to the boat.

"There he is. Shoot!" They each fired once before Charlie could get his gun up ready to fire. Charlie fired quickly, emptying the clip in the direction of the guards. Then he moved away before the guards aimed at the flashes. But they didn't fire. "I'm hit," said one guard. "Get me out of here."

Charlie couldn't see Jake. Was he dead under the water? *Oh, God. Let him be okay.* Charlie reached the trees, looked back, and saw the guards, one helping the other walk toward the house.

RENNIE HOWARD

"Charlie, here," Jake groaned. Charlie found him leaning back against a tree. "They got me."

"Where?" Charlie, relieved that Jake was alive and talking, thought he could fix anything else that might be hit.

"My left shoulder is all, but it hurts like a bitch."

Charlie got to him and shined the flashlight on his shoulder. An entrance and exit wound were evident at the base of his neck on his left shoulder. The bullet had entered the trapezius in back and exited above the clavicle, missing the major arteries and veins, but still bleeding from the front and back, while forming a large hematoma under the skin. Charlie took off his and Jake's stocking caps and fashioned a crude dressing over both wounds to hold pressure. He helped Jake back to the boat, got him in, and began paddling back toward the camp. They were almost around a bend when several other men appeared, shouting and shining flashlights out over the water and in the cypress grove. Charlie pulled over near the shore where thicker, taller brush gave better cover, and they crouched low in the boat out of sight.

"Did you get a look at them?" asked one voice.

"They were dressed in black, but I'd swear one was a white guy and one was black. Never got close enough to see faces." They looked around a while, then left. When they were far enough away, Charlie rowed until he was out of earshot, then started the electric motor and rode back to the camp.

Inside the camp house Charlie got a better look at Jake's wound. He had good pulses in his arm, and no loss of sensation or motor function. The hematoma was probably from muscle bleeders, which would stop on their own. He cleaned and dressed them with supplies Doc kept at the camp.

"Charlie, we gotta talk," said Jake, putting on dry clothes and looking at Charlie with an "oh shit" look on his face. "What do you think we should do?"

"Let's see what we got," Charlie said. "First, we were trespassing and also broke into and entered a posted house. Second, I shot a private guard who was doing his job. I may have killed him. At least we didn't steal anything." Jake failed to see the humor in that. "Why didn't you shoot back at them, Jake?"

"When I first hit the water, I tripped on a stump, hit a tree with my arm, and dropped my gun in the water. The dogs were coming fast enough, so I didn't try to find it in the muck. Then I saw them shooting at you and didn't see you surface, so I thought you were probably dead and they were coming after me. Say, I didn't know you took a gun."

"I thought you'd treat me like Andy did Barney and either not let me take one at all, or give me just one bullet, so I didn't tell you."

"I'm glad I didn't know, but seeing you come up out of the water and empty your gun on those guys was one of the prettiest sights I ever did see." Jake looked out the window at nothing in particular, wondering what to do next. "I guess we have to report this."

"Why?" asked Charlie. "They don't know who we were. If they report it to you, you can investigate. At least until we find out what is going on. If they don't report anything, that'll tell us something too. If they do, you'll have a reason to look at things in the daytime." Charlie then added, "And if that guard I shot dies, I hope that will be one killing that goes unsolved. Just sayin'."

Jake was quiet for a few moments. "How will I hide this wound?"

"Put on a neck brace. Tell anyone that asks you have a bad crick in your neck. Keep a dressing under it. I'll get a tetanus shot for you at Dad's office tomorrow and a dose of antibiotics. The ER wouldn't do anything more than that. Then let's just play it by ear. I don't think there is an instruction book for this circumstance."

"How do you feel about shooting that guy? In my twenty years of law enforcement, I have never shot or killed anyone. I've only had to pull my gun once."

"It hasn't sunk in yet, I guess. It felt like self-defense except that he wasn't shooting at me, he was shooting at you. Also, in my twenty years of practicing surgery, I probably have contributed to someone's demise, unintentionally of course, but they're still just as dead."

Jake looked strangely at Charlie. "Hadn't thought of it that way."

Delphine was waiting up when Charlie came in. "How'd it go?" she asked, standing with her hands on her hips and her head cocked to one side. Her question sounded more like an accusation than an inquiry.

"Okay," said Charlie, certainly not wanting to go into details. He preferred to let Jake tell his mother in the morning. "It's late so I dropped Jake off at his house. Good night, Delphine, I think I'll hit the sack."

"Charlie, you're not telling me everything. Is Jake okay?"

"He's fine. He hurt his shoulder, but it'll be okay."

Delphine thought that would have to do. There was probably more, but she'd find out tomorrow.

CHAPTER NINE

THURSDAY, JUNE 8

Charlie lay in bed and stared at the dark ceiling, unable to sleep. Not only was he wound up from the evening's events, but so many things had happened in the last three days that he couldn't organize it in his mind. It was as if he had been picked up by a tornado, whirled around, thrown about, and had no idea where it would put him down. Tomorrow he would go see his dad and meet his lawyer in New Orleans. Needing some help to relax, he went downstairs, poured a glass of bourbon, and sat in his dad's chair, hoping it would impart some wisdom. He drank some of the bourbon and fell asleep in the chair, spilling the rest on his sweatshirt. He dreamed of alligators and water moccasins. He heard a man scream and saw blood shooting out of his mouth. Then he was breaking into a house when the alarm went off. It kept ringing even though he ran out the door.

Slowly he awoke, realizing that the phone was ringing on the table beside the chair. Reaching for it he knocked the receiver off onto the floor. He retrieved it and said sleepily into the mouthpiece, "H-hello."

As his head cleared, he heard Jim's voice. "Charlie, you there?"

"Yeah, Jim, sorry. Guess I was in a deep sleep. If you

said anything already, you'll have to repeat it. I'm awake and listening."

"Got a problem here and I need your help. Somebody dropped off a man at the back door of the hospital and left. The guy has been shot in the abdomen and is too unstable to transfer. We can't find Kaiser and I promise I tried. Will you come have a look?"

"Be there in a minute." Charlie stumbled out of the chair, noting a wet spot on his sweatshirt. He ran upstairs, put his slacks and shoes on, got in the old jeep, and was at the ER in less than ten minutes.

A crowd had gathered outside the trauma room. X-ray was there to take portable films, as were the EKG and lab techs. One nurse was putting a Foley catheter in the patient's bladder, and Jim was starting a second IV. Charlie squeezed through. An ER nurse gave him a funny look as he went by. Charlie met the man's eyes. Thankfully, he showed no sign of recognition, but was breathing rapidly and looked scared to death. "How did you get shot?" asked Charlie.

"I work as a guard at Vidrine's. Couple men broke into the old house. Me and my partner went to check it out, and they started shooting at us."

Not exactly, thought Charlie, *but certainly no time to argue.* Charlie reached over and palpated the man's abdomen. He grimaced and went rigid, reaching to push Charlie's hand away. "Is the OR crew here?"

"We called them when we called you," Jim said as he was putting the dressing on the second IV. The x-ray tech came back with his abdominal film. The entrance wound was just to the left of and a little above the umbilicus. The bullet was also on his left side, the lateral film showing it embedded in a large back muscle.

"You need an operation to fix whatever the bullet damaged. The incision will be down the middle from here to here." Charlie pointed to two places above and below the umbilicus, indicating the incision would be about eight inches long.

"I don't care where you make it or how long it is. Just fix it. I can't take this pain." The man looked pleadingly at Charlie and grabbed his wrist. "And please hurry. Don't let me die."

While anesthesia was putting the man to sleep, Charlie was scrubbing his hands, thinking it was a helluva way to get cases, maybe a first but, in this particular situation, not reportable. *If he dies, I could be charged with murder—attempted murder with the gunshot and finishing him off at surgery.* Charlie wondered what the charge might be if he lived. Add that question to all the others. Right now he had to concentrate only on performing a good operation; then the chips would just have to fall.

After the patient was prepped and draped, Charlie made the long midline incision. There were blood and bowel contents free in the peritoneal cavity. Charlie eviscerated the bowel, then followed the bullet track. It went through the left colon mesentery, missing the colon. He elevated the colon over to view the retroperitoneum. The bullet was below the left kidney and had barely missed the ureter. There was a hematoma where the bullet was imbedded in the back muscle, but it was not actively bleeding and the hematoma was not expanding. He would deal with the bullet issue later. There were six holes in the small bowel. These were debrided and sutured closed with single layers of silk suture. One mesenteric bleeder required a suture ligature. He then irrigated the peritoneal cavity with two liters of normal saline. The patient was doing well.

Now about the bullet. Ordinarily one would not bother to remove the bullet if it were not easily accessible. If he removed it, it would be evidence and the ballistics would be checked and matched. If he left it in, it might be removed if the man didn't make it and be used as evidence. Maybe he could remove it and throw it deep into the bayou. He looked back at the hole. He put his finger in the hole to see if he could feel it. He couldn't. Removing it would cause more damage than leaving it. Medically, leaving it was the right thing to do. Decision made. He left it as he always had before. Charlie returned the intestine to the peritoneal cavity, arranged it in an orderly fashion, closed the fascia with a large nylon suture and the skin with staples. He thanked everyone for their help again and went to the recovery room to dictate the operative note and write post-op orders. He looked to see if anyone was in the family area to hear about the operation, but nobody was. The clock read 0400. Sleep had been hard to come by lately.

Charlie made it home by four thirty and slept until six. Scrambled eggs, bacon, and toast with mayhaw jelly were waiting when he went downstairs.

"So, what did y'all find that was so important, riskin' your lives like that?" Delphine still wasn't happy.

"Not sure, Delphine. I know. It might not have been the smartest thing we ever did." He was glad Delphine didn't know the half of it. She was still quiet when he left for the hospital.

Beau was dressed and ready to go. The IV had been discontinued. Ellie was there, although she had spent the night at home. "It's okay for him to shower with that dressing on. Just

leave it on and I'll come by next week and take out his stitches."
He walked with them to the front door, Beau in a wheelchair
per hospital policy. "I'll give warning before I come by, but call
if you have any problems or questions before then. You still
have my cell number?"

"I have it," said Ellie. "You think you might check on him
sooner?" She smiled at him teasingly.

"I'd feel a lot better if I saw it again the next day or two.
I'm going to New Orleans this morning on business and to
check on Dad, but I'll call tomorrow."

Beau, listening to this conversation, said, "Dr. Leveau, we
have a game tonight. I know I can't play, but would it be all
right to go?" He looked hopefully at Charlie. "We're facing this
pitcher who is almost unhittable. He's got a ninety-mile-per-
hour fastball and a curve that falls off a table."

"Sure, I don't have a problem with that. I'd like to see him
pitch myself if he's that good. What time is the game?" Charlie
hadn't seen a good baseball game in a long time.

"Starts at seven thirty."

"If I get back from New Orleans in time, I'll see you there."
He waved as they drove away, then went to the ICU to check
on his patient.

"He's been very stable, Dr. Leveau," said the nurse. "His
urine output is good, and he is waking up. He pushes the PCA
pain pump regularly, and it seems to control the pain." She
walked over to the patient's bedside and pulled back the covers. "He has some bleeding on his dressing that has been there
since he came in from the recovery room. I drew a line where
it was, and it hasn't gotten bigger."

"Thanks," said Charlie. "I'll be in New Orleans for most of

the day. I don't expect him to have any problems. I'd like him to get out of bed at least in the chair today and walk some if possible. You have my cell number if you have any questions, and please don't hesitate to call."

Charlie walked to the cafeteria to get a cup of coffee. Dr. Kaiser was sitting at a table in the corner eating breakfast. Charlie walked over with his coffee and sat down opposite him, thinking he would ask about Dr. Solomon's patient. "Hi, I'm Charlie Leveau. Been looking forward to meeting you."

"That right?" Dr. Kaiser looked up briefly but continued to eat his breakfast, annoyed that his quiet time had been interrupted.

Not really, thought Charlie. "Have you enjoyed being in Bayou Belle?" he asked, trying to find a way to break the ice.

"It's okay." Dr. Kaiser was not an accomplished conversationalist.

"I heard you came here by way of Africa." Charlie thought he might get more of a response.

"That's right." He reached for the beeper on his belt. "It's the nurse on the floor. Better get to rounds. Good to meet you." He left his sausage and eggs only half eaten.

It was time to leave for New Orleans. Charlie didn't want to be late. He would have to apologize to Dr. Solomon for not getting to ask about his patient. Hopefully, Dr. Solomon had been able to arrange a transfer.

CHAPTER TEN

THURSDAY, JUNE 8

Charlie arrived just before noon in front of Brennan's after a two-hour drive from Bayou Belle, wearing comfortable slacks, loafers, and a purple polo shirt. Linda George arrived two minutes later, carrying a briefcase almost as big as she was and wearing a business suit that easily distinguished her from the tourists. They were seated at a table for two in a private section.

"I know you haven't reviewed this. I'll drink my coffee while you look it over." She handed him a thick chart and reached for the sugar and cream.

Charlie read through the double-spaced document quickly, skipping to what was alleged in the complaint. The incident began to come back to him as he read.

He had been consulted by an OB-Gyn to place a subclavian IV in a pregnant woman suffering from hyperemesis gravidarum, which is extreme nausea and persistent vomiting during pregnancy that can lead to severe dehydration. She had been vomiting so much that she was not only dehydrated; she was hypotensive, disoriented, combative, and in grave danger of losing her baby and her own life. Her veins were so collapsed the nurses were unable to start a peripheral IV. With the patient thrashing around seizure-like in bed, Charlie was able by some miracle to find and stick her right subclavian vein after several tries. Saline was flowing through it easily, and there was a good blood return. Charlie remembered being pleased and greatly relieved. A portable chest film showed that instead of going into the superior vena cava as intended, it had crossed over into the smaller left subclavian vein. The patient was already being rehydrated and her baby would be safe. Trying to relocate it would risk pulling it out and not being able to restart it.

Charlie had made the conscious decision to leave it alone, thankful that under the circumstances he hadn't caused a collapsed lung. A few weeks later, the patient delivered a healthy baby girl. Two weeks after the baby was born, the patient came to the hospital complaining of left shoulder pain and a swollen left arm. Venous studies revealed a clot in her left subclavian vein, assumed, probably correctly, to have been caused by the catheter that Charlie had placed. Charlie had not been consulted about the clot and was not aware it happened. She was instead admitted to the vascular service, where she received anticoagulation therapy and antibiotics. The offending clot dissolved, her arm returned to normal size with treatment, and after a few days she was discharged home to her husband and healthy baby. She had suffered no long-term consequences of the phlebitis. She was suing because of pain, suffering, and the inconvenience of having to be hospitalized away from her family all because of a misplaced catheter. After reading the complaint, he handed the document back across the table to Ms. George.

"What do you think?" she asked.

"I can't believe it," said Charlie. "I mean, her life and that of her baby were saved by the IV fluids. Then she gets a complication that completely resolves, and she sues for pain and suffering. If you ask me, she experienced a lot less pain and suffering than she would have at her baby's funeral. I really just can't believe it."

"Well, it's true," replied Ms. George matter-of-factly. "She sees a chance to make some money to pay for her baby. Her lawyer tells her it won't cost you anything; that your insurance will pay and he won't collect any money from her unless he wins the case." She looked down at her food for a moment, then looked back up at Charlie, who was shaking his head, his lip tight. "And, Dr. Leveau," she added, "I have to tell you, she has a case."

"Seriously?" asked Charlie.

"I know you have a lot going on right now. This would not be a high-dollar settlement, and you could put this one thing behind you by offering a deal."

Charlie couldn't believe what he was hearing, yet Ms. George looked very serious. "Why would I even consider settling if I did nothing wrong and, in fact, did a great job saving two lives with one IV under very difficult circumstances?"

Ms. George answered, "I have represented many doctors facing malpractice suits. Most are settled for a lot less than originally demanded, and there are some incentives to settle." Charlie could hardly sit still. "One, it won't make the newspaper, and if the settlement is as low as I would expect it to be, it might not be reported to the National Data Bank."

"I would never settle something like this," argued Charlie. "The whole malpractice crisis has been financed by exorbitant malpractice premiums, then doctors settling frivolous claims to keep their names off the news." Charlie hesitated, then looked Ms. George squarely in the eye, making sure he had her full attention. "I definitely will not settle. The question is, are you prepared to represent me, or do I need to request another lawyer?" Charlie was rising out of his chair as if ready to leave before eating his lunch.

"Hold on now, Dr. Leveau." Ms. George held up her hand to get Charlie to slow down. When it looked like he had cooled off enough to hear what she had to say, she continued. "I had to ask the question and give you the option. It's part of my job, informed consent, if you will. I should also tell you that I showed the x-rays to a young staff surgeon at Baylor Hospital, and he said that it was wrong to leave the catheter where you did."

"Ordinarily, I wouldn't leave it there either, but under the same circumstances, even if I knew she would develop phlebitis, I would do exactly the same thing again." Charlie's voice was rising as he spoke. Restaurant patrons glanced in their direction, probably thinking the two were having a lover's quarrel.

"That is exactly what I wanted to hear you say," stated Ms. George. "We will fight this together, and I think we have a good chance to win. We'll need a credible expert to agree with us. You might be thinking of someone you know who would be good. Their expert's deposition is here in New Orleans next week. You are welcome to attend if you would like."

"Wouldn't miss it," said Charlie. "Who is their expert?"

"He is an older surgeon who learned central line placement in the army. He has a private practice at Touro Infirmary, and his office is on St. Charles Street near Tulane. I'll let you know more details when I know them." They finished the rest of their meal. Ms. George got out her credit card, but Charlie insisted on picking up the tab. Had he known how much her law firm was likely to make from his insurance company for defending him, he would have let her pay, then stayed for dinner.

After lunch, he went to see his dad. The LSU Medical Center was on Perdido Street across from the old residence hall where Charlie and Jan had lived during medical school, located on the former site of the Jolly Bunch Social and Pleasure Club and Busy Bee Saloon. Jazz funerals, returning from the cemetery, accompanied by a Dixieland band and dancing mourners twirling parasols would end at the Jolly Bunch, and the party would begin in earnest. Charlie went to the neurosurgery ICU and was directed to his dad's room. Doc's eyes were closed and he lay still with an endotracheal tube in place and a ventilator controlling his respirations.

"Why does he still need to be intubated?" Charlie asked the nurse. "Is he still that unconscious after surgery? I thought he was getting better."

The nurse replied, "He was beginning to come around, but his oxygen levels haven't. He still needs ventilator support."

"Why?" asked Charlie. "He doesn't smoke and he's never had any trouble with his lungs."

"I heard the doctors talking about him on rounds today. They think he aspirated. His x-ray shows a pattern like aspiration pneumonia. We can't get his O2 over ninety percent when he breathes on his own even with forty percent oxygen running."

"So is his unconscious state due to his head injury or the sedation required for the ventilator?" Charlie had been encouraged by Dr. Janetta's report but was now as worried about his dad's lungs as he was his brain. The nurse didn't know the answer. He spent the rest of the afternoon at his dad's bedside, again sleeping in the chair.

Later that afternoon, Dr. Janetta came in, followed by an entourage of medical students. After examining Doc Leveau and looking at his chart, he said to Charlie, "I think he'll wake up when we are able to get him off the ventilator." Then he went on to explain, "It's impossible to say right now how much deficit he will have, but I continue to be optimistic. Some of the best pulmonologists in the city are on consult. We'll just have to wait and see."

Charlie felt somewhat better after talking to Dr. Janetta because of his optimism, which Charlie thought was real and his expertise obvious. It would be days before they would know more. He couldn't do anything more, so he headed back to Bayou Belle. His dad hadn't even known he was there.

As Charlie was getting on the elevator to leave, Vinnie, dressed in scrubs and a lab coat, was getting off.

CHAPTER ELEVEN

THURSDAY NIGHT, JUNE 8

Approaching Bayou Belle, Charlie saw lights on at the baseball field. Hungry, not having eaten since lunch, he drove toward the lights, hoping the concession stand still served the same hot dogs. It did. The scoreboard indicated the game was in the third inning and scoreless. He walked to the fence along the third baseline to watch while he devoured a hot dog and a Coke. The pitcher for the visiting team looked unhittable. But after watching two innings and gulping down another hot dog, he had him figured out. He walked toward the bleachers and ran into Billy Jack.

"Glad you made it. It's still nothing to nothing." He pointed up in the stands. "Beau and Ellie are up there. I'm going for a hot dog. Want one?" Charlie thanked him but said he'd already had a couple. Billy Jack nodded toward the field. "Beau's team is missing his bat. Come on up and sit with us."

Charlie sat between Beau and Billy Jack, Ellie on the other side of Beau. "We have never been able to beat this pitcher," said Beau. "Already has a scholarship to LSU next year. I was looking forward to this game, but this way I'll have a few less strikeouts and a better batting average."

"You can hit this guy." Charlie pointed at the pitcher. "He tells you what he is throwing."

"What do you mean?" Beau looked doubtful.

"He calls his own game," explained Charlie. "Watch. If he shakes off a sign, he throws a curve. If he doesn't, he comes with his fastball. Just watch."

"That helps," replied Beau, "but you still can't hit that curve, even if you know it's coming."

"Just watch," said Charlie again. "He hardly ever throws the curve for a strike. Your guys are swinging at bad pitches. If you know a curve is coming, decide ahead of time you're going to take the pitch, even if it comes in for a strike. Wait for the fastball, which he throws when he doesn't shake off a sign."

Beau watched closely the next inning. He caught on and a light came on in his eyes and a smile graced his face. "Excuse me," he said and went down to the fence and motioned for Jeremiah to come over. Charlie saw them talking.

Ellie asked, "Charlie, what did you tell him?"

"I'll let him tell you. Let's see what happens." Charlie smiled. Ellie smiled back, but for some reason looked uneasy.

It was the bottom of the last inning and Jeremiah was up first. The score was still zero to zero. The visiting team had left many runners on base, but their pitcher was pitching a no-hitter. Jeremiah was a good fastball hitter. He also could hit the ball a long way. His problem was the curve. Beau was on the edge of his seat. The next inning his team would have to go with a relief pitcher who threw batting practice speed. They had to do something this inning. The opposing pitcher had gotten stronger with each inning and showed no signs of tiring.

Before taking his place in the batter's box, Jeremiah looked up at Beau and gave him a thumbs-up sign. The pitcher shook off a sign, then threw a curve ball that hit in front of home plate. Jeremiah took it, making the count one ball, no strikes. The pitcher didn't shake off a sign, and the next pitch was a fastball that came in high and inside, brushing Jeremiah back from the plate. The count was 2-0. Jeremiah stepped out of the batter's box and rubbed some dirt on his hands and bat, then stepped back in to the batter's box. The pitcher shook off another sign. This time the curve came over for a strike. Jeremiah took it. Count 2-1. Again, the pitcher shook off a sign, but this time the curve hit in front of the plate. Jeremiah took it, never getting the bat off his shoulder. The count was now 3-1. Surely the next pitch would be a fastball. Sure enough, the pitcher did not shake off a sign, and Jeremiah was ready. The fastball came down the middle about waist high. Jeremiah had it timed, and it was like watching in slow motion. Making a now familiar metallic sound striking the aluminum bat, the ball sailed 400 feet over the centerfield fence for a walk-off home run. The pitcher never looked back, just walked toward the dugout with his head down. Beau jumped so high when Jeremiah hit the ball that he grabbed his right side. Ellie frowned. Charlie gave her a reassuring glance.

When Jeremiah was rounding third, Billy Jack leaned over and said to Charlie, "I need to talk to you after the game. It's important."

"All right," said Charlie. "Everything okay?"

"Don't leave without talking to me."

"I won't." Charlie wondered what BJ had on his mind and worried that he might not want to know.

Jeremiah and Beau were whooping it up and went with some other teammates to the A&W root beer stand to celebrate. Ellie worried about letting him go, but Charlie said it was fine. She didn't say much as they walked to his car, where Billy Jack was waiting. They all got in the Wagoneer, Charlie and Ellie in front, and Billy Jack in back.

"Charlie, we got trouble." Billy Jack jumped right to the point.

"What's that," asked Charlie, trying to look unconcerned, but not succeeding.

"I was on my porch last night and heard a lot of shooting down the bayou. A little later you and Jake pulled up to your camp in Doc's boat. You helped Jake out and took him in. The lights came on and stayed on for about half an hour. This morning at Julius', Jake came in for his coffee wearing a neck brace and looking like warmed-over shit. He told us there had been a break-in at Vidrine's and one of their guards was shot. He went on to say that you had been called in and operated on the fellow. He said it looked like the patient would be okay and that he was on his way to Vidrine's to investigate. Before I left to go to the game this evening, Julius called and told me that a nurse from the hospital had come in and announced that the man died."

Charlie's mouth dropped open as he jerked his head toward Billy Jack. "What?" He couldn't process it. "Why? How? That doesn't make any sense. Tell me what you know." Ellie remained quiet and just looked at Charlie.

Billy Jack continued. "He must have gone bad in the intensive care unit. Kaiser rushed him back to the operating room, and he died during surgery. The word is he bled to death because you missed an aortic injury. Ruben Martin has been looking for you. Just wanted to give you a warning." Ellie was still just looking, waiting for Charlie to comment on what her dad had said.

"I don't know what to say," said Charlie, feeling like he might lose the hot dogs. "Something very strange is going on here in Bayou Belle. Jake thinks Dad was assaulted, that his head injury was no accident. We were trying to find out more when things got out of hand. I'm in a lot more trouble than I bargained for, or that I ever imagined could happen. But I promise both of you, I have not intentionally done anything wrong, and my patient did not have an aortic injury."

"Charlie," said Billy Jack, "Doc hinted to us that he was on to something but was still trying to get information and wasn't ready to say. He may have found out more and that's why they got him. You could be in danger too."

"Come home with me, Charlie." Ellie reached over and put her hand on his forearm. "I have a couch in the parlor. You can sleep there and nobody will know where you are. Leave your car here. We'll get it in the morning."

Charlie didn't want to involve Ellie, but she was persistent, as was Billy Jack.

When they were in Ellie's car, she looked over at Charlie and asked again, "Just what is going on?"

He might as well tell her. She would just keep asking, and besides, he wanted to tell someone. "When Jake came and got me yesterday, he showed me evidence that Dad's fall had not been an accident. There was also evidence that someone from Vidrine's may have done it. We flew over the company yesterday to see where planes had been flying in and out. Then we went back last night without a warrant to see what was in the old buildings. Well, we got caught. We were running to get away when they started shooting. Jake was hit and dropped his gun. One of the guards was aiming at him, about to fire again, when I started shooting at him. The guard went down, his partner ran, and Jake and I rowed back to the camp." He went on to tell her about getting called by Jim to help with the gunshot victim. "I operated on him knowing of course that I was the one who shot him. There was no aortic injury. The tract of the bullet didn't go close. I looked at the aorta. It wasn't hit." He then said with less confidence, "I think I'll be able to clear that up in the morning."

Ellie parked under her carport and they went in through the back door into the kitchen. She apologized for the dirty dishes in the sink from dinner just before she and Beau left for the game. The house looked like Ellie. It was bright and open, with white kitchen cabinets and a small butcher block table with two chairs. She led him into a cozy parlor. Charlie looked around while Ellie went for a blanket and pillow. The sofa looked comfortable if not quite long enough. It was arranged with two chairs facing the television. An Audubon print of a large white crane decorated one wall, and a bookshelf on another wall contained many recent best sellers and several family photographs. Charlie was looking at the pictures when Ellie came back in with the blanket. "That's a picture of our family just a month before Clay died," she said as she put the pillow down and walked into the kitchen. Charlie was still looking at the picture, thinking what a beautiful family it had been and how much Beau looked like his father when Ellie came back in with a bottle of wine and two glasses.

They sat on the sofa. Charlie uncorked the wine and generously poured two glasses of Pinot Noir. "What'll you do? I mean, breaking and entering, burglary, trespassing, use of a gun while committing a felony, and now maybe murder. Maybe you should clear out of here for a while and hide."

"I can't do that." Charlie sat staring straight ahead, slowly shaking his head in disbelief. "No, I just can't do that. I need to know what happened to my dad. For what it is worth, our main law enforcement officer was with me, and he will be in charge of the investigation. That should allow a little time to dig into this further if somebody doesn't kill me first."

They talked about all sorts of possibilities, none of which sounded plausible, and then discussed more pleasant things, like what had happened to old friends they both knew and where they were now. They were finishing their second glass of wine when Ellie said, "Charlie, thanks for trusting me and telling me what happened. I'm on your side and you know I'll help any way I can." She stood up to leave. Charlie, the gentleman, stood also. She came over and hugged him. The hug lasted longer than friendly allowed. They looked at each other for a long moment without saying a word when the front door flew open and Beau came through it.

"Charlie is sleeping here on the couch tonight." Ellie's face was red and her words were awkward. "His a-air-conditioning isn't working"

"Cool," said Beau. "Man, did Jeremiah hit that ball or what? It was still going up when it cleared the fence. I just hope nobody tells the guy we figured him out. Thanks, Dr. Leveau. Mom, anything to eat?"

"I bet I can find something." She smiled with relief at Charlie and went to the kitchen to fix a sandwich.

Beau sat down in the chair across from Charlie and they replayed the game. Ellie let Beau eat his sandwich in the living room. Then they all agreed that it was getting late and time for bed. Ellie and Beau turned in, but Charlie couldn't sleep. His mind went back over the laparotomy on the guard. Could he have missed an injury? Anybody is capable of making a mistake. Doubt began to creep in. An hour later he was convinced that he had missed an injury. The jury would think he had missed it on purpose. When he finally dropped off to sleep, he dreamed he was in the operating room and everything he touched bled. He couldn't stop it. Then he was trying to run from someone, but his legs wouldn't move. He awoke with a start, concerned that he may have yelled out in his sleep. It was three o'clock before he was able to rest.

CHAPTER TWELVE

FRIDAY, JUNE 9

Charlie woke up wondering for a second where he was. The smell of coffee brewing drew him to the kitchen, where Ellie, in her bathrobe, was cooking bacon and eggs.

"Good morning. Sleep well?" she asked.

"I did." Charlie didn't see any point in recounting his nightmares. He was glad that she hadn't bothered to put on makeup or fix her hair. She was a dream, the kind he preferred over the ones from the night before. He walked over and without thinking about it put his arm around her shoulder and gave it a squeeze. "Hope you're not fixing this breakfast for me."

She looked back over her shoulder and up at him. "Don't flatter yourself. There's a teenager who'll be here in a minute. I swear he has a hollow leg. Pour yourself some coffee. Milk's in the fridge." She motioned with her head toward the refrigerator as she turned the bacon. Charlie was on his second cup when Beau came in yawning and stretching, gave his mom a kiss on the cheek, said "Morning" to Charlie, dished up his bacon and eggs, and poured himself a glass of milk. The morning conversation was again about baseball and the result of last night's St. Louis Cardinal game.

After breakfast, Ellie took Charlie to his car and he drove home to clean up. As he turned in to his driveway he noticed a Ford sedan parked down the street in front of a house for sale. A man was sitting in it, looking at Charlie. Once inside, Charlie went to a front window to get a better look at the man and the car, but they were gone.

Putting it out of his mind, he showered, shaved, and drove to the hospital, intending to clear his name. Charlie went first to the ICU. The shift had just changed. The nurse who had been taking care of the guard who died was back at work. She tried to avoid Charlie and called the supervisor to come to her rescue.

"I want to know what happened." Charlie was frustrated by their reluctance to talk to him. The nurse supervisor said to Charlie, "These nurses are busy and need to be taking care of their sick patients. You will have to talk to administration."

"Administration doesn't have a clue what happened. Why are you all stonewalling me?" Charlie stalked away, slammed through the automatic doors before they had time to open, and moved in a run toward the operating suite, the supervisor right behind.

"Dr. Leveau." The supervisor was trying to catch up.

Charlie stopped and turned around. She almost ran into him.

"What?!" He could barely contain his anger.

"Come with me." She walked ahead of him to an empty patient room down the hall from the nurse's station. She opened the door to the room for him to enter, then looked back down the hall to see if anyone had seen them go in. "Sit down for a minute, cool off, and listen to me."

Charlie sat, but he wasn't cooling. "I just want to know what happened to my patient. I operated on him and fully expected him to do well. I wouldn't have left town otherwise.

Everyone's being so obtuse."

The nurse went to the door and looked out again. Satisfied that they were alone, she sat opposite Charlie in a straight-back chair. Holding her clipboard in both arms against her chest, she leaned forward and said after glancing at the door one last time, "We have all been instructed not to talk to you. I'm surprised you got this far. Word is that they're waiting for you to arrive to fire you. If Ruben Martin knew that I was talking to you, I would be summarily dismissed. So I just have a minute to talk."

Charlie was all ears. "I'm listening."

"Yesterday, your patient was doing well. You were gone, so Kaiser said he was supposed to check on him. He went in your patient's room and in a minute came running back out. When he took the dressing off, he found the wound had opened and the man was losing a lot of blood. Before the lab tech could get there, your patient went into shock. Kaiser rushed him to the operating room. He found an aortic injury that you missed. The poor patient bled to death before Dr. Kaiser could get control." She went back to the door one more time to look down the hall. "You need to talk to the OR nurse, but they also were told not to talk. Rumor has it you had been drinking and botched the case. They don't want lawsuits against the hospital, and we can't bring the patient back, so they just want you gone. That's the gist of it."

"Thanks for telling me," Charlie said sincerely. "I won't tell anyone that you talked to me."

"I need my job, but something isn't right. I've been a nurse a long time. None of this smells right. They're waiting for you in Martin's office, just so you know." She took one more look out the door, nodded at Charlie, and left.

Charlie walked to the OR. He was told that the nurse who helped Dr. Kaiser do the re-operation had the day off. The anesthetist involved was in a case and couldn't be disturbed. Charlie gave the OR supervisor his cell number and asked her to give it to the anesthetist and have him call. She said she would. He knew she wouldn't.

Time to face the music. The door to Martin's office was open. Charlie walked in. Seated around Martin's desk were Martin, Hubert Polk, and Dr. Kaiser. They all remained seated. Charlie took the offensive. Pointing his finger at Kaiser, he asked, "Why the hell would you operate on my patient without calling or consulting me?" He glared at Kaiser, waiting for him to look away. "That's a serious ethics violation." It sounded lame, but it was the best Charlie could come up with.

Remaining seated and calmly looking back at Charlie, Kaiser replied, "The man was dying. He was bleeding to death and needed my help. There was no time to call, and the nurse said you were out of town anyway. Wouldn't you have done the same thing?" He sneered at Charlie. "And speaking of ethics, why did you leave town with a critically ill patient in the hospital and no coverage?"

Ruben Martin piped in. "We aren't here to discuss Dr. Kaiser. We are here to talk about you. So I will make this short and simple, Dr. Leveau. Your services are no longer required at Bayou Belle hospital. As a matter of fact, your privileges were over before you botched the operation."

Showing great restraint, Charlie stood still and listened, thinking to himself, *Steady now, just stay calm and listen to all of it before you respond.*

Hubert shifted uncomfortably in his seat.

"We have here a notice indicating that you are being sued for malpractice in Texas. You withheld this information from us when we granted you temporary privileges. We also hear that your wife is divorcing you because you have a drinking problem." Charlie started to object, but Martin held up his hand. "Let me finish. Last evening you operated without hospital consent on a patient, missing a major blood vessel injury. As a result that patient is now dead. If that were not enough, word is that there was a strong smell of alcohol on your person when you came in to see the patient. The very idea of operating on a patient in a drunken state is unconscionable." Ruben Martin was gloating, sure he had slammed the Bayou Belle door closed on another Dr. Leveau, but he went on. "Then you drive off to New Orleans on a personal matter, leaving a critically ill patient uncovered, and have the audacity to attend a baseball game before checking on that patient when you get back to town."

"Are you finished?" Charlie looked at Kaiser. "As you know, I was not on call and operated only because Dr. Kaiser could not be found. You should also know that the patient did not have an aortic injury. I dissected the entire aorta along the bullet tract, and the bullet didn't come close. So," he said, looking directly at Kaiser, "you are lying, you lowlife son of a bitch." Charlie was so angry tears were in his eyes and he was having trouble catching his breath. "You killed him, and I will prove it at the postmortem exam. When will that be?" He looked at Ruben. "He's surely a medical examiner case, and I would like to be present at the autopsy." Charlie had them now.

Ruben smiled his evil smile. "Dr. Kaiser is the medical

examiner in Dr. Leveau's absence. His operation sufficed as the postmortem exam. The body has already been cremated. The family did not want to see it in its mutilated condition. Just so you know, if the family sues, the hospital will take their side to keep from being named as a co-defendant." Then he added unnecessarily, "You'll be all on your own with this one."

Charlie was stunned; it was like being hit by a 300-pound tackle. He backed up, sat down in a straight-back chair, and looked at Hubert. Hubert looked down, not wanting to meet Charlie's eyes. The superior, gloating look on Ruben's face made it impossible to take. "I see" was all Charlie said. Anything else would have sounded defensive. They had all the cards. He got up and turned to leave, but Martin wasn't finished.

"We are obligated to report all this information to the state medical board and national data bank. You'll never be able to apply anywhere else without divulging the entire story. You will also have to enter an alcohol rehab program if you ever hope to practice surgery again."

It was the smirk on Martin's face that caused Charlie to snap. He had started to leave but turned back at the door, and when he saw it he broke in a run toward Martin, murder in his heart. He was about to leap across Martin's desk when the huge form of Hubert Polk stepped in the way. "Hold it, Charlie. Don't make it worse."

It may have been the best legal advice that Hubert Polk had ever given. Charlie stopped, his heart pounding in his chest. He might one day be thankful to Hubert, but all he felt now was hatred mixed with embarrassment, hurt, and pure un-adulterated rage.

Charlie shook himself off, stared at Ruben Martin, and

said, "For whatever reason, you have it in for me. I haven't fig-ured it out yet, but I will. You may have won today, but you've begun something that one way or another I will finish."

"You all heard him. Is that a threat from the good doctor?" Ruben laughed, still sneering at Charlie.

"Call it what you want," said Charlie. "I'd consider it more a statement of purpose." He continued. "And don't worry about your back. When you get yours, you'll know where it came from." He looked at Dr. Kaiser. "I hope your surgical judgment improves, because right now it's no better than your choice of friends." Then looking at Hubert, he said, "Thanks for protect-ing me from myself." With that he turned and this time made it out the door without looking back.

Charlie walked to Julius'. Billy Jack was there sitting with Mr. Julius. Charlie signaled for a cup of coffee and slumped in a chair at their table. "I walked here from Ruben Martin's of-fice." He lamented, "I think I miss my dad more now than ever. I was already in the toilet, and Ruben Martin just flushed it."

"What in the world happened?" Mr. Julius looked concerned.

"They say I missed an aortic injury and the patient bled to death. I know I didn't miss an injury like that, but who would believe it? They cremated the man before a post was done, counting his second operation as the autopsy." Charlie was staring at his shoes, shoulders slumped.

The group was quiet for once, not knowing what to say. Pete Charlet finally asked, "Could you have missed the injury?" Upset with himself for asking, he quickly added, "Or is there another reason for him to bleed like that, like maybe a blood clotting problem?"

Charlie looked up at the group: All were staring back at him. He could sense they were thinking that he had screwed up and wouldn't admit it. "I think Kaiser murdered him." It sounded ridiculous and Charlie immediately regretted saying it.

"Well, somebody shot him," Mr. Julius said. "Do they have any idea who it was?"

Billy Jack spoke up, protecting Charlie. "Jake is conducting the investigation. From what he told me, there aren't any clues yet." Then he changed the subject to the ballgame the night before. "Jeremiah knocked that ball a country mile. He was waiting for that fastball and caught it perfectly. Charlie, you got credit for the win."

That's life, thought Charlie. *One gets both undeserved credit and blame.* His cell phone rang, a Riverton number showing on the dial. "Hello."

"Charlie, it's Harry Morris. I have divorce papers from Jan's attorney in Houston. For some reason, they're in a hurry to get this done. When can you come by the office?"

Charlie explained that he was in Bayou Belle seeing about his dad but could be there tomorrow. They made an appointment for ten o'clock, giving Charlie time to make an early morning flight. Tomorrow was Saturday, but Harry agreed to see him before his tee time.

The cell rang again. Thinking Harry had forgotten to tell him something, he picked it up and said, "Yeah?"

"You are a dead man." The voice was as menacing as the words. "You killed my brother. I'm warning you because I want you to worry and have to look over your shoulder. I won't make you wait long." Then he repeated, "You are a dead man," and hung up.

CHAPTER THIRTEEN

FRIDAY, JUNE 9

Charlie walked back to the hospital, peeking around every corner and looking behind him every few seconds to be sure he was not being followed. A strange car came down the street when he was halfway to the hospital, and Charlie ducked behind a tree, imagining a machine gun coming out of the car window and spraying a barrage of bullets in his direction. The car, carrying a family of five, passed without incident. He made it to his car, drove home, and made sure all the doors and windows were locked, then called Jake to report the threat. He cleaned and reloaded his gun, then lay down and took a nap. He got up to eat supper before going to the town hall meeting, more determined than ever to make an appearance and show he hadn't been scared off. He would try not to look as jumpy as he felt.

The courtroom was full. People were standing along the sides. A few who couldn't get in milled around outside. Charlie sat near the back next to Jim and Betty. Jake was standing in front, like a bailiff, to maintain order. Concerned citizens carried signs, some dignified, some not. "Keep Local Control," "Don't let them steal our hospital," "Great Northern Sucks," "Great Northern is an Oxymoron." One hundred and fifty years later, for some the Civil War had never ended.

Ruben Martin and Hubert Polk entered from the judge's chambers and took their places behind a table set with microphones. They were greeted with applause and several boos. Hubert banged down the gavel and the noise increased. Raucous laughter issued from a back corner. Jake stood in front and raised his hands. He pointed a big finger at a couple of noisemakers and the auditorium quieted.

Hubert called the meeting to order, then gave a canned spiel about the benefits of a new full-service hospital that would be owned and run by Great Northern. He introduced Ruben Martin, who pointed out in a very organized and convincing way that small hospitals all over the country were finding it advisable to join with larger hospital groups to insure future viability. Ruben seemed extremely confident, spoke clearly, and had the crowd in the palm of his hands. He explained well how many small hospitals that remained independent had fallen on hard times and were eventually taken over out of necessity rather than choice. Those hospitals and communities didn't get as good a deal. He pointed out that Bayou Belle Hospital was still very healthy and could demand a good price. The community would also benefit from all that a larger hospital system could offer.

The mayor, Dave Abernathy, then spoke on behalf of Great Northern and how much better the hospital would be for the town as it grew. Marie Bond, president of the hospital auxiliary, carried on for a few minutes about how good the local hospital was and how much had been spent on a recent renovation that would now be wasted. Loss of local control was emphasized as a major deterrent to a takeover. The takeover crowd seemed to be carrying the night when Tom Bradshaw stood, turned toward Charlie with an apologetic look on his face, and said, "I think we should hear from Dr. Charlie Leveau. He practices at a hospital in Texas that was recently acquired by a large hospital corporation. He can give us some perspective on what we might expect to happen."

Charlie reluctantly stood and addressed the gathering. "There are good and bad things about joining with a large corporation, but in my opinion and in the opinion of all the doctors in Riverton, Texas, the bad things outweigh the good."

"Why is that?" hollered someone from the back.

Charlie looked back toward the woman who asked the question. "The main drawback is what has already been said, that the community no longer gets to decide the direction of the hospital. Right now, the emphasis of the hospital is doing what is best for the people of Bayou Belle and the surrounding area. On the other hand, the emphasis and priority of Great Northern will be their financial bottom line. If a service doesn't make a profit, they will likely discontinue it whether the community needs it or not. For instance, the policy of treating everyone in town regardless of their ability to pay would come to an end. Great Northern will find a way to send those folks to a charity hospital in a larger city."

"That's not true," yelled Martin.

"It's true in Riverton, Texas," retorted Charlie, "but perhaps Great Northern would be different."

A man sitting close to the front then stood and pointed a finger at Charlie. "There is something you all should know," he announced loudly in an accusing tone. "Last night at our local hospital, young Dr. Leveau here botched the surgery on a friend of mine, and my friend died. Dr. Leveau had been drinking before the operation. Also, some say he's fooling around with a widow lady here in town even though he's married. We don't need his kind in this town, and we sure don't need his advice."

There was a loud "amen" from the back. Charlie's eyes met Ruben's. He was smiling. Then he looked over at Ellie. Her head was down. He was sorry she had heard that. She certainly didn't deserve to be dragged into his problems. With nothing else to add, Charlie sat down, his head suddenly throbbing, wanting desperately to be anywhere else. When the meeting was over, several old friends came over to shake his hand and lend support. He wondered what they might really be thinking. Nobody had stood up and spoken in his defense.

Ellie's car was gone before Charlie made it out the door. He drove home to an empty, quiet house. Really wanting a drink, he picked up the Blanton's, then had second thoughts. Right now he needed a clear head. The back door opened and Charlie whirled around, wishing he had his gun.

"Charlie?" Ellie's voice was a pleasant surprise. When she saw him she ran over and wrapped her arms around him. "I'm so sorry. I could wring Ruben Martin's neck."

"Thanks for coming by, but are you sure it's a good idea? I don't want to ruin your reputation any more than I apparently already have."

"Charlie, I've checked around and can't find anyone who knows who that man was. He must have been a plant." She pulled away from him but stood close, looking up. "How can he get away with saying things like that? You should sue him for slander." She led him by the hand to the sofa and sat down. "Now I want to know what happened today. What did you find out at the hospital?"

Charlie looked at her for a long time, an easy thing to do, and considered telling her. "Ellie, I may be in a lot of trouble. Actually, I am in a lot of trouble and maybe in really serious trouble."

"I'm listening."

Charlie was glad he had Ellie to talk to. He told about his experience at the hospital with the nurses, what the supervisor said, and almost verbatim the meeting in Ruben's office. He explained how it could be career ending.

Ellie sat back on the couch, drew a deep breath, and was quiet for a while, deep in thought. "What do we do?"

Charlie appreciated the "we."

"As much as I appreciate the support, there is no 'we' here. I'm the one in trouble, and I don't want you to be collateral damage."

"Whether you like it or not, there is a 'we.' That man at the meeting saw to that. So I'll ask it again, what do we do?"

"I have to go to Texas tomorrow to meet with my lawyer and take care of some other things. I'll probably be gone two or three days. When I get back we'll talk about it. Don't be doing any sleuthing while I'm gone."

Charlie's cell rang.

"Charlie," Hubert Polk sounded panicked, "I need to talk to you right away. It's important."

"Come on over. I'm at home."

Ellie stood up to leave, but Charlie grabbed her wrist and signaled for her to sit down.

"I can't be seen at your house. I'm calling from the parish's only pay phone because I'm afraid my phones are tapped."

Hubert's voice was shaking.

"Hubert, I'm leaving early in the morning for a couple of days. Can it wait 'til I get back?"

"I guess it'll have to. Actually, it might be very good that you'll be gone. Does anyone know where you're going?"

"I'm going to…"

Before Charlie could finish the sentence, Hubert interrupted him. "No," he almost shouted into the phone. "Don't tell me. I don't want to know, and if I were you I wouldn't tell anyone else. Your life may be in great danger, and that's all I have time to say. Let me know when you get back, but don't call on my phone."

This was very intriguing. "Tell you what. First morning I'm back, I'll go to Julius' at nine o'clock. Be watching for me. I'll meet you there. That sound okay?" He winked at Ellie.

"Okay, Charlie. I'll be watching." Hubert sounded in a hurry to get off the phone. "See you then." And he hung up, not waiting for Charlie's good-bye.

Charlie looked at his phone. "That was very strange."

"I heard," Ellie said. "Hubert's voice carries. Now I have something to do. I can be the messenger. Do you think I need a special code name?" she teased, then added more seriously, "I don't think you should come back at all until you find out what Hubert has to say, for sure not if your life is really in danger."

"Hubert really sounded scared." Charlie looked at Ellie, a frown on his face.

"I'll make an appointment to see him, using Beau's medical bills as a reason. Maybe he will tell me and I can pass it on to you by phone. What do you think?"

"I still don't like it. You just sit on your hands until I get back. I'll call you to give you a heads-up when that will be." He looked at her, feeling like he wanted to protect her from harm, and certainly not cause her any.

Ellie didn't agree or disagree. She just changed the subject. "So you're leaving early tomorrow?"

"I have a ten o'clock appointment in Riverton," answered Charlie, aware that she hadn't agreed to his instructions. "Say, how about a cup of coffee."

"I better get going. Beau went to a movie and will be home soon."

Charlie walked her to her car and stood and watched as she drove away. Then he latched the doors, turned out the lights, and before turning in, put his reloaded nine millimeter on the bedside table and a chair in front of the bedroom door.

He had just dropped off to sleep when a loud thud hit the house right beside his upstairs bedroom window. He grabbed the gun, rolled out of bed, crawled to the window, and looked over the window ledge just in time to see a Ford Mustang filled with kids hightailing it down the street, passing under a street light. Charlie drew a deep breath, sat on the floor a moment while his heart slowed down, and chuckled to himself remembering the cherry bomb under Mr. Watson's truck. *Sure enough*, he thought, *what goes around comes around.*

CHAPTER FOURTEEN

SATURDAY, JUNE 10

Before leaving town, Charlie went by Jake's office to check his wound. "What have you found out so far at Vidrine's? Any clues about the shooter or what the shooter was looking for?"

"I've been out to the scene a couple of times." Jake opened his desk drawer, took out a bullet, and handed it to Charlie. "This is the bullet Kaiser took out of the patient. Looks like a nine millimeter. Who do you know that shoots one of those?" He asked it with a straight face.

"I have one," Charlie replied. "I thought of getting rid of it, maybe throwing it in the middle of the bayou, but with these death threats, I'd prefer to keep it with me. I'm flying to Texas this morning, not running away, you understand, just going to see my lawyer about one of the other irons in the fire that has become my life."

"Glad you'll be gone. One less thing for me to worry about." Jake leaned back in his chair, his hands behind his head. Then he came forward and put his elbows on the desk. "There is one thing, Charlie. I wasn't going to tell you, but you should know."

"What?" He wondered why Jake would keep anything from him.

"First of all, when I checked in the old house, there is now photo equipment in the room with the gas tanks and OR equipment, so maybe they are making movies." Jake hesitated, not wanting to scare Charlie, but he had to be told. "The guard who is still alive reported that there were two people there, one white and one black. The bullet that hit the guard came from the white guy because the black guy didn't shoot after they hit the water." Jake hesitated, then added, "Death threats would be unusual directed toward a doctor who was thought to be at least trying to save a life, even if he failed." Looking Charlie right in the eye, he concluded, "Makes me think the threat may have come from someone who knows who the shooter was."

Charlie sat down. "Maybe I should bypass Riverton and fly on to Mexico, maybe set up housekeeping there." He was serious. "They might be happy to have a new surgeon somewhere south of the border. Maybe too it's time to get the FBI involved. This is getting out of hand fast, and the real story might sound better coming from us."

"Not yet," said Jake. "It will be much better for all if we can handle it."

And much worse for all of us if we can't, thought Charlie. But he said, "I trust your judgment, and I'll be back in a couple days."

Charlie was much better rested for the return flight to Riverton. He had slept surprisingly well considering the jumble of problems bouncing about in his brain, and rocks bouncing off his house. He tried to use the time alone in the plane to contemplate his situation and how he planned to deal with it, but the black eyes and impish smile of Ellie Boudreaux were a distraction, not to mention her well-put-together frame and the way she moved about, pleasingly unaware of how much a distraction she was.

His plane touched down at the Riverton airfield a little after nine o'clock. Page was there to meet him.

"You look like you're about to pop," Charlie teased.

"Thanks a lot," Page replied sarcastically. "How is Granddad?"

"Holding his own for now. We'll know more in a few days about how much function he will recover. Say, thanks for taking care of things here. Have you talked to your mom?"

"I talk to her every day. She asks if I talk to you, and she asks about Granddaddy. Dad, I know she feels guilty about leaving the way she did, especially with everything that has happened since. Have you talked to her?"

"No," Charlie admitted, "I tried once and she didn't answer. She said she wouldn't, so I didn't try again." He looked over at Page. "She could always call me. She's the one that left, and I have a strong feeling that she won't be coming back. She's been working up the courage to leave for a long time."

"I know," said Page. "I have the same feeling. I don't know how to say this, but when I talk to her she sounds happier than she has in a long time." Page wasn't sure how her dad would take that.

"I'm sure she is. We had been slowly drifting apart for years, but when you guys left home, there wasn't any reason for us to stay together. She got more involved in her community work, and I hid behind a busy surgical practice. It's like the tired old story. Time passed. The gulf widened. Your mother, aided by the last blow of my missing her big event, had the guts to leave and start a new life. I'll always love and care about her as I think she will about me, but I don't blame her for wanting something better." Page was staring straight ahead at the road. "How do you feel about it?"

"Neither Chuck nor I are surprised. I guess we would have preferred to have grandparents together for Thanksgivings and Christmases, but we had a family while we were growing up, and that is more than a lot of folks can say. Are you really okay with it, Dad?"

"I guess I'll have to be. I feel like such a failure, and I really hate that feeling. It's not one I'm accustomed to. I had convinced myself that I was a wonderful husband and father and provider. Deep down I knew things weren't exactly like that, but I couldn't face the fact that I was failing at something; it wasn't a simple hernia repair. I will say one thing, though; we had wonderful kids, and neither she nor I could be any prouder of how you and your brother turned out."

They arrived at the house. The window had been fixed. Page had taken the rest of Jan's clothes to her in Houston. Some of the family pictures were gone. The familiar smell of Jan and her cosmetics was still there but fainter. Charlie walked from room to room, each one holding special memories.

"Sweetheart, we may sell this house so we can divide the estate. Do you think you might want to live here and sell your house?"

"I would love that, Dad. This house is home. I'd hate to see someone else living in it. Paul and I have talked about needing a bigger house for our growing family. But if there is a chance you and Mom might get back together, I wouldn't want that to influence what you do."

"If by some miracle that happens, we'll have everyone here

for the holidays. But I think it may be you and Paul having us all here for those holidays." He held her for a minute, both arms around her shoulders and his chin resting on the top of her head. "May I borrow your car to go see Mike and Harry? I should be back by noon and we'll get lunch. Or you could drop me off and have the car, whichever you want."

"You go ahead and take the car. I'll call you if I really need to, but I'll plan to see you at lunch."

Charlie made the ten o'clock appointment with Harry, but he went first to his old office, which was open until noon on Saturday. His staff was shocked, but glad to see him. Joyce had been with him since he opened practice. She came over, hugged him, and then admonished him for not keeping in touch. "We know you've had a lot going on. Page brought that letter by to fax, and we know your dad was injured. We were just so worried that something else had happened. You've always been so good at keeping us up to date." She also knew Jan had left but didn't say that.

"Sorry 'bout that," said Charlie. "Just got really busy." They didn't know the half of it, and he didn't have time to tell them. "I'll try to do better. Is Mike here?" Mike had been his partner for the last ten years. They were also friends.

"He's back in his office."

Mike rose when Charlie walked in. "Great to see you back, Charlie. Too much here for one guy to do. Your dad okay?"

"I think so. Still in a coma but partly drug induced. They say we'll know in a couple of days how full his recovery will be. I really want to thank you for covering for me on short notice."

"Glad to do it. I'll get you back one day." Mike sat back

down and Charlie sat across the desk from him. "By the way, all your patients did well and are home but one. The big gunshot wound is still with us. He's out of the ICU and up walking. His colostomy has pulled back some, but I think it's viable. It hasn't started to work yet. Mrs. Jones worked me for a couple extra days, but she's okay. Are you back to stay?"

Charlie looked around the office he and Mike shared. He'd been gone a week, but it seemed like a year. "Just for the day, Mike. I have to see Harry Morris about helping me with the divorce. I guess you heard."

"Yeah." Mike looked embarrassed. "My wife told me. She heard it at church."

Good place for gossip, thought Charlie. "Honestly, I don't know when I'll be back or even if I'll be back." Mike's look turned from embarrassed to surprised. "I've run into a bit of trouble in Bayou Belle that I have to clear up before I come back, and I don't know yet how long my dad will need for me to be there."

"You mean you may leave Riverton?" Mike studied Charlie, sensing there was a lot he wasn't being told.

"That's a real possibility. Meanwhile, I don't expect my salary to continue if I'm not contributing. Look at the contract and see what severance pay is and let's start that. If I come back, we'll just pick up where I left off and I'll repay the severance." Charlie hesitated a second before bringing up the other reason he came by the office. "And Mike, one other thing, I may need a character witness before long, maybe before the medical board and maybe even in criminal court. Hope I can count on you for that."

Mike was flabbergasted. He'd never known Charlie to have

any kind of legal or moral problems and couldn't imagine what might be going on. "You mean you want me to forgive you for always giving me the fat patients and the crocks." Mike could always get him to laugh, but Charlie just smiled. "Charlie, I can tell you have more going on than you're telling me, and you must have your reasons. Just let me know how I can help you and I will."

Good old Mike, thought Charlie. *He really is a good friend.* "As soon as I know anything for sure, you'll be the next to know." They shook hands and Charlie bade Joyce and the front office folks farewell, then drove to Harry Morris' office.

Harry and Charlie had played golf at the country club in the same foursome on Wednesday afternoon for several years. Both maintained handicaps of around ten and both dressed better than they played. A lot of money had changed hands over the years, but Charlie figured after all that time they were about even. Harry was probably missing a Saturday morning tee time to meet with Charlie.

Harry stood up and came around his desk when Charlie entered his office. "Charlie, good to see you." They shook hands and Harry motioned for Charlie to take a seat. "Wish it could be at the club and under different circumstances. You holding up okay?"

"Fine," Charlie lied. "Actually, I'd much rather be playing golf also. Have you heard anything from Jan's lawyer?" He jumped right to the point, not wanting to take up any more of Harry's Saturday than necessary.

"I got the letter and we have talked on the phone a few times." Harry fumbled with some papers on his desk. "They have come up with a proposal, but before I tell you what it is,

I'd like to hear what you think is fair."

Charlie hadn't given it much thought. His talk with Page about the house was the first time he had even considered property settlements. "I would keep it simple and give her half of everything. Somebody reputable could appraise her jewelry. We could decide how to divide things up so that we each get half the value. I don't know. Does that seem reasonable?"

"It does to me. Unfortunately, things usually get sticky."

"Is it possible to keep things friendly? I don't think I could stand a knock-down, drag-out fight right now."

"It's possible, but doesn't usually happen. What they propose is similar to what you say, but she wants twenty thousand dollars a month in alimony."

Charlie could now see how these cases could become unfriendly in a hurry. "I don't make much more than that after taxes. What does she expect me to live on?"

"They know they won't get that much, but it's a starting point. What do you say?"

"I'd like to sit down across a table, the four of us, and work it out face-to-face. I don't think she could look me in the eye and ask for everything."

"You might be surprised. I have dealt with her attorney before, and I know she'll be well coached." Harry wasn't exactly encouraging.

"What if I give her two-thirds or three-fourths of everything but no alimony. Right now I don't care that much about property, but I can see a huge cash flow problem coming." Charlie was staring at the floor, thinking he might have to find a new career that would not be nearly as lucrative as the practice of surgery. Maybe he could live in his dad's house and wait tables for Mr. Julius or be a deputy for Jake. He did have some experience in that area now. Then again, he might end up in the jailhouse. In that case he would at least be housed, fed, and clothed, but the prison laundry was not likely to provide much money for alimony. Coming out of a trance and back to the present, he heard Harry's voice.

"I'll feel them out on that and get back to you. I'll also try to arrange a face-to-face as we get closer to a deal."

It was almost eleven when Charlie left Harry's office and drove home to have lunch with Page. She had prepared ham and cheese sandwiches from food still good in the fridge. Out of all Charlie's problems, the one most on Page's mind was the impending divorce of her parents. He told her what he could, careful not to be too encouraging or too discouraging. Having completed what he came to do in Riverton, he was thinking about flying back to Bayou Belle when it dawned on him what to do next. It was better not to be in Bayou Belle right now anyway.

They finished lunch and while washing the few dishes together, Charlie told Page he was going to fly on to Small River, Oklahoma, that afternoon.

"What on earth for?" Page asked, a puzzled look on her face as she dried the last glass.

"That's where Ruben Martin was before coming to Bayou Belle. I'd like to talk to some of the people there and see what they thought about him. Maybe I can find out more."

"You're not a detective, Dad, and this baby needs a granddaddy." She patted her stomach. "Don't go getting yourself in trouble."

"I may not be a doctor much longer either, sweetheart. I'm

already in trouble over my head. But don't worry about me. You just see to keeping yourself and my grandbaby healthy." Then he added, "And thanks for helping with the house and the car and the bills. I knew I didn't have to worry about those things with you in charge."

Page wasn't so sure about his flying off to Oklahoma, but arguing with him had never gotten her anywhere. "Just be careful, you hear?"

"I will, hon. I promise." *When do children begin to worry more about their parents than the other way around?* he wondered.

CHAPTER FIFTEEN

SATURDAY MORNING, JUNE 10

Jake was walking to Julius' for a cup of coffee when he heard a plane overhead and looked up to see Charlie's Cessna gaining altitude, heading west toward Texas. He had been to Vidrine's on Thursday and Friday and interviewed employees. Yellow police tape was still around the old house and grounds. Now that it was Saturday, he did not plan to go back. Forensics was examining some of the scant, unrelated "evidence," and he wouldn't have the report back for a few days. He had not sent the bullet, still trying to think of a way to lose it. He got his coffee, walked back to his office, put his feet on his desk and relaxed. He read the morning paper, dozed a few minutes, and was enjoying a third cup of coffee when his phone rang.

"Sheriff," said the voice on the other end, "this is James Vidrine. I was wondering if you were coming back out this way today because if you are, I'd like for you to stop by my office and see me."

"Mr. Vidrine, I hadn't planned to unless something came up. Right now I'm just waiting for the reports from the forensics lab on the things we sent them. Don't know when for sure they'll be back. But if you need to see me, I'll come back out." Vidrine sounded friendly enough and Jake was curious. "When would be a good time?"

"I've just got some paperwork to do, so come on out anytime."

Jake, not wanting to sound anxious, said, "I'll be there in about an hour. That okay?"

"See you then, Sheriff," Vidrine said and hung up.

The guard at the gate was expecting Jake and directed him to Vidrine's office. Vidrine greeted Jake at the door and ushered him into his inner office and motioned to a chair for him to sit in. Vidrine sat behind his desk. "So, how is the investigation going, Sheriff?"

"A few leads," replied Jake, "but not much to go on yet." Then he innocently asked, "I understand you're making pornographic movies out here. Is that right?"

"That's right," replied a smug James Vidrine. "Private property. No law against it. These folks fly in here on Sundays when we're not busy, get their work done, and clear out before we start work on Monday. They pay well and they don't like being disturbed. Hence, we keep the place well guarded."

"What about the guns and shooting that people have heard?" asked Jake.

"Those are blanks of course. Some of the movies can be violent. It's not all porn." Vidrine seemed to be enjoying the give and take. "Last week and this week the movie takes place in a hospital, so they brought in a lot of medical equipment."

"And that big thing in the corner of the outbuilding?" asked Jake. "What is that?"

"That's a large industrial oven. We have lots of stuff to burn out here. Saves on trash costs. No hauling trash on highways, no smelly trash Dumpsters, and the air pollution is negligible. I got a good deal on this one because it was used, so I bought it." Vidrine was on a roll, but it was time to discuss the real purpose of the called meeting.

Smiling in a way no longer friendly, Vidrine reached in his desk drawer and held up a 1911 A1 government issue Colt 45. "We found this in the muck of the bayou mud. The surviving guard said he saw something drop out of the black guy's hand as he was running, and we were able to locate it with a metal detector."

Jake was staring at the gun he had owned for years. Suddenly nervous, he asked, "Why didn't you tell me this at first? This is real evidence." He was hoping his voice, a little higher pitched than it had been, was not giving him away. "I can get the serial number run and find out whose gun it is."

"Nice try, Sheriff. You're pretty good. We might be able to use you in one of the Sunday night films." Vidrine was smiling wider now. "We already had it run. Seems I have some influence in certain police departments. Unless I miss my guess, I now have a great deal of influence in the Bayou Belle sheriff's office too." He leaned back in his chair, his fingertips all touching, his index fingers against his chin, and his smile continuing to grow wider and more evil.

"Don't suppose it would do any good to tell you that I lost that gun two years ago when we were fishing." Jake knew it was a stupid response, but he was otherwise at a loss for words.

"It might, except that it hadn't been under water that long. I suspect that the white guy with you was Charlie Leveau." He looked at Jake and hesitated for a moment, waiting for a response. When Jake didn't bite, he continued. "But so far I have no proof of that. Pretty good trick he pulled. He shoots the guy but doesn't kill him, then operates on him to finish the job." Vidrine paused again and let that sink in. "Tell you what, Sheriff, I don't give a damn about that guard who was killed, but I don't want any more snooping around on my property. I'm keeping your gun. The day will come when I need a big favor, and I expect that you'll be happy to accommodate me. Are you catching my drift?" Jake sat quietly, his life passing before his eyes. "Meanwhile, before I ask for that big favor, I expect to be kept informed of all police matters that might concern me, my company, or my family. Is that clear?"

Jake was able only to nod. His voice wouldn't work.

"One other thing." Vidrine sat forward in his chair. "The man who was killed is a brother of a hit man for the New Orleans mob. If he got a clue who shot his brother, well, I don't have to tell you. Just tell Leveau to watch his back. If he does anything to piss me off, I'll tell Vinnie personally that Leveau did it, even without proof. That's the nice thing about being on my side of the law. I don't worry about proof." He sat there a while longer for effect, then said, "You can go. But if I call, I expect the phone to be answered on the first ring." Then he added, though it wasn't really necessary, "And I know where you live and the usual whereabouts of your wife and son." He made a shooing motion with the back of his hand indicating that it was time for Jake to leave.

Jake drove slowly back toward town.

CHAPTER SIXTEEN

SATURDAY AFTERNOON, JUNE 10

The flight to Small River was a little bumpy, and Charlie had to fly around some clouds. It was almost dark when he spotted the small airport. The runway lights came on when he clicked the call button. He announced his approach on the given frequency and landed on the second bounce. *Must be tired*, he thought. *Probably overdid the solo flying today.* He tied the plane down where he was instructed.

"Good thing you got here when you did," said the old attendant. "I was about to leave for supper and wouldn't have been back 'til tomorrow morning. You need gas?"

"Not 'til tomorrow," said Charlie. "I'm going to stay here in Small River for the night. Are there any cars to rent?"

The old man cocked his head, rubbed his chin, and said, "Naw, and the only taxi closed at five. Not much need for rent cars 'round here."

"Any hotels?" Charlie was thinking he probably should have researched these things before striking out.

"There's a Motel 6 near town and they usually have vacancies." The old man was locking the door to the small airfield office.

"How far is town?" Charlie had seen a few lights from the air and thought it wasn't too far if he had to walk.

"A couple miles. Come on, I'll give you a ride."

On the way to the Motel 6, the old man asked, "So what brings you to Small River? Most planes we have are locals, and we don't get much out-of-town traffic."

Charlie thought fast. "I'm a freelance writer working on small-town stories." Then they passed Small River Hospital on the right. "Nice hospital," said Charlie.

"Yeah, it serves about four counties. Kind of in the middle of all of 'em. That's why it's so big. Probably the biggest business 'round here."

"Do folks like the hospital?" asked Charlie innocently.

The old man looked over at him with a questioning look. "Guess so," he said. "What's not to like about a hospital?"

Good point, thought Charlie. The old man pulled up in front of the motel and dropped Charlie off. "Many thanks," said Charlie. "I don't know for sure when I'll be leaving, but could you fill up my tanks in the morning? I'll probably leave sometime after noon."

The old man saluted. "I'll do that," he said. "If you're looking for a place to eat, there's a diner in the middle of town. Sara does a good job cookin'."

"Thanks again," said Charlie. "See you tomorrow." He checked into his room, which was clean, small, and comfortable, with a working television. The décor reminded him of his aunt's house, which hadn't been updated since the 1970s.

After washing up he walked down the street to Sara's Diner. Before Charlie sat down, Sara, walking over with a menu in her hand, said, "I got pot roast with mashed potatoes and gravy and string beans for the special, and we got a little left. What would you like?"

"That sounds real good to me," said Charlie, and it did. "Do you have sweet tea to go with it?" He realized how hungry he was.

"I do that." Sara looked like she had enjoyed her own cooking for many years. Her cheeks were so full it took an effort to open her eyes enough to see over them. But she moved like an athlete. Several others in the diner were already enjoying the dessert special, chocolate pie. Everyone was with someone else, so there was no way to politely engage in conversation tonight.

Charlie enjoyed his dinner and when taking the last bite of chocolate pie, he said, "That was all delicious." She smiled at the compliment. "How long have you lived in Small River?"

"All my life," she said. "My dad was raised here, and when the depression hit and a lot of Okies went to California, we stayed behind and made a go of it. I wasn't here then, but I heard tales. My dad always said, 'At least we weren't eatin' those grapes of wrath.' Didn't know what he meant 'til I got to high school and had to study Steinbeck."

"Anything interesting happen in Small River?" asked Charlie.

Sara laughed. "We get an occasional tornado, but Small River isn't the place to be if you're looking for excitement. Why, you writing a book?"

"How did you know?" Then he backtracked. "Actually, I occasionally submit human interest stories to magazines about small-town America. I figured a place with a name like Small River would have some good small-town stories."

"About fifteen years ago, Terry Bradshaw came through here and ate right where you're sitting. He was on his way to a football game in Norman. That's about it. I stay pretty busy cooking and feeding folks, and I'm not good at remembering, but most mornings Freddie Burrows comes in here, and he might have something interesting to tell you."

"What time do you open?" asked Charlie, thinking he may have flown a long way and spent a lot of money on expensive airplane fuel for nothing.

"I get here at six, but Freddie doesn't get here generally 'til around seven thirty."

"I don't know how hungry I'll be after your pot roast, but I'll see you in the morning for breakfast. And Sara," he added as he was getting up, "that was really good." Charlie was sincere. She smiled a knowing smile. He paid the bill and over tipped Sara since she stayed late for him and had been helpful.

"Hey, thanks a lot," said Sara and waved as he walked out the door and back to the motel.

Linda George called just as he was getting to his room. After exchanging a few pleasantries, she said, "The date for the deposition has been set for this Monday, day after tomorrow. The plaintiff's lawyer wasn't going to be able to do it for another few weeks otherwise, so I took it. I hope that's okay? It's short notice and I know you wanted to be there."

"Absolutely, I'll be there. Where do I go?"

"It will be at his office on St. Charles right near Tulane. Two o'clock."

"Fantastic, can't wait to get this over with. Then I'll see you day after tomorrow in New Orleans. Oh, what is the doctor's name?"

"Now don't laugh, or if you are going to laugh, get it over with before you get there. His name is Robert Dingleberry."

"No."

"Oh yes," said Ms. George. "And Dr. Dingleberry is apparently a little touchy about it. We should try not to piss him off."

"Okay," said Charlie. "Thanks for a laugh anyway." He hung up and tried to imagine what Dr. Dingleberry looked like before turning in for the night.

CHAPTER SEVENTEEN

SATURDAY, JUNE 10

When he left Vidrine's, Jake intended to go back to his office, but the car seemed to drive itself to Doc's house and then stopped in front. He wanted some motherly advice for the first time in years. Delphine was dusting the downstairs when Jake went in.

"Jake, what in the world? You look almost white. Come on in the kitchen and sit down. Ain't much to do 'round here with Doc gone."

Jake told Delphine the whole story, from his and Charlie's night raid on Vidrine Trucking and Porn Industry, through the meeting he had just left with Mr. Vidrine at his office. He didn't leave anything out.

"Charlie doesn't know yet that the man he shot was the brother of a mafia hit man. Momma, I worked so hard to get where I am. I was so glad to make you proud of me and be able to support my family better than my dad ever did. Now I've got to be afraid for their lives. Vidrine owns me."

Delphine had walked over to the kitchen sink and was looking out the window, seeing nothing but red. Her hands clenched the countertop. She could kill anybody who made her son feel that way. She trusted that Jesus had died for her, and paid for her sins, and rose again, proving he was indeed

God himself. She accepted that and believed it with her whole heart. It was the only thing that made any sense in this world. But right now, she could kill James Vidrine and laugh.

"Momma, you okay? You hear what I said?" Jake's elbows were on his knees, his hat in his hands, looking at the back of his mother's head, tears in his eyes.

Delphine turned slowly around. "Jake, they think they got you because they think everyone thinks like they do. We don't think like that. I didn't raise you that way." She walked over to him, sat in the chair facing him, and took his hands in hers. "We're not playing their game, but we'll let them think we are. We need some help. Let's call Ellie over here. I think she knows what's going on as much as we do. She'd be the best one to call Charlie."

Delphine called Ellie. Her morning history class had just concluded. She was on her way home but would be glad to stop by and see them. They were still sitting at the kitchen table when she came through the back door. "What's going on?" She could tell there had been a dramatic new development by the looks on their faces.

"Sit down a minute. Jake has something to tell you."

Jake then related the same story he had just told Delphine. She had already heard it from Charlie, but listened again to see if Jake added anything that Charlie might have unintentionally left out.

"Charlie told me a lot last night after the town meeting, but he doesn't know that his patient was the brother of a hit man, or that Vidrine has your gun and knows you all did the raid."

"I think the reason Charlie is getting death threats is because Vidrine told the hit man who shot his brother. This whole thing just doesn't make sense." Jake stood and paced back and forth in the kitchen. "Why is making dirty movies reason to kill someone like Doc? There's got to be more to it."

"I don't think they'd try to kill Doc for that either," Ellie piped in. "Jake, Hubert called Charlie last night and sounded panicked, wanting to meet with him. They're planning to talk when Charlie returns. Maybe Hubert knows something. Charlie thought he sounded scared to death."

"Why don't you pay him a visit, Ellie?" He stopped pacing and sat down for a moment by Ellie. "I can't go talk to him now or it would blow everything up. Call me or come by my office after you talk to him." Jake wasn't at all sure where this was going, but it seemed like a start, like they were doing something.

Ellie didn't even go home first. Even though Charlie made her promise not to get involved, she drove straight to Hubert's office, hoping to catch him before he started his afternoon. His secretary was out to lunch, and the door to his office was locked. She was sure someone was in there because she had heard noise when she first entered the waiting room. She knocked but got no answer. Then she called, "Hubert, it's Ellie. If you're in there, let me in. I need to talk to you." Still there was no answer. She went to the secretary's desk and wrote a note for him to call her when he came back. She slipped it under the door. He might not want his secretary to know. Before she got back to the main door, Hubert's office door opened and Hubert peeked out. "Ellie, come on in. I was catching a few winks," he lied. He walked over and locked the main door, commenting that his secretary was supposed to do that before she left. "What can I do for you?" He ushered Ellie to a chair and then sat across from her.

"I was with Charlie when you called last night. We were talking about how the town meeting went. He thought you sounded desperate and was worried. It turns out he may not be back for a few days more, so he asked me to find out if there was anything he could do from a distance." She had decided on this story on the way over and hoped it made sense.

"No," said Hubert. He would have denied knowing anything, but Ellie already knew. He used a pay phone to keep anyone from listening in, and somebody else heard anyway. "There is nothing I can tell you. I can't believe he would send you. I think it might be better if you left now before someone finds out you're here. Trust me. You don't want to know any of this stuff." He stood to show her to the door.

"Wait a minute, Hubert. I already know a lot more than you think. We may have related information that is not the same but put together might mean something. What were you going to tell Charlie? I can pass it on to him and meet back with you if that is necessary. I know this is dangerous stuff, but I'm already involved. If I come again, I'll make an appointment with your secretary and tell her it's about Beau's medical bill. Okay?"

Hubert looked doubtful, but he'd known Ellie all her life and he trusted her. "Before the town hall meeting I saw Ruben talking to the man that stood up and cut Charlie to shreds. He basically was telling him what to say. I wouldn't have been too surprised about that, knowing Ruben, but then I heard him say, 'Make it bad enough that he'll leave town voluntarily, because if he doesn't leave, we'll have to make sure he permanently leaves, and they might start getting suspicious after Adams and

Doc Leveau.' Then I walked in the room just off the stage, and Ruben looked at me and I knew he knew I heard. During the meeting he leaned over to me and said, 'That's what that hundred grand is for. I'll swear you knew all about it.' Then after the meeting was over, he called someone on the phone and with me listening said, 'We have to get rid of Charlie Leveau. He will poison the whole deal.' So, Ellie, I'm in over my head. If he knew I was talking to you, we'd both be in grave danger, so I probably shouldn't have told you. But Charlie needs to know before he comes back. This hospital business is mean stuff. I never would have believed it."

Ellie looked at Hubert with a new respect. She knew what it took for him to tell her. She wasn't sure what he meant about the hundred grand, but whatever it was terrified him. "Thanks for telling me. I'll call Charlie and let him know." She was standing to leave before the secretary returned when there was a loud, aggressive knock on the door. Hubert's face paled and he jumped out of his chair, hitting the desk. "Stay here. I'll see who it is."

Ruben Martin's unmistakable voice said, "Hubert, we have to talk." Ellie looked desperately for a hiding place. There were no closets and the curtains didn't go all the way to the floor.

"What do you need?" she heard Hubert ask.

"Let's go in your office, I don't want this to be heard by anyone else."

"My secretary won't be back for another half hour. We can sit here. It's a little more comfortable."

"Are you crazy? Come on." And Ruben walked in his office. He sat in the wingback he had enjoyed since meeting Hubert six months ago. Hubert went around, sat in his chair. Ellie was curled up where his large legs would ordinarily go.

Hubert was trying to look comfortable and nonchalant with his feet on the desk. "What do you want?"

Ruben looked at him, shaking his head, thinking Hubert was trying to look relaxed when it was obvious to anyone that he wasn't. "It's about what I said to you the other night. Perhaps I came on a little strong. It's just I was upset and I can't afford to have anything get in the way of this hospital deal. You can keep your hundred grand. But if I ever find out that you told somebody what you heard, not only would I have you disbarred for betraying an attorney/client privilege, your life wouldn't be worth a plug nickel. You understand?"

"I think I already knew that. To be real honest, Ruben, I wish I didn't have that hundred grand, and I wish I'd never gone to New Orleans and met you. Now I have to deal with what I have done." He wanted Ruben to leave before Ellie sneezed or coughed, but he had to know. "Why is the hospital takeover, especially a small hospital, such a big deal?"

Ruben laughed his evil laugh. "You really think this is all about the hospital? You poor, dumb, naïve bastard. It's better you don't know. You'd just soil your pants. Just remember, you're still my and the hospital's lawyer. Act like it."

After he left, Ellie slowly came out of her hiding place. "Wow," she said. "Well, Hubert, if anything happens to you, I'll be a witness against him. He won't get away with it."

"Thanks a lot," Hubert replied sarcastically. "Now I feel so much better." He walked over to the window and watched Ruben get in his car and drive away before he let Ellie come out of his office.

"I'll call Charlie and fill him in. If you need to talk to me, just leave a message saying something about the hospital bill. I'll do the same with you."

He nodded agreement.

Ellie was walking down the stairs when Hubert's secretary came in. She asked, "Will he be in this afternoon? I needed to talk to him about a hospital bill for my son, but I'll call back later." The secretary said that would be fine and went on up the stairs.

CHAPTER EIGHTEEN

SATURDAY AFTERNOON, JUNE 10

Ellie sat in her car for a minute, deciding what to do. She had to tell Charlie what she had found out and make sure he didn't come back to Bayou Belle. She knew he would be upset with her for getting involved when he made her promise not to. But she wanted to do something with this new information, so she went to see Jake.

After Jake left Delphine he went to his office, mechanically going about his work, his heart not in it. His mom made him feel better and he was glad they were doing something, but he couldn't shake the queasy feeling in the pit of his stomach that he knew would not leave him until the Vidrine issue was resolved.

He looked up when his office door opened and Ellie walked in, looking a little shaken. He just pointed to a chair and she sat. "What happened?"

"I was talking to Hubert when Ruben Martin showed up. I had to hide under Hubert's desk, trying to listen and remember everything said while trying not to sneeze." She shook her head at the memory. Then looking up at Jake, fear in her eyes, she said, "Ruben threatened Charlie's life. They mean for him to leave town dead or alive. He also told Hubert that he didn't know everything, and if he did he would soil his pants, and something about a hundred grand that I didn't understand."

"Did he say anything that could be tied to Vidrine Trucking?" Jake knew in his heart there was a connection. He just couldn't figure out what it might be.

"Not a word about that," said Ellie, "unless that's what he was talking about when he said Hubert didn't know as much as he thought." Ellie shifted in her chair, her head down. Looking up at Jake, she asked, "Would you call Charlie and tell him? Just don't tell him how you found out. I promised him I wouldn't do anything until he got back."

"Under the circumstances I think he would much rather hear from you. I know Charlie. He'll understand. We're all playing this by ear."

Ellie agreed to call Charlie with the latest news and plead with him to stay gone a while longer. Ruben Martin seemed capable of anything. Certainly the mob was.

At the end of the day Jake was the only one in the office and was closing up to go have supper with his family. So much had changed in the last few days. He was turning out the lights when there was a quiet knock at his back door. Jake drew his replacement gun, a 40 cal H&K, and moved toward the door. "Who is it?" He stood to the side away from the door.

"Sheriff, it's Donnie Myers. I see you at the hospital some-time. I work on the housekeeping team there. I have something to talk to you about."

Jake, not really sure who it was, said, "I'm just closing up. Can this wait 'til tomorrow?"

"It's about Vidrine." Donnie was talking quietly.

Jake kept his gun drawn, then cracked open the door just enough to see. He recognized the man as one he had seen at the hospital, so he opened the door to let him in, reholstering his gun only after he was inside and the door was locked. "What's this about Vidrine?" Jake eyed him curiously, wondering what this man could possibly know that would be helpful.

"First let me tell you who I am so you might be more likely to believe me," Donnie began as he sat before being offered a chair.

"I'm listening," said Jake, still standing but moving over to sit on the corner of his desk.

"My real name is Donald Henderson. I'm an FBI agent out of Chicago assigned to follow up on some information concerning the takeover moves of Great Northern Hospital Corporation. They are involved in some shady dealings that involve interstate commerce, hence the involvement of the FBI. Ruben Martin has been at the center of many of these acquisitions. He does it by hook or crook or bribery and sometimes threats and blackmail. Anyway, that's why I'm here, but I think a lot more than a hospital takeover is happening in Bayou Belle."

"What's this about Vidrine?" Jake asked, eager for the FBI agent to get to the point, wondering how he was going to deal now with Vidrine, the FBI, danger to his family, and possible criminal charges. Maybe Donnie could provide the link between the hospital and Vidrine Trucking that he had suspected.

"I got myself hired as a housekeeper because I thought it might get me into offices without sneaking around. I put a bug in Martin's phone and I listen to it every evening. He is usually very careful to avoid saying anything incriminating over the phone, but this morning he got a call from James Vidrine."

Jake thought, *I'm dead. Mr. Henderson, an FBI man, already knows what I did, and now I'm caught in a whipsaw.* "What did he say?" Jake asked the obvious question.

"The essence was that he had you where he wanted you, that he had found your gun, identified by serial number, in the swamp behind his property where a burglary took place a couple nights ago, and where a man was shot and has since died."

"Is Vidrine connected to the mob?" Jake asked. "There have been rumors around here for a long time."

"He is, loosely."

"That's all very interesting," said Jake, "but what do I do with the information?"

"I'd say nothing for right now. But I have your back. I know your motives for going to the company were clean, even if your method was awkward at best. Just don't do anything stupid if Vidrine asks you to. It will be intended to make you more indebted to him. We have to figure out what is going on out there and get the right people in here to do something about it. Here's my cell number if you need my help." He wrote his number on a Post-it note on Jake's desk and handed it to Jake. "For right now I'm going to keep my job at the hospital and my ear to the ground." They shook hands and he eased himself back out the door.

Jake felt relieved, with a new spring in his step. After all, the FBI knew of his escapade and he was still walking free. Just maybe this would all work out, but he had to get to the bottom of it soon.

Mary had meatballs and spaghetti ready when Jake got home. "Running a little late tonight. Everything okay?" She worried more about her husband every day. Jake had finally told her about getting shot. After getting over the initial shock, she had been furious. "Jake, your job is dangerous enough as it is without doing stupid stuff." He had to agree.

"Somebody came by as I was closing up and wanted to talk, so I stayed and listened."

"Anything important?" Mary was plating the spaghetti for both Jake and Jeremiah.

"About some of the goings-on at Vidrine's." He told the partial truth.

"What do you think is going on?" asked Mary. "People been talking for months about jet planes in and out on Sunday nights, about the sound of gunshots and things."

Jake looked at Jeremiah, wondering if he should hear this, and decided that he was almost a grown man. It probably wasn't anything he hadn't heard before. "The best theory is that they are making pornographic movies. They fly people in and out on Sundays so nobody around here is involved. It's private property and not really against the law. I saw a lot of moviemaking equipment when I went out to investigate the shooting."

Jeremiah was a bit embarrassed by this line of conversation but thought he should participate to show he was listening, and hoping to hear more. "Do these people come all the way from Hollywood?"

Jake laughed. "I doubt any of the stars of these movies would be recognizable, not their faces anyway. No telling where they come from. Since they are so sensitive about security, they may also be running some kind of prostitution ring, flying in high-class call girls and high rollers who don't want to get caught where they live. Or there could be gambling. Lots of possibilities. Just don't say anything about it. It's an ongoing investigation, and you two know nothing about any of it, right?"

"Right, Dad," said Jeremiah. "Reckon they need any teenage stars?" Jeremiah lowered his head and looked at his dad with upturned eyes, trying not to laugh.

Jake drew back his hand like he was about to hit him with a backhand, but instead reached over and tousled his hair. "Very funny. Don't let me catch you anywhere near that place. I have reason to believe there are some very dangerous people out there."

Mary smiled, looking back and forth between the two men of her house, so proud of both. "You did hear your dad, right?"

"Yes ma'am. I guess I'll have to be older to be a porn star." Jeremiah laughed, then added to his mother's increasing consternation and wide eyes. "Just think, I could live at home and work locally."

Mary started to laugh but wondered, *How does he know about porn stars?*

CHAPTER NINETEEN

SATURDAY NIGHT, EARLY SUNDAY MORNING
NEW ORLEANS, LATE JUNE 10, EARLY JUNE 11

Just before midnight a paneled van turned off Canal Street into the French Quarter and pulled to a stop behind a large black limousine, flashing its lights twice. Two burly men got out of the limo, opened the back door, and dragged a young man out. He was dressed in an open neck white silk shirt with gold chains around his neck, handcuffed, and his mouth duct taped shut. They unceremoniously threw him in the back of the paneled van, then got back in the limo and drove off.

Two blocks over, a homeless man was leaning against the wall of an old barred-up furniture store, asleep, drunk, or both. The driver of the van and his partner, both dressed as police officers, approached the man quietly. The homeless man didn't wake up before his mouth was taped shut and his wrists were bound. He, too, was tossed in the back of the van.

The van's next stop was near Tulane. They had been given the address of a Chinese exchange student who had arrived in New Orleans the week before to take summer school classes before enrolling as a full-time student in the fall. He had no family in the States, and the language barrier prevented him from making friends. He lived by himself in a small apartment off Broadway. The two men knocked on his door. He answered the door rubbing his eyes, turning on the front porch light.

He never had a chance. He also was taped, cuffed, and in the back of the van in less than a minute. Nobody would notice that he was gone.

CHAPTER TWENTY

SUNDAY, JUNE 11

The bed was hard, as were the pillows, but Charlie was able to sleep. He arose early, showered, shaved, put on some jeans and a clean shirt, and walked to Sara's. He got there right at 7:30. A man at the counter with a two-day growth of whiskers leaned over his bacon, eggs, and toast. Sara nodded toward him, looking at Charlie to indicate that this was Freddie. Charlie sat two stools down, not wanting to crowd him but also not wanting someone else to get between them. Freddie looked up as Charlie sat down and nodded a hello.

"Mornin'," said Charlie.

Freddie continued to eat.

Sara smiled and said to Charlie, "This is Freddie. He must have had a bad night. Hasn't uttered a peep since he came in. He's more friendly after a couple cups of Sara's coffee."

"I see." Charlie was hoping she was right. Freddie continued to eat.

Others drifted in and gradually filled the diner. There was a lot of camaraderie in Small River, much like Bayou Belle. Folks who grow up and live in big cities might see a lot, but they also miss a lot. Charlie was enjoying his grits and toast and watched as Freddie finished his second cup of coffee. When Freddie put the cup down and signaled Sara for a refill, Charlie asked, "Freddie, much happening around here exciting?"

Freddie looked at him for a long moment, picked bacon out of his teeth with a toothpick, then said, "Naw, can't say anything of note has happened here in years." Freddie stared off into space and, remembering something he had seen when he was a kid, he said, "We had this kid one time, a strong left-hander, name of Lefty Donaldson. Best pitcher anybody'd ever seen. Unhittable. Threw a hundred-plus miles an hour and his face was meaner'n a snake. Anyway, he pitched for the local semipro team back when Mickey Mantle was playing ball in Commerce. They came here to play one night, and the whole town turned out to see if Mantle could hit Donaldson. Mantle batted right-handed, which was his natural side, against Lefty. Lefty refused to throw curves to keep Mantle off balance. He said up front he was throwing heat and Mantle couldn't hit it if he knew what was coming. Sure 'nough, he struck Mantle out first three times he come up. Mick couldn't even foul one off. Fourth time, Mantle worked it to a full count and Lefty told him out loud another fast ball was comin' and the Mick was ready. He threw a ball— musta been going upwards one hundred ten miles an hour—that went over the inside cor-ner of the plate. Trouble was, the ump called it a ball, and Mantle walked. Lefty got so mad he threw his glove down and stomped on it. When they threw him back the ball, he mouthed something to Mantle, then to the ump, and turned and threw the ball on a straight line over the centerfield fence. He was ejected from the game, but before he left the mound, all the Major League scouts in the stands—and there was a bunch all licking their chops—left and were in their vehicles going home. The newspaper caught up with one scout before he got away and asked him about Lefty. 'He's got a million-dollar arm and a ten-cent brain.' Then he got in his car and drove off. Mick went on to play for the Yankees. Lefty was pumping gas at the Gulf station last time anybody saw him, before he was kilt in Vietnam."

"Interesting," said Charlie. "Anything else?"

"Brenda Lee Darling left here 'bout fifteen years ago to become a star on Broadway. She could sing. Boy, could she sing." Freddie looked up at the ceiling remembering the last time he saw her in a high school play portraying Nellie Forbush in *South Pacific*. "Turns out though, lots of girls can sing. When she got to New York, she couldn't get anyone to listen, so she ended up in a travelling troupe doing *Annie Get Your Gun*, 'cept she wasn't Annie. Last we heard she had got herself married to a Ford dealer in Kokomo and had about five kids."

Good stories, thought Charlie, *but not exactly what I came for.* He tried a different tack. "I passed by that big hospital coming in last night." Charlie added more salt and pepper to his grits. "It looked impressive."

"Yeah, it's a good hospital." Freddie took a sip of his third cup of coffee. "I was in there with the DTs a while back. They told me if I didn't stop drinking I was going to die. I told them I did stop drinking and that's why I was in the hospital." He chuckled. "If I'm gonna die, I'd like to die happy and about the only time I'm happy is when I'm drunk. So there. Make sense to you?"

Charlie considered this for a minute and thought, actually, it did make sense in a convoluted sort of way. "Who owns that hospital?" he asked.

"These four or five counties did own it, but I think it's

owned now by some big corporation."

"How'd that happen?" Charlie wondered if he were talking to the most reliable person in Small River.

"I don't rightly know," said Freddie. "They got this guy to run it, and a few months after he got here, the board sold it. Beats me why. Then the guy ups and leaves. Lots of folks around here weren't happy, but it's still a good hospital, and I got well when I went there." Freddie thought for a moment and added, "I would've gotten well a lot sooner if they'd given me some whiskey. It works a lot faster than them pills."

"Why did the guy leave?" Charlie was fishing, hoping for a big fish in a very shallow pond.

"What guy?" asked Freddie.

"The guy who sold the hospital. You know, the one who was only here a short while." Charlie was thinking he had really wasted his time.

"Don't rightly know," said Freddie. "Happened pretty fast. One day he was here and the next he was gone. The company that bought it had a name reminded me of toilet paper, can't remember what it is. Anyways, they sent someone else to run it, and it seems to be doin' okay. Why do you want to know that?"

"No reason," said Charlie, "just looking for good small-town stories to write about, and usually there are good stories connected to hospitals."

Someone hollered from a booth by the window, "Hey Freddie, tell him about the undertaker. That was big news just last year."

"Aw, that looks bad for Small River. Why should I tell him that?"

"What about the undertaker?" asked Charlie.

"Well, he opened this crematorium a few months before. Lot of folks these days been getting themselves cremated, when they die of course, 'stead of buried. He was trying for that business. Well, the West family who owns the hardware store lost their son in a hunting accident and decided to have him cremated. Old Mr. Kirkpatrick, the undertaker, was going to take care of it. He told them he would have the ashes for them in a few days. They selected an expensive urn, still a lot cheaper than a gold-plated casket. The next day they changed their minds when their other kids got home. They wanted him buried with an open casket at the funeral home, and went to see Kirkpatrick to tell him. Well, Kirkpatrick pitched a conniption fit, said it was too late, the papers were signed and cremation arrangements made and paid for. But the Wests insisted and demanded to see the body to be sure it hadn't already been burned up. They forced their way back into the morgue and opened the storage vault. Lo and behold, the boy's eyes was gone along with a lot of his skin. It was like some horror movie. Well, Mrs. West, she passed right out and had to be hospitalized. There was going to be this big investigation, but before it got started they found poor Mr. Kirkpatrick hanging from a light fixture in his embalming room. He had put a casket he liked under it so when they took him down, he would be in it. It was the most expensive casket in the place, but he got it wholesale. Guess he didn't want to trouble nobody. Left a note, but all it said was that he was sorry and couldn't believe he had been talked into such a thing. And that was that."

"And when was that?" asked Charlie.

"Just last year," said Freddie. "Hasn't been that long. Caused quite a bit of stir, but since the folks think so much of Mrs. Kirkpatrick, they don't say much anymore."

"Where does Mrs. Kirkpatrick live?" Charlie thought he might try to pay her a visit.

"Right behind the funeral home a couple blocks over," said Freddie, "but she don't like company much, and I'd hate for you to bother her on account of something I told you. Okay?"

"Okay. Thanks, Freddie. You know, Sara was right. You are a different person after a couple cups of her coffee. Maybe you should just stick to that."

Freddie just looked at him as he left.

"Come back," said Sara. Charlie waved as he went out the door.

After leaving Sara's, he wandered down the street toward where he assumed was the funeral home. As he approached the Kirkpatrick home, he noticed an elderly woman working in her flower bed. "Pretty flowers," said Charlie and they were. Her garden was full of many varieties of roses.

"Why, thank you, young man," said the woman.

First time in a long time I've been called a young man, thought Charlie. *Must be the blue jeans.* "Are you Mrs. Kirkpatrick?"

"Yes, I am," she said. "How can I help you?"

Charlie could think of no other way than to just ask the question. "Can you give me any information on a man named Ruben Martin?"

The woman stood straight up, raised the hoe as if she were going to strike him with it, and said, "Get out of my yard and out of my sight. I never want to hear that man's name spoken again in this lifetime. Out! Get out!" She moved toward him with the raised hoe.

Charlie held up his hands while backing up. "Hold on now. I didn't mean to upset you. But I am investigating some dealings he had in Chicago, and I hope I can put him behind bars for a long time." He was still backing up. "I thought you might be able to help."

Mrs. Kirkpatrick lowered her hoe but kept her eye on Charlie. "My husband dedicated his life to taking care of families and their loved ones at very difficult times. He had a wonderful reputation, made a good living, and supported and loved his family. It all came to an end because of that horrible man whose name I still cannot bring myself to say."

"Can you tell me what happened?" Charlie sensed she was warming up. "I won't use any names. I just have to know the facts."

She hesitated, studying Charlie for a long moment, then said, "You seem like a nice young man. Come on up on the porch and I'll get us some iced tea." They sat in rocking chairs, facing each other, enjoying their tea as she related the story of how Ruben Martin came to town and made a big deal about selling the hospital to Great Northern. Then he visited Mr. Kirkpatrick several times and tried to get him to do some illegal things. Mr. Kirkpatrick was horrified at first but saw an opportunity to help with his grandkids' expensive college educations, so he relented. Nobody was to ever know, and nobody ever knew for sure whose ashes were in what urn... She stopped talking, looked down at the floor, and sobbed.

Charlie could tell she was trying to justify her husband's actions. He could appreciate that.

"Why did he do it? We were so happy." She seemed to be talking to herself as much as to Charlie. "We didn't really need anything. That Mr. Martin. There, I said it. I despise him. My husband was caught red-handed. He committed suicide because he was so distraught, and this horrible Martin fellow," she made a disgusted face, "just walks off scot-free. And it was his idea all along."

"Mrs. Kirkpatrick, thank you for telling me this. I know how hard it was for you. But I promise you that Ruben Martin is about to get what's coming to him." Charlie wished he were as sure as he tried to sound. He thanked her again and said he would be sure to let her know what happened. She said she would look for his article in a magazine.

Charlie caught the only taxi back to the airport. He thought about eating at Sara's one last time, but was now in more of a hurry to get home. He was to be in New Orleans for the deposition tomorrow.

After thanking the old gentleman at the airport again for his help, he began the flight home. He landed in Pittsburg, Texas, to refuel and grab some lunch. He was eating his second order of hot links when his cell phone rang.

"Charlie, where are you?" Ellie sounded frantic.

"I'm at a hot links joint in Pittsburg, Texas, eating lunch. What's up?"

"I'm so glad you answered. I've left a couple of messages and was afraid you would get here without me contacting you first. When are you coming this way?" She was so relieved to be talking to him without having to leave another message he might not get in time.

"I just stopped here for gas and some food. I'll be home later this afternoon. Why? Is there a problem?"

"Yes. Charlie, you can't come home. It's not safe. I can't say too much more over the phone. Where else can you fly close enough that I can drive to meet you this afternoon?"

"How about Ville Platte? That's a half hour or so away. I should be there about five o'clock."

"I'll be there to pick you up at five. Be careful."

"See you then." Charlie finished eating and went back to his plane, wondering what had changed. He would find out in Ville Platte, but he felt a new sense of urgency to get home.

CHAPTER TWENTY-ONE

SUNDAY EVENING, JUNE 11

All the way to Ville Platte the plane seemed to be bucking a headwind. Charlie determined to upgrade to a more powerful, retractable-gear, faster airplane at his first opportunity. He touched down at five thirty, just as some clouds were coming in from the southwest, obscuring the sun. Ellie and Beau were there to meet him. He tied the plane down and made arrangements to park it there for a few days. They drove downtown to The Pig Stand, a Cajun barbecue restaurant, to eat an early supper. It was not crowded at this hour so they were seated near the front. Not wanting to discuss the situation in Bayou Belle in front of Beau, the conversation turned naturally to baseball. Beau was more animated than Charlie had seen him. He was definitely feeling better and eager to play.

"We have a game next week. Do you think it'll be okay to play?"

"I think so," said Charlie. "I want to get a look at that wound again and get your stitches out first."

"I know I can hit and run. I've been swinging a bat and it doesn't hurt." Ellie's eyebrows went up with this statement, but she didn't say anything. "I just hope I'm at a different place in the batting order."

"Why is that?" asked Charlie. "I thought you were already

batting fifth."

"I was and that would be okay. It's just that I have died on third so many times the last couple of years. You wouldn't believe how many times I've been on third base and watched Billy Don strike out."

"That's funny," Charlie said, thinking maybe Billy Don needed his eyes checked. "It reminds me of something that happened when I was in college. We had this guy, Knotty LeBlanc was his name, who had come from a junior college and had a lot of baseball savvy. We were playing a team that had a tall fastball pitcher, and the score was tied going into the last inning. Well, Knotty managed to get to third base with two outs. Unfortunately, Speedy Fontenot, a big football player who played baseball to get out of spring football practice, was next up. He was one of those hitters that could drive a ball 500 feet but usually got his three swings and came back to sit in the dugout. The pitcher wasn't pitching from a stretch windup, so Knotty got his attention by sitting down on third base." Charlie smiled just remembering it. "When Speedy swung and missed for a second strike, Knotty stood up and yelled to the pitcher that he was stealing home on the next pitch. The pitcher chuckled and rolled his eyes. But when he began his windup, Knotty took off for home, screaming at the top of his lungs and not having a prayer of getting there in time. He got a good jump from third base and was halfway down the line, too far off to turn back, when he stopped dead still. The pitcher was so flustered he stopped in the middle of his windup."

"You mean he balked?" Beau grinned.

"Bigger than Dallas he did." Charlie laughed as he remembered the reaction of his coach running toward the umpire, hollering, "He balked, he balked, he balked."

"I'm not recommending that, but sometimes you have to give yourself a chance and try something unorthodox."

Another life lesson taught by sport, thought Charlie.

They finished their meal. As they were walking out, they saw lights on at the ballpark even at this early hour. There was a light mist and the night air had cooled. Beau asked if they could go to the game for a while. "We may be playing these guys in the playoffs."

"Good idea," said Ellie. It would give her a chance to talk to Charlie about something besides baseball. Hopefully the rain would hold off long enough to catch Charlie up.

Beau went up in the bleachers while Charlie and Ellie stayed in the car, windows down and a light, cool breeze blowing through. "Thanks for coming to get me," said Charlie, leaning against the passenger door with his arm on the back of the seat. "I've been dying to know what happened and why I can't go home."

Ellie still gripped the steering wheel and looked out the window for a moment before turning to face Charlie. "Charlie, the guard you killed is a hit man's brother, so the death threats are for real." She had considered how best to tell him, but when the moment arrived, she just blurted it out.

Charlie sat for a moment without saying anything, a stunned look on his face. "No kidding?" He was assimilating what he thought he had heard. "I didn't kill him, and I sure don't like the way that sounds."

"You know I didn't mean it like that, and I haven't finished the story." She reached over and took his hand in both of hers.

Charlie acted like he didn't hear, but he didn't take his

hand away. He looked past her out the driver's side window at nothing in particular, then mused, "So it looks like I'll either be killed by the mob or face a murder charge." He looked back at Ellie. "And how did you find this out?"

Still holding his hand and trying to get him to look her in the eye, she continued. "You probably hadn't even landed in Texas before Jake got a call from James Vidrine to meet him at the trucking company office." She then told him in detail about Vidrine's having found Jake's gun and the threats directed at Jake. "He knows you were the white guy and the shooter." She told him Vidrine wasn't interested in prosecuting the murder, but he couldn't speak for the guard's brother. "And now he is blackmailing Jake, who feels like the sword of Damocles is hanging over his head."

"That tells us Vidrine is mob connected," said Charlie. "How else would the hit man know and already be making death threats?"

"Jake went to see his mother after his visit to Vidrine. They called me because they didn't have your cell number. They wanted to warn you so you wouldn't come home to a trap." She dreaded telling him the next part because he had made her promise not to snoop around, but there was no choice.

Charlie could hardly sit still and objected several times as Ellie related her experience under Hubert's desk listening to Ruben's repeated threats and the implications that he had ordered Ken Adam's death and the attack on Doc.

"Are you sure Ruben didn't know you were there?"

"I'm sure," Ellie said with a confidence she wasn't sure she felt.

Charlie wasn't sure either. He looked at Ellie. "There's a backseat in that Cessna. How 'bout you, Beau, and me disappearing somewhere in Mexico?" He meant it to lighten the mood, but as he thought about it a little more, it sounded like the best idea.

Ellie tried to laugh, but it came out as a groan.

Charlie didn't share anything he had learned in Small River. He had not come to any sure conclusions yet and didn't want that information out. Changing the subject, he said, "I have to go to New Orleans tomorrow for a deposition. I guess I'll rent a car here and go, but I was thinking you might like to go with me? I'd sure enjoy the company. We could get some lunch beforehand. I could check on Dad. Then we'll have a good dinner in the French Quarter afterward. What do you say? I'd also like for you to be somewhere besides in Bayou Belle." Charlie wanted to be persuasive, but was fearful that she may reject him if she thought his intentions were more than friendly. "We can review all we know, take notes, and organize our thinking."

"I'd love to go." She smiled at Charlie. "Beau could stay with Jeremiah. They're always asking him over. He'd be safe at Jake's house." She thought for a minute. "Tell you what. Don't rent a car. I saw a Hampton Inn as I was driving in. You could stay there tonight. I'll come back in the morning and we'll take my car to New Orleans. That be okay?"

"That would be great, if you're sure you don't mind. We'll need to leave here by nine if we want to get lunch. The deposition is at two o'clock."

"I'll pick you up at the hotel at nine, then."

Charlie went to get Beau. The game was almost over, and he had seen what he came to see. They dropped Charlie off at the hotel, then drove back to Bayou Belle.

CHAPTER TWENTY-TWO

MONDAY, JUNE 12

Charlie was waiting outside the Hampton Inn when Ellie drove up. Delphine had gotten his suit cleaned and gave it to Ellie to bring with her. She waited in the car while he changed. "You dress up well," she said when he came back out. He also looked rested for the first time since she had seen him at the ER door a week ago.

"Thanks," he said, looking at her approvingly. "You dress up pretty well yourself." Ellie was wearing a white silk blouse and beige pants that fit extremely well. Pearl earrings and a necklace dressed it up, but she had on comfortable shoes for walking in New Orleans; a nice combination of dress and comfort, which she pulled off well. He couldn't imagine her looking bad in anything, remembering the first time he saw her in a sweat suit.

"You want to drive?" she asked, holding out the keys.

"Sure." He folded his coat and put it in the backseat. He chose a scenic route that took them past bayous and marshland, sugar cane and cotton fields. He went a little out of the way to the River Road past Oak Alley, crossed the river at Vacherie, then passed San Francisco Plantation and Destrehan, and followed the river into New Orleans. Charlie called ahead for reservations at Dante's Kitchen. The weather was pleasant enough for them to eat outside in the courtyard. Ellie enjoyed the mignon trois, and Charlie ordered their famous roasted chicken under a brick. They shared a bottle of red wine that complemented both their meals. Charlie said at one point, the wine about gone, "If we have to we can take the trolley to the deposition." They talked about history and Ellie's classes and students. They discussed movies, music preferences, and favorite authors. Time passed very fast, and it was after one o'clock before Charlie paid the bill and they left to find Dr. Dingleberry's office.

Linda George was sitting in a waiting room chair, looking over her papers when Charlie and Ellie walked up. Introductions were made. "How long do you expect this deposition to last?" asked Charlie.

"I would say about two hours, depending on how long-winded the doctor is. I have enough questions to last over an hour anyway."

Charlie turned to Ellie. "There's no need for you to wait around here. I have your cell number and I can call you when we're finished." He looked toward St. Charles Street. "You might want to take a trolley ride down St. Charles. Or the Audubon Park Zoo is across the street."

"Don't worry about me for a minute. I'll be fine. It's a beautiful day and I love New Orleans. I'll go on now so you two can review your case." She shook Linda's hand and walked toward the trolley stop.

"Tell me about this doctor," said Charlie.

"He is a surgeon in private practice and has been for over thirty years. He is affiliated with Tulane as an adjunct professor of surgery but is not a full-time member of the Tulane staff.

It may be difficult to sit there and hear him say what you did wrong, but that is what I want you to do. Don't say anything. Remember, we just want to hear what he has to say so we know what we have to rebut."

Promptly at two o'clock, Linda and Charlie were escorted into Dr. Dingleberry's private office, where he sat with the plaintiff's attorney. A few pleasantries were exchanged, but they soon got down to business. This was indeed not a social call. Charlie regarded Dr. Dingleberry as an enemy. After the preliminary statements about who was present, what their credentials were, acknowledgment about the session being recorded, and the swearing in of the witness, the deposition got under way. Linda was thorough in her questioning. Charlie was pleased by her knowledge of the subject. The gist of the testimony was that Dr. Dingleberry believed Charlie had committed malpractice when he left the tip of a subclavian catheter in the left subclavian vein instead of replacing it into the superior vena cava where it belonged. "I would never" (and he stressed never) "leave a catheter where Dr. Leveau did because of the risk of blood clot, which is indeed what happened." Dr. Dingleberry learned how to place central lines while in Vietnam and had done many over his career, but had not done any for several years because as he said, "The younger surgeons do most of the emergency work."

The deposition lasted a little more than an hour. When it was over, they all shook hands and Charlie walked Linda back to her car.

Linda asked, "So what did you think?"

Charlie had listened without commenting and was finally able to speak his mind. "I thought he was very credible and a likable person. I would say he is a nice guy, but he is wrong."

"I thought he was very credible too," said Linda, "and he will be believed by a jury if it comes to that." She stopped and faced Charlie before they arrived at her car. "Charlie, you should know this. I have asked two different young surgeons in Dallas associated with the medical school about this, and both said it was wrong to leave the catheter where you did. So far I haven't found a good expert witness for our side, and we have to find one soon. Do you have any suggestions?"

Charlie felt his chest tighten. "I'll give it some thought." He hesitated for a long moment, looked down at the sidewalk and across St. Charles toward the zoo, then back at Linda, who had a puzzled expression. "There is something else that, as my lawyer, you should know." He wanted to avoid the subject, but he didn't want her to hear it from someone else. He already thought she doubted him, and this would make that worse.

"What is that?"

"I've had some trouble since going to Bayou Belle, a lot of trouble." Linda looked at him, waiting for him to go on. Charlie was staring at his shoes, his shoulders slumped. *Where to start?* He shrugged his shoulders and dived in. "I may be involved in another lawsuit, this time a wrongful death malpractice suit. It happened very recently, so there has been no notice. I might even be charged with murder." When he looked up, Linda was staring at him, her mouth open and an unreadable expression on her face.

Linda, somewhat annoyed that he had not notified his carrier, asked, "Do you think you were wrong or guilty of malpractice in that case?"

"Not at all," said Charlie.

Linda rolled her eyes. She had not known many doctors who thought they were actually guilty.

"Not only that," said Charlie, "they are accusing me of drinking before performing the operation that eventually resulted in the death." He neglected to mention that he also was the one who shot the patient. He wasn't sure that his lawyer wouldn't throw up her hands and run off down the street screaming. Besides, she wasn't a criminal defense attorney. She was a malpractice attorney.

Linda cocked her head to one side and with raised eyebrows asked, "Had you been drinking?"

"Yes," said Charlie defensively, "but it was just one drink, and it was two hours before being called to the hospital and three hours before the operation. So it had no effect. I had gone to sleep in a chair and some spilled on my shirt, which is probably what somebody smelled."

"Oh my," said Linda, a worried expression on her face, "this could be bad. This could be real bad."

"Wait," Charlie continued, wanting to get it all out. "It gets worse. The hospital CEO is kicking me off the staff and reporting me to the state medical board."

"Can he do that?" asked Linda.

"Well, actually he just refused to consider me for permanent status. I was granted only temporary privileges to do one case, and it wasn't that case. I didn't actually have privileges to do the case in question."

"Oh my," said Linda again, thinking she might need some help with this one.

"I may also be recommended for mandatory rehab in order to keep my license to practice. You can't imagine what that does to a surgical practice. Surgeons build a reputation, not a practice. Internists see the same patients over and over again, but surgeons have to continuously get new patients who, after surgery, go back to their internists and family doctors."

"Unfortunately, Charlie, I do know what it does. It goes without saying that you should have thought about that before having that drink. Any application you fill out for hospital privileges or any application for malpractice insurance will require all this to be explained. So, Charlie, this makes an even stronger case for settling this lawsuit. That would at least keep it out of the newspapers. Since the damages were not that great, I think we can settle for less than one hundred thousand dollars and may not have to report it to the national data bank. Sounds like you have enough going on without having to worry about this."

Charlie considered this for a moment. "Hell no. If I'm going down, I'm going down fighting. Most of this is trumped up anyway, whether you believe it or not. And, Ms. George, I'll completely understand it if you don't want to do it that way. You can hand it over to someone else with no hard feelings on my part, but I want my day in court, and I want you to be my lawyer. If I never practice surgery again, I'll at least be able to live with myself."

Linda looked at him and took a moment to reply. "Charlie, you are my client and hopefully will be for the duration. If you are in it for the long haul, then I'll be there with you. You have to understand that if I question you, it's because I have to know everything. I can't give you good advice if I don't know all the facts. Also, the questions you will get from the plaintiff's attorney will be much harder. It doesn't hurt to practice.

Shake?" And she held out her hand. "We'll be okay," she said, with what Charlie thought was less confidence than she had before. "Now, where can we find an expert witness for you?"

Charlie asked, "Who would you say is the most respected vascular surgeon in Dallas?"

"That's easy," said Linda. "It would be Dr. Ron Davis, who's been practicing out of Baylor Hospital for many years."

"Then get him to listen to the story, then look at the x-rays and see what he says."

"Charlie, he is very busy, and even that much would be considered expert testimony and would result in a huge fee." Linda looked doubtful. "Dr. Davis is often asked to be an expert, and because he is so busy with his own vascular practice, he asks three to four times the going rate for experts. Since the insurance company has already paid two experts, I'm not sure they will spring for another, especially one as expensive as Dr. Davis."

Charlie thought fast. "Just ask him. Here's the deal. If he listens to the story, studies the x-rays, and says I was wrong, then I will pay his fee personally and will agree to settle the case. But if he agrees with me, we will use his testimony and fight the case in court."

"I don't see how the company can refuse that offer," said Linda. "Paying Dr. Davis would be a lot cheaper than paying the plaintiff."

"Good. Then it's settled. The deal that is, not the case." Charlie was relieved. "Call me after you have a chance to meet with him." He thanked her and shook her hand as she got into the cab for the ride back to the airport. Charlie watched her drive away, then reached for his cell to call Ellie.

"How did it go?"

"Okay, I guess," said Charlie. "It's very humiliating, though. Where are you?"

"On the trolley, just leaving Canal Street on the way back. I thought your deposition would take longer so I rode it to Canal Street and went in the Roosevelt Hotel. My parents used to talk about it. They would drive in and go to the Blue Room and dance to Leon Kelner's band. And I have always loved St. Charles Street. It's magnificent. I can only imagine how it was in its heyday." Charlie tried to imagine Billy Jack dancing to a big band. *You never know all there is to know about people.* He enjoyed the thought.

Charlie walked past Tulane, then wandered back to the trolley stop just in time to meet Ellie. She waved as the trolley rolled to a stop. Charlie walked over and helped her down. "I want to hear all about it," she said.

"Okay, but while we have a chance, let's enjoy the city. I promise to tell you everything if you really want to hear."

"Sure," said Ellie. "I got the 'most understanding award' in high school."

Charlie laughed, surprising himself. They walked to the car and did a driving tour of parts of the city. They drove past Commander's Palace, then back down St. Charles to Poydras, then went by the Superdome. Charlie showed her LSU Medical School and what was left of Charity Hospital after Katrina. He drove down Canal to the river, turned down Chartres, and parked in a lot by the Mississippi River beside the old Jax Brewery. They walked past Jackson Square, and got a cup of coffee at Café du Monde. Charlie tried to get Ellie to sit for a portrait on the square. She cheerfully but adamantly refused. A Dixieland band played in front of the Cabildo. They strolled down Pirate's Alley to Royal Street. Ellie found the antique shops fascinating but too expensive. It was early for the Preservation Hall Band, but Charlie hoped there would be time to come back later. It was five thirty so they went into Pat O'Brien's, sat in the courtyard and enjoyed hurricanes, then strolled on to Bourbon Street. A long line had formed outside Gallatoire's. Needing to check on Doc Leveau and not wanting to waste time in line, they walked a couple of blocks to Canal Street and hailed a cab for a short ride to the Bon Ton.

Still early, there was no problem getting a table. They enjoyed the wine recommended by the waiter and ordered. Ellie, not hungry after a big lunch and a hurricane, ordered the bayou jambalaya off the appetizer menu. Charlie opted for the Bon Ton Salad and then shared his shrimp étouffée with Ellie. For dessert, they drank dark roast coffee and split the bread pudding with whiskey sauce. The meal was excellent, the conversation easy and uncomplicated. Charlie was afraid he bored her with his recount of the deposition, but Ellie insisted that she wanted to hear all about it. It was the most enjoyable day Charlie had spent in a very long time.

While drinking the second cup of coffee, Ellie asked, "I've had a wonderful day and thank you so much for asking me along, but I have to ask, what will your wife say when she finds out you spent the day in New Orleans with another woman, even if she was a former batboy?"

Charlie was relieved that she broached the subject. He looked at his coffee, hoping he could find the right words. "Ellie, I haven't been completely truthful with you and I apologize, but I will tell you now what I left out before." He looked across the table. Her coffee cup was halfway to her mouth, but it stopped when he said that. "When I told you that my wife had gone to visit her sister in Houston, what I didn't say was that she is not coming back." He hesitated a moment before continuing. "She hired an attorney and has filed for divorce. I went to Texas to meet with my attorney. I went on to Oklahoma after the meeting." He looked at his coffee, took a sip, and added, "This all happened the same day that Dad was hurt and the same day I found out about this lawsuit."

Ellie reached over and put her hand on Charlie's wrist. "I'm sorry, Charlie. I didn't mean to pry. We've just become reacquainted for a week, so I can't expect you to spill your whole story all at once. You have no obligation to tell me anything at all."

Charlie looked at her with a worried look. "I have enjoyed seeing you, and I hope this won't make a difference."

"Of course not." Ellie was somewhat ashamed that she was elated by this revelation. "How do you feel about the divorce?"

"I guess I feel like a failure for not being a good husband. I worked too hard trying to be a good and successful surgeon and did not spend enough time nurturing a marriage. I know that now, but several years too late. We just gradually grew apart and were living together out of convenience, necessity, and habit. Tell you what, let's not ruin a great day with unpleasant conversation. It's time to go check on Dad before we go home."

As they were preparing to leave, the manager of the Bon Ton came over to make sure they enjoyed their meal. Assured they had indeed enjoyed the food, he asked where they were from. Charlie told him they lived in Bayou Belle without giving more details.

"Bayou Belle?" The man looked like he was trying to remember something. "You are the second table I've had recently from Bayou Belle. A few months ago I had a diner from there. He was a very large man. I remember it well. He came in by himself but was joined soon by another man whom I don't think he was expecting. Anyway, I watched the table. They were in an intense conversation."

Charlie asked, "What did the other man look like?"

"He was tall with a long nose and small, close-set eyes. The big man was alarmed at first but seemed very happy when they left, which made me feel better." The man shrugged his shoulders with a "surely you understand" look on his face. Then, as if remembering something else he had forgotten, he continued. "After they left, this other man, who had been sitting by himself, came over to me and asked where the big man was from." The manager seemed pleased with himself for remembering.

The evening was cool so they walked arm in arm down Magazine Street, across Canal back to Ellie's car, and drove to LSU Medical Center.

CHAPTER TWENTY-THREE

MONDAY NIGHT, JUNE 12

A guard was posted outside Doc Leveau's room. He checked Charlie's ID and allowed Ellie and him to enter. Charlie was glad for the security. Jake arranged it when he was convinced that Doc had been assaulted. A nurse was taking his blood pressure and looked up when they walked in.

"Dr. Leveau, looks like you have some company." She smiled, introduced herself as Maria, and went about her duties.

Doc opened his eyes and when he saw Charlie, his face, somewhat confused at first, suddenly broke into a wide grin. He held out his arms and Charlie went over for a big hug. "Hi son, so good to see you." Doc looked so much better. For the first time Charlie felt like he would make a complete recovery. "Ellie?" Doc asked with a confused look, like he was trying to remember.

"Hi Dr. Leveau," said Ellie. "Glad you're doing better."

Charlie interrupted, "You look great, Dad. I was afraid we might lose you there for a while." Then he turned to the nurse and asked, "Is he doing as well as it seems? I mean, this is a remarkable turnaround."

"He really is. His strength is returning, and he can walk. However, he's frustrated by his loss of memory. He has total amnesia about the day he got hurt." She patted Doc on the arm as she took off the blood pressure cuff. "I think it'll all come back gradually." She put the stethoscope around her neck and walked toward the door. "You folks stay and visit. I've got some other patients to see to. Maybe visiting with you will help him remember."

They pulled up chairs to the side of Doc's bed. Charlie told him that all the patients he left in the hospital had done well and were all discharged. He recounted the well-wishers and what they had said, especially the coffee group. Then he broached the subject.

"So, Dad, you don't remember anything about that day? What is the last thing you do remember?"

"I think it's starting to come back, but not much. Can you tell me what happened?"

"Don't let this upset you, but Jake thinks you were assaulted at the camp. Billy Jack found you when you were still actively bleeding from the head wound. He may have scared somebody off and saved your life."

"Is that right?" said Doc. "Well, I'll never hear the end of that. Are you sure he didn't bring me some moonshine and I didn't have money to pay him so he hit me?" He winked at Ellie.

Ellie laughed. "I can't wait to tell him that theory."

"You give him a heartfelt thanks from me. He's the best friend I have, and now I really owe him one."

"What's the last thing you do remember, Dad?" Charlie was eager to find out all he could before his dad tired.

"It seems like I was going fishing. I had left my fishing gear in Ken Adams' old office and went to get it. It all gets fuzzy from there. I'd swear I had words with Ruben Martin, and I remember being uncomfortable about it. Can't say why."

"Well, if that much came back," said Charlie, "maybe some more will. At least physically you're recovering fast. You'll be home soon. Delphine is ready for you to come home." Charlie laughed. "She needs someone to appreciate her cooking."

"How is Delphine?" Doc asked, but before Charlie could answer he continued. "Don't know what I'd do without her. I might have had to get married again, and pickings are pretty slim in the Belle." He laughed again and Charlie was overjoyed that his dad had maintained his old sense of humor.

They talked about the kids and Beau's appendectomy and happenings in Bayou Belle. Charlie didn't say anything specifically about Jan and Doc didn't ask. If he sensed anything wrong, he didn't show it. A little while later, Charlie looked at Ellie and said, "I think it's about time we got going. We have a good drive back to Bayou Belle." They were walking toward the door when Doc stopped them.

"Charlie, there is one thing that for some reason keeps coming back to my mind."

Charlie turned around. "What is it, Dad?" He walked back toward the bed. "It might mean something. Anything might help."

"This is really silly, but I seem to remember putting something in my fly rod box. No idea what it might be. Not much room for anything big. Anyway, it's just a thought. If I remember anything else, I'll give you a call. Good to see both of you." As the door was closing he hollered, "Ellie." She stuck her head back in the door. "Thank your dad for me. I really do owe him one."

"I will," she said, "and glad you're doing better, Dr. Leveau."

As they were getting on the elevator to go down, Vinnie was getting off. Before the elevator door closed, he turned back around and met Charlie's eyes.

Charlie hadn't said much on the way to the car. As they were getting on the interstate for a quicker ride back to Bayou Belle, Ellie said, "A penny for your thoughts."

Charlie, realizing he had been deep in thought and not communicative, said, "My thoughts are worth a lot more than that." And he smiled over at her. She was leaning against the passenger door, looking at Charlie. "I was thinking about Dad. He seems so much better and looks like he will recover fully even if he doesn't remember that day. In some ways it might be better if he didn't. The mind works in strange ways."

"What else are you thinking? Maybe about the fly rod box?" Ellie asked innocently enough with eyebrows raised.

Charlie grinned. "How'd you guess? I'm going straight to the camp and open it. I'll drop you off first if you need to get home. I know it's been a long day."

"Are you kidding? I've never been so interested in looking at a fly rod in my life."

They arrived at the camp house a little after eleven o'clock. Charlie went straight to the storage closet where his dad kept his fishing equipment, retrieved the fly rod case, carried it to the dining table, and opened it. At first all they saw was the old fly rod in a worn cloth cover. Charlie lifted it out of the box, uncovering some old flies and extra line and leaders. He was frustrated and was closing the box when he spotted an old-fashioned portable recorder. He picked it up and looked at Ellie. In great anticipation they rewound the tape and pressed "play." Doc's voice came through loud and clear. He was dictating patient notes as he was making rounds at the hospital. Charlie recognized the patients' names that he had visited for his dad. They were listening to the fourth patient report, thinking this wasn't evidence. Charlie was about to turn it off, but Ellie said, "Wait. There has to be something else." Just then they heard someone else's voice. It was garbled and difficult to understand but sounded like the voice of Ruben Martin. Doc had obviously recorded a conversation that he wasn't supposed to hear. Perhaps a crime lab could make sense of it, but Charlie was certain this was connected to the attempted murder of his dad.

"Dad is in more danger than I thought. If his memory returns, he could tell us what he heard. Ruben must know he heard and that's why Dad was attacked." He looked at Ellie. "What do we do?"

"Call Jake."

Jake and the boys were watching an extra inning game between the Cardinals and the Cubs. "You back? The game is still on. Ask Ellie if Beau can just spend the night here."

Charlie looked at Ellie. She nodded her assent. "Sure. That's fine. But that's not why we called." Ellie took over the conversation. "We have a tape we want you to hear. And it needs to be tonight. Dr. Leveau may be in more danger than we realized."

"I'll be there in ten minutes." Jake told Beau he would be spending the night so he could finish watching the game, then said he had to go to work and left.

They listened to the tape. Jake couldn't understand either but agreed that something more had to be done to keep Doc safe. "They're not trying to just get him out of the way.

He heard something and they don't want him talking. He's in more danger than I thought."

Charlie considered driving back to New Orleans and sitting beside his dad's bed himself.

Ellie, sensing Charlie's fear, said, "Why don't we pull a Tom Sawyer?"

Charlie and Jake looked at each other with frowns and shrugs. "What do you mean?"

"I mean we fake his death and make it look real. Then we hide him out somewhere. To make it more convincing, we stage a fake funeral so all the people who want him dead will believe he is." Still looking at blank stares, she continued. "You know, Aunt Polly thought they were dead so they had a funeral. Tom and Huck were at their own funeral."

Again Jake and Charlie looked at each other and shrugged at the same time. Charlie said, "I sure don't have a better idea. It might work. It would take the whole New Orleans Police Department to protect him from the likes of the mob. How do we do it?"

Jake volunteered, "I have a friend who may be able to help us out." With Charlie and Ellie looking on, he dialed the number that Donnie had given him.

Thirty minutes later Donnie arrived at the camp. Charlie recognized him as the housekeeper at the hospital. "Well, son of a gun." Charlie was amazed.

They sat around the camp house great room and considered a few options, then decided that Ellie's idea about the fake death and funeral was the best idea. It just had to be done fast and well.

Donnie took over. "I'll arrange the death and transfer of

the body. It will be better if none of us knows where they hide him. Kind of a temporary witness protection, but with a guard and whatever medical care is still needed. It may take a day to set up since we don't even have a destination. But I'll get started right now. Meanwhile, starting now, we'll double the guard on Doc's room."

Donnie got on his phone and began making the arrangements. Charlie would get the word out that Doc was worse and then wait for word of his death and transfer before making arrangements for a Saturday funeral in Bayou Belle. Jake would begin plans for a raid on the Vidrine Trucking Company for the next Sunday night. It felt better having a plan.

They were leaving the camp and Ellie said, "Charlie, I'm way too tired to take you back to Ville Platte. Would you drive my car back, or if you want you can sleep at my house tonight."

"Sure was a great day and I hate to see it end, but I probably should go back. I'll come back early in the morning so you'll have your car."

There were no cars on the street when Charlie drove up to Ellie's house. He parked in the carport, went around and opened the car door for Ellie, and helped her out.

"Come on in and I'll make a pot of strong coffee. Don't want you going to sleep and wrecking my car." She laughed.

Ellie put on a pot of coffee, but it never got drunk.

"Beau is at Jeremiah's all night." Ellie had her arms around Charlie's neck.

"Good thing," said Charlie. "I'd hate for him to catch us doing what I have in mind."

They almost didn't make it out of the kitchen and then left a trail of clothes through the living room, knocking over a straight-back chair on the way upstairs to Ellie's bedroom.

At five AM Charlie got up and began to dress, trying not to wake her. Ellie was sleeping sweetly on her back, her face framed with thick black hair splayed around it on the white pillowcase. She must have sensed that he was looking at her because just then she opened her eyes and looked at Charlie, disappointed that he was leaving. She sat up and the sheet covering her fell away. He sat down beside her and they held each other. Charlie stood up to leave. "Sure you can't stay another half hour or so," she asked and grabbed him and wouldn't let go.

It can't be said that Charlie fought hard. "Well, maybe a little while longer," and he got back in bed. An hour later, the dawn of a new day was announcing itself through the window. Charlie got dressed, kissed her again, and left promising to call later. The morning was warm and bright with the smell of freshly mown grass. His car was still at the airport and so, tired of hiding and with the confidence of a plan, he struck out down the street heading for Julius'. There was a new spring in his step, and halfway down the block he realized he was whistling.

CHAPTER TWENTY-FOUR

TUESDAY, JUNE 13

Hubert was standing at his window and saw Charlie go into Julius'. *He must not have talked to Ellie or didn't take the warning seriously. I have to let him know.* He sat down at his desk and quickly scribbled a short note that said, "You're in great danger. Believe Ellie." He told his secretary he'd be back in a minute as he rushed out of his office.

Charlie entered the café with his head down, ready to begin his acting career. Putting on the saddest face he could manage and with his shoulders appropriately slumped, he walked slowly over to the village statesmen seated at their usual table in the back. His look did cause some alarm amongst the group.

"What in the world's wrong, Charlie," asked Mr. Julius. "You look like your dog died." Then Mr. Julius realized what may have been the reason for Charlie's demeanor and said, "Oh no. I'm sorry, Charlie. Something happen to Doc?"

Charlie felt guilt for deceiving his dad's dear friends, but it was necessary, and one day hopefully they would understand if it all worked out. Charlie, trying to muster tears that just would not come, slowly nodded his head up and down, still without saying anything.

This got everyone's attention and they all looked worriedly at Charlie. "What happened?" asked BJ.

"His doctors think he re-bled into his brain." Charlie hesitated a moment for effect. "He's paralyzed on one side and can't talk." Charlie thought if word got out that Doc couldn't talk, it would make it less likely they would try again to kill him. "The way it looks, I doubt he makes it much longer. They called from the hospital just a while ago and said I should come back if I wanted to see him again, but that he wouldn't know I was there." The mere image in his mind of that happening almost brought the wanted tears to his eyes. "So I'm just going to stay here and wait for word. I doubt he makes it through the day." He was able to get a sobbing sound out at the end of the sentence, good enough that Mr. Julius stood up quickly and put his arm around Charlie.

"So, so sorry," was all Mr. Julius could say and was all that needed to be said. Charlie thought of the advice he had been given about what you say to families who have lost a loved one. That advice was to say as little as possible.

The front door jingled and Hubert walked in. He saw the sad group gathered in the back and went over. "Charlie's just told us that Doc probably won't make it through the day. He's taken a turn for the worse." Mr. Julius looked back and forth between Charlie and Hubert.

Hubert was devastated. His big body visibly wilted and his head sagged. He felt responsible for what had happened to Doc. "I'm so sorry, Charlie." Hubert was indeed sorry, genuinely and profoundly, and almost forgot why he had come. Remembering, he shook Charlie's hand, leaving the note behind. "If there's anything I can do, please let me know." Hubert excused himself to go back to work.

"You forgot your coffee," Mr. Julius reminded him when

he was almost to the door.

"That's okay. I just lost my taste for refreshment, and I have to get back to work anyway." And Hubert was gone.

"You think he really has that much work to do?" Billy Jack tuned in. "I think he just likes to say that. Still pictures himself a big city lawyer." Billy Jack was as usual trying to brighten the atmosphere.

"Give him a break, Billy Jack," Mr. Julius chided. "He looked really upset with the news."

Charlie, wanting to avoid any more questions, said, "I need to get out to the airport to pick up my car. Anybody going that way?"

Billy Jack spoke up and said he'd be glad to give him a ride. On the way to the airport, Billy Jack asked, "Where is your airplane?"

"I left it in Ville Platte." Before he could be asked, he added, "Ellie and Beau came to pick me up there. At the time I didn't think it was safe to come home. It's probably not safe now, but there's a lot that needs to be done, and I have to be here to do it."

"So, you went to New Orleans yesterday to see Doc?"

"And for a deposition I needed to attend. Ellie went with me and we had a couple of good meals."

"I wondered where she was. I didn't hear from her yesterday and she usually calls. You know, your kids never stop being your kids." BJ glanced over at Charlie.

"Billy Jack, I need to tell you something, but I'll wait 'til we get to the airfield because I don't want you to drive off the road." They were almost to the airfield anyway.

"Charlie, you're a grown man and Ellie is a grown woman.

What you two do is no business of mine," Billy Jack said as he pulled up and parked.

Charlie looked over at Billy Jack with a puzzled look on his face and said, "That's not what I'm talking about, Billy Jack."

"Oh?"

"No, it's not." Charlie thought this was awkward enough as it was. "I'm not saying nothing is going on, but what I need to tell you is something else." He then related to Billy Jack that Doc was really doing well and they planned to fake his death to protect him and go as far as have a funeral with all the family coming in. "But we need a place to meet where nobody would suspect. Some plans need to be made."

Billy Jack looked incredulous. "Of course," he finally said. "What kind of plans about what?"

"That's what we'll get together to decide." Charlie added, "And late tonight would be the best time for the first meeting. How about your place?"

"I'll wait up with the lights on."

Charlie got out of the car, leaned back in the window, and said, "Thanks for the ride. See you tonight 'bout eleven."

The Wagoneer at first didn't want to start. Charlie flooded it, then had to wait. More careful the next time, it started on the second try, sounding like it might not make it back to town. But it did. On the way in he made a decision that he hoped was wise. He drove to Ellie's but her car was gone. *Of course, she had classes today.* He drove to the school and ran up the stairs to her office. The door was closed and there was no answer to his knock. He was still standing there when an older professor with glasses on the end of her nose, a bun on the top of her head, and two books cradled in her arms walked by.

"May I help you?" she asked.

"I'm Charlie Leveau and I was wondering what time Mrs. Boudreaux would be back in her office."

"I know who you are, Dr. Leveau. I was at the town hall meeting the other night. I agreed with you. I couldn't believe the audacity of that man who was given the floor and said what he did. It was a real low point for Bayou Belle. I assure you most of the town would side with you. Anyway, Ellie's class will be over in just a few minutes and she'll come back here then. I'm sure you'd be welcome to go in and wait for her inside." Then she said good-bye and smiled a conspiratorial smile as she walked down the stairs.

Ellie's office was not more than a large closet but it looked like her. A bookshelf held copies of her favorite books, including John Winters' *The Civil War in Louisiana*, T Harry William's book on Huey Long, Robert Penn Warren's *All the King's Men* and several other works of fiction, including *Huckleberry Finn* and Hemingway's *The Sun Also Rises*. Portraits of Gen. P.G.T. Beauregard, Lou Gehrig, and Jean Lafitte hung on the wall alongside a picture of Andrew Jackson at the Battle of New Orleans. Charlie was admiring a dated family portrait of Ellie, her late husband, and Beau when she walked in. She closed the door behind her, turned back to him, smiled sexily, and said, "Couldn't wait for me to get home? Have that much fun last night?" She walked over to him, put her arms around his neck, and kissed him.

"How'd you guess? Might be a little awkward in here, but we can clear some of this stuff off your desk to make room. You'll have to promise not to make too much noise."

She backed up, hit him on the arm, and said, "Me make

noise? Mrs. Fisher came over this morning and asked me if some man was in my house yelling. I had to tell her I went to sleep with the television on." They both laughed.

Getting more serious, Charlie told her he had seen Hubert at Julius'. He told her about the note as well. "We are going to meet tonight at your dad's house at eleven o'clock." Ellie's eyebrows went up. "I thought it would be a place nobody would be watching and nobody would notice. And he agreed. We can trust your dad. I couldn't think of another place," Charlie explained, afraid that Ellie might be upset.

Ellie frowned but nodded in agreement. "Actually, Dad used to do this sort of thing in the military, but he never talked much about it. He's a great choice."

"He may be doing it to protect his lovely daughter."

Ellie blushed. "You told…?"

"I didn't have to. He had already surmised it."

"Oh well," she said. "I should know. There are no secrets in a small town."

"Up 'til now there's been a big secret being kept at Vidrine's, but this august committee will soon put an end to that."

CHAPTER TWENTY-FIVE

TUESDAY NIGHT, JUNE 13

The LSU hospital was understaffed for the night shift. Most activity took place during the day. A lot of night nursing was expensive babysitting. Maria was the nurse in charge of the neurosurgery floor tonight. She had been contacted at home and informed of the plan to move Doc in the early a.m. Records were to show that he had suffered a stroke and died. She was sworn to secrecy. The FBI and Donnie hated to involve her, but with such short notice, there was no other way. At supper time she told Doc about the plan and how he was to leave with his face covered and to lie quietly until safely in the hearse. Doc didn't know what all the fuss was about, but he could tell that Maria was serious and needed his cooperation.

The night before, Vinnie had planned to finish his work, but each time he checked, a New Orleans policeman, requested by Donnie, was sitting with John, and he couldn't get in Doc's room. He was also afraid the policeman would recognize him. He had, after all, made several guest appearances at various New Orleans precincts. He just had to hope he wouldn't be here tonight or he might have to punt the whole thing and try to disappear. At seven thirty Vinnie went up the stairs to the Neuro floor, looked down the hall, and saw John, one of the night guards, sitting by himself. The police were shorthanded due to a riot in the French Quarter, and couldn't supply a guard until after midnight. Any attack would be expected after midnight, so they hadn't hired an extra private-duty cop.

Vinnie was aware of Ruben's growing impatience and, if he failed again, would likely end up at Vidrine's on Sunday night like some of his former friends. He walked to a restaurant and bar down the street to eat dinner and kill time while John got tired sitting in his chair.

In Bayou Belle, the team gathered at Billy Jack's, staggering their arrival times to lessen the chance of drawing attention. Charlie and Ellie arrived first. He left the old jeep at her house and rode in her car. Earlier in the day, Ellie had called Hubert's office and insisted on an emergency appointment. The secretary gave her a rather cold look when she walked through the office. Ellie told Hubert where the meeting would take place, but gave him no details about who would be there or what it was about. All Hubert knew was that he would see Charlie there. Hubert arrived about five minutes after Charlie and Ellie, surprised to see Billy Jack in his own house. Donnie rode with Jake in his patrol car.

Billy Jack, acting the good host, arranged chairs in a circle in his big room. The lights were low. Coffee and snacks were not being served. Jake took charge of the meeting.

"We got us a situation here in Bayou Belle that includes at least blackmail and murder. The FBI is involved." Jake turned toward Donnie and motioned for him to speak.

"What the sheriff said is true. I have been investigating Great Northern and Ruben Martin's means of acquiring hospitals, but this has turned into more than that. Ruben's real name is Ruben Martinelli. His father, Dino Martinelli, is one of New Orleans' crime bosses, the don of the Martinelli family. He wanted his offspring to get out of the organized crime business, so he sent Ruben off to get a degree in hospital administration. The old man is on the national board of Great Northern and had some influence getting Ruben a good starting job. However, Ruben managed to get into enough trouble that Great Northern wanted him out of Chicago. He found a niche in the takeover of smaller hospitals, helping the expansion and national growth of the company. He shortened his name to Martin so nobody would be suspicious. But Ruben couldn't play it straight. He used bribery and other illegal means to facilitate the takeovers quickly. Great Northern apparently wasn't aware of his methods, but they appreciated the results. The FBI was concerned that organized crime was gaining a foothold in the hospital business. Any questions so far?" Donnie looked around the room. Hubert had sunk a little lower in his chair.

"Why did he or Great Northern decide to target Bayou Belle hospital for takeover?" Billy Jack considered his town a little too obscure to be noticed.

"Good question." Donnie continued. "Turns out, Ruben's sister is James Vidrine's wife. Mr. Martinelli arranged her marriage to Vidrine, who at the time ran a successful and legitimate trucking business. Martinelli would be able to send legal business his way and make it even more successful and provide his daughter with a good lifestyle outside the family business but still be close to her old man."

Hubert asked, "So Ruben just wanted to come here to be close to his sister?"

"I think it was more than that," said Donnie. "I believe Vidrine is ambitious and he and Ruben cooked up some illegal means of making a lot of money using some of Ruben's contacts. We don't know what they're doing out there for sure, but it probably involves drugs or prostitution or both. Jake will tell you he saw some camera equipment, so they may be involved in making movies, legitimate or not. The reason we're here tonight is to put all our information together." Donnie looked at Jake. "That's all I have for now."

"You look so familiar to me," said Hubert. "Where have I seen you?"

"I was sitting at the next table at the Bon Ton eavesdropping on your conversation with Ruben."

"I knew it. I knew I had seen you. So you already know he paid me a hundred grand to help him with the takeover of Bayou Belle Hospital."

"He did what?" Billy Jack was almost coming out of his chair.

Hubert, with his head down, continued. "That's right. He met me in New Orleans and told me what Great Northern planned and put the money in Hibernia Bank in my name to help get it done. He made it sound like it would be doing the community a lot of good, and I would be a hero besides being a good bit richer. Now I see what I've done. I'm responsible for what happened to Doc." His voice trailed off, his head still down, shaking it slowly side to side.

Ellie went over, sat next to him, and put her arm around his shoulder. "You weren't the cause of Doc getting hurt, Hubert. You couldn't see any of this happening. Besides, you came and told us before we found out another way." Ellie then looked up at the group. "Hubert called to warn Charlie after something he heard Ruben say. It would have been very tempting for any of us to accept money for what we thought would be a good thing for Bayou Belle. Anyway, we're all on the same side now. Hubert, tell us what you heard."

Hubert looked back up and continued. "After the town meeting I overheard Ruben talking to someone on the phone. Ruben said something like, 'We made our point, but we have to get rid of Charlie Leveau permanently. He could poison the whole deal.' Then he said, 'We can't do it like we did Adams and Doc Leveau. It'll look too suspicious.' He threatened me with my life and that of my family if I ever told. Said he had enough goods on me to put me away for years or to have me killed." His confession somewhat easing his conscience, he looked back up and around at the group. "Being here may sign my death warrant should he find out, but I couldn't let it go. Doc Leveau was one of the finest people I ever knew, and no matter what you say, I am partly responsible for what happened to him. I want somehow to make things right, if that is still possible."

Charlie spoke up. "Hubert, as far as I'm concerned, it's forgotten. Like Ellie says, you couldn't have known. So forget about it and help us figure out what to do."

"For crying out loud," opined Billy Jack, "it'd be one thing to be fighting a small-town trucking company gang trying to solve a local problem, but it's another thing altogether to be up against the whole New Orleans mob."

"Maybe," said Donnie, "but I'm not sure how much the New Orleans people know about all of this. My contacts in New Orleans haven't gotten wind of anything going on in Bayou Belle. This could be a scheme cooked up by Ruben and James Vidrine. Ruben may be using some people he knows from the mob, but my sources don't think it goes to the top."

Jake broke in. "Vidrine sure thinks he owns me." And he looked at Donnie, who nodded for him to go ahead. Jake then told the story of his and Charlie's misadventure and Vidrine's men finding his gun, but being willing to drop the mess if Jake would cooperate with him when needed. "He also knows Charlie is the one who shot his guard, who later died. Turns out that guard is a brother to one of the mob hit men, maybe even the one who attacked Doc."

Hubert was now sitting straight up in his chair looking at Charlie. "You mean you shot the man, then operated on him and he died?" Hubert shook his head harder. "I thought I had troubles."

Just before midnight, Vinnie rode up the elevator and slipped down the hall to where John was sleeping in his chair, leaning back and propped against the wall. Vinnie thought about knocking him out and leaving him in his chair, but Ruben was insistent that this still had to look like an accident. Vinnie touched John lightly on the shoulder. John jumped, the chair started to slide out from under him, but Vinnie caught him to prevent a fall. "Sorry, man," Vinnie laughed, "didn't mean to scare you, but if they catch you sleeping again, you may lose your job."

"That's okay. Thanks." John shuffled over, looking down the hall to see if any of the nurses had noticed. Relieved that he had once again gotten away with a snooze, he shook his head to wake up and said, "Wife had me shopping all day and didn't get to take my nap. They warned me to be very awake and alert tonight, but so far, nothing out of the ordinary has happened." Then he opened Doc's door and looked in just to be sure nothing had happened while he was dozing. He turned back to Vinnie with a relieved look and a deep sigh.

"Say, John, if you sit back down, you're just going back to sleep. While the nurses are in report, why don't you go down to the cafeteria and get some coffee or walk outside and get some fresh air. It might help keep you awake."

"I better not do that. I'd get fired for sure if I left my post. I'll just stand up till I wake up a bit."

"Suit yourself, but I would be glad to watch the door for a few minutes if you'd like."

"But you don't even have a gun." John was weakening.

"Believe me, if anyone starts down this hall, I'll scream bloody murder, loud enough to have the whole New Orleans police force here in no time."

John laughed at the thought. "I'll be back in five minutes max. Thanks, Billy."

Vinnie was glad John had reminded him that he was Billy. He couldn't remember how he had introduced himself several days before.

John rounded the corner out of sight, and Vinnie wasted no more time. He slipped quietly into the room. Doc was asleep and snoring. He was no longer connected to IVs and the breathing tube was gone. Vinnie picked up a pillow at the foot of the bed, and holding it in front of him with both hands, he leaned over to place the pillow squarely over Doc's nose and mouth. In doing so he leaned against the bed, setting off the bed alarm, there to alert the nurses if a patient tried to get out of bed. The loud noise woke Doc up, and when he saw Vinnie holding the pillow, his eyes got big and he mouthed the word "You" as Vinnie brought the pillow down on his face. Doc struggled mightily, but Vinnie was too strong. When Doc realized he couldn't win, he stopped struggling, hoping that Vinnie would think his job was done and let go. Vinnie still held tight. Doc felt himself blacking out, hungry for air, sucking in but getting only a mouth full of pillow.

Maria was with another patient when the bed alarm went off. For a moment she paid no attention. There were so many false alarms. Then she noticed it was from Doc's room. She went out of the room and looked down the hall just as the oxygen saturation alarm also went off. John was not there. She screamed for help and ran down the hall. Maria crashed through the door, surprising Vinnie, who momentarily looked up and loosened his grip on the pillow, but Doc didn't move. Vinnie knocked Maria against the door as he ran out and down the hall.

John hadn't turned the corner when he saw Vinnie run by and heard the commotion down the hall. He thought, *I should just go home now, rather than face the music*, but he didn't. He dejectedly made his way back to his duty post.

A medical response team was busily resuscitating Doc Leveau. His EKG showed no acute changes, and he was now breathing on his own with a rebreathing mask at 100% oxygen. After a few minutes of catching his breath, Doc was stable.

There were no apparent signs of damage. Thank God for pulse oximeters and patient bed alarms.

When Maria came out of Doc's room, John was standing there sheepishly with his hands in his pockets. "John, quit playing with yourself and get ready to use that gun if you have to. If anything else like this happens on my shift, I won't have you fired, I'll kill you with my bare hands. Do you understand?"

John understood. She sounded like she meant exactly that. All he could do was take his hands out of his pockets and nod his head.

Jake was still talking when Donnie's cell rang. Donnie held up his hand for quiet. Maria was calling from LSU. With a worried look on his face, he looked over at Charlie, holding up his index finger, signaling to hold on for a minute. Donnie asked, "Is he okay?" Charlie got out of his chair and walked toward Donnie, holding his hand out for Donnie's phone. Donnie held up his hand, asking Charlie to wait a second while continuing to talk to Maria. "Okay, we'll get right on it. Put another guard at the door. We'll make the transfer by 0500." Looking at Charlie, he then said to Maria, "I'm here with Charlie Leveau, Doc's son. I'll give him the phone so you can tell him what you just told me. Thanks, Maria, you're wonderful." He gave the phone to Charlie, then told the group: "They had to call a code on Doc because some guy got to him, but he's okay and we're moving up the transfer. Trouble is, now all pretenses are off. The bad guys don't have to make it look like an accident anymore and could walk in there and shoot him and the guard. But they've also done some of our work for us, long as we make it look like they finished the job. We'll just have him out before sunrise."

Charlie thanked Maria, hung up, and gave Donnie back his phone. He was reassured about his dad and, since he already had the floor, recounted what he had learned in Oklahoma. "A couple days ago I went back to Riverton, Texas, to take care of some business and went on to Small River, Oklahoma, where Ruben was before he came here. He successfully engineered the buying of their hospital before leaving. One thing I found may be a key to this whole thing." Charlie then recounted talking to Mrs. Kirkpatrick in Small River and what had happened to her husband.

"So what do you think all that means?" asked Donnie and Billy Jack at the same time.

"I wonder if they're running some sort of organ-selling ring. When Jake and I were in the house on the Vidrine property, there was the setup for an OR, complete with nitrous tanks and OR lights."

"They told me it was for a movie set," said Jake, "some *sex in the OR* story."

"That could still be, but I don't think they would be so willing to kill to keep that from being discovered." Charlie looked at Jake. "You remember we saw that large oven in one of the outbuildings?"

Jake nodded. "Yes."

"What if they're harvesting organs in that little OR, selling the parts, then cremating the remains so it can't be discovered." Charlie raised the question to the group. "There is a big black market for organs. Thousands die every year waiting for organs. Many will go to extraordinary means to procure a needed organ for a loved one."

"Wouldn't you need live organs for the big money?" Hubert was beginning to get nauseated.

"They can sell skin, bones, corneas, and some other things from cadavers. For hearts, kidneys, liver, or lungs, they'd need live donors."

Ellie spoke up. "Charlie, while you were in your deposition in New Orleans, I picked up a *Times Picayune* on the St. Charles Trolley. There was an article on the front page about the unusual number of missing person reports and how most of them are still missing. Fifteen to twenty people are still missing without a trace."

This brought quiet to the gathering. The silence was broken when Billy Jack said, "Geez. Right here in our quiet town. What can we do?"

Charlie spoke back up. "They must be bringing in a team of nurses or doctors or both on those planes that come in on Sunday night. They do their thing, leave the bodies to be cremated, and fly off with the salable organs. Unless I miss my guess, the organs are sold before they are harvested, and the hearts are flown by jet to a prearranged destination. They have to be there within six hours after harvest."

Donnie, rubbing his chin, said, "That explains what Ruben said the other night on his phone." All eyes were on Donnie. "He said things were getting hot and they should call it quits for a while 'til things cooled off. Vidrine said he had already been paid for three hearts, so they had to deliver."

Now even Charlie's mouth dropped open. "Vidrine said that?" he asked incredulously.

"Sure did and I still have the recording. Just had no idea

what he meant 'til now."

Jake said, "Letting this thing go another week would mean more lives lost. We have to do something now."

"Even with the tape evidence and everything everyone has heard, we need to catch them red-handed. We've got time to get a small army in here and raid their place Sunday evening. It'll have to be timed well enough so that they don't know we're coming, and early enough that they won't have killed anyone else." Donnie was already turning over in his mind the best way to go about it.

"How do you think Kaiser fits into all this?" asked Hubert.

"I've got a theory," said Charlie, "but I don't know. I know he was brought here by Ruben, and Ruben is using him."

The meeting came to a close as initial steps were proposed. Donnie and Jake would come up with a plan of attack. Meanwhile there was a funeral to plan for Saturday. Ruben wasn't watching Donnie, so any news that needed to be communicated would go through him. He gave them all his cell number and home address. They could also find him with broom in hand at the hospital.

Vinnie had run halfway down the block when he remembered that his car was parked in back of the hospital. He doubled back to it after all the police cars had gone by, unlocked it, and sat watching the door to see if he could get an indication or proof that Doc was dead.

Two hours passed before a hearse pulled up. A stretcher with a sheet completely covering the face of the rider was wheeled out the back door. They rolled it to the back of the hearse. One of the accompanying guards was John, enough evidence for Vinnie that the corpse was indeed Doc Leveau.

Vinnie wanted to catch a little sleep, then get out of town. He would report to Ruben and get his money. He started to follow the hearse, but drove instead to Bayou Belle, intent on killing his next victim, the doctor who had killed his brother.

CHAPTER TWENTY-SIX

EARLY WEDNESDAY, JUNE 14

Vinnie left New Orleans, heading toward Bayou Belle a little after three am. The police would be looking for him with a good description from Maria and John, so he best get out of town. If he could get to Bayou Belle before sunrise, he should have time to set up a line of fire to kill the younger Dr. Leveau when he came out of the house to get into his car. Then he would report to Ruben.

He arrived in Bayou Belle at five-twenty in the morning and drove slowly by the Leveau home. The old jeep was parked in front. The house across the street was still for sale and no lights were on. Vinnie drove around the block and parked in front of a wooded vacant lot. Still dark but with a faint glow showing on the eastern horizon, Vinnie opened the trunk, put on his gloves, and retrieved the case holding his rifle and scope. Looking around and easing the trunk closed, he raced across the lot toward the backyard of the house for sale. He approached the back of the house, drawing his pistol out of his shoulder holster. He was prepared to kill whoever was there. The back door had a dead bolt. Quickly looking around, he used his elbow to break out a pane of glass. Gun drawn, he waited to see if any lights came on. After none did, he reached through the broken glass and opened the door from inside.

He searched the house thoroughly and found nobody home. Walking room to room he chose a window in front that gave him the best view of the Leveaus'. He raised the window slightly, put the gun together, and adjusted the scope. Now all he had to do was wait. Ruben would want a report soon, so Vinnie hoped it wouldn't be too late when young Dr. Leveau left the house. He would have preferred to kidnap Charlie so he would know who killed him and why, but there was no time. Better not to take a chance going by the hospital. With his work done, he would disappear. Ruben could wire him his money.

Charlie slept later than usual. It had been a long night. His dad should be wherever they were hiding him by now. Charlie had no idea where that was. Donnie thought the fewer people who knew the better. His job today was to make arrangements for the funeral and to call his family. He would ask Page to write the obituary and put it in tomorrow's paper. It would have to be really good because, unlike with most obits, the subject and still-breathing honoree would get to read this one.

Delphine had bacon, eggs, and grits ready when Charlie came down. He walked over and poured himself a cup of strong coffee and put his arm around Delphine's shoulder. "Delphine, I'll be straight with you this time. I have a secret that you have to help me keep. Okay?"

"Charlie, surely you know you can tell me anything, as many secrets as I kept from your parents." She looked up at him and winked. "Do you even have to ask?"

So Charlie told her the whole thing in abbreviated form. "We're going to have a funeral for him on Saturday. I'm making the arrangements with Charlet's. Family will be coming in probably starting tomorrow. They will all have to think he is dead, so we can't let on, not even to Page or Chuck or Jan. That's why I wasn't going to tell you at first. Can you do that?" He was looking at the back of her head, waiting for a response.

"If it means helping to save Doc's life, I can do anything. Just let me know what I can do. If it's just cooking and cleaning and taking care of the out-of-town folks, that's okay. I won't say a word."

"I know that," said Charlie, "and I'm glad you know. I'm not a good enough actor to hide it from you. Hope I'll be good enough to fool the others." Charlie sat down and was enjoying his breakfast. He looked at his watch. It was almost nine AM. He needed to get to Julius' soon. He thanked Delphine for the breakfast, got up, and walked toward the front door.

Vinnie had almost dozed off a couple times. Amazing how one can be sleepy even if he is about to kill someone. He saw the front door open and Charlie Leveau start to come out, then turn around.

"Charlie, you come back here and have at least one of Delphine's biscuits. Some of my mayhaw jelly is open on the table." Delphine had buttered two biscuits, and a teaspoon was in the jelly. Charlie sat back down, ate the biscuits, and wondered how men could live happily without good biscuits and mayhaw jelly in the morning.

"Damn," Vinnie said out loud. He had hoped to be on the way out of town by now. He knew Charlie was dressed and it wouldn't be too long before he came out, so he kept his gun trained on the door. His best shot would be just before Leveau got to the car. He preferred a head shot, but better a sure thing and go for the chest. As he was thinking this, the

BAYOU COCKTAIL

front door opened again and Charlie Leveau walked out in a starched white shirt. He stopped momentarily at the door and looked up and down the street, as if he suspected something, then walked fast toward the car.

Charlie was about five steps from the car, still looking around.

Vinnie had the crosshairs on the left side of Charlie's chest. The man was walking fast but slowed as he neared the car. Vinnie was waiting until he came to a full stop, wanting to take no chances of a miss. The sight steady on Charlie's left front pocket, Vinnie gently squeezed the trigger, and his hand gradually tightened around the handle. Charlie stopped and reached to open the door. Now, Vinnie squeezed the trigger, but as he did a piece of glass from the broken window crashed to the floor, startling Vinnie and causing his hand to jerk slightly just as the shot fired. Charlie twirled, grabbed his left chest, took three steps toward the house, and fell face first to the ground.

Vinnie quickly dismantled his rifle and put it back in the case. One more glance out the window assured him Leveau was on the ground lying perfectly still. Vinnie raced to his car and drove out of town. He called Ruben. "I got 'em both," was all he said when Ruben answered.

Ruben, awakened by the phone and disoriented, asked, "Who is this? What are you talking about?"

Vinnie repeated himself. "I got the old Doc last night, and I killed his son just a minute ago coming out of his house."

Ruben, still trying to clear his head, was now up sitting on the side of the bed. "You crazy bastard! Nobody told you to do that!" he screamed into the phone, holding it away and looking at it like it was an alien creature.

"You didn't have to. After I saw the old man leave in a hearse, I came here on my own to collect my money and kill the SOB that killed my brother. That part was my doing."

A throbbing ache was forming behind Ruben's eyes. He rubbed his forehead, hoping he was still asleep. "Don't come anywhere near me. Get out of town and don't look back. I'll send the money to wherever you end up."

Vinnie, pleased with himself, headed west with no plans of returning.

CHAPTER TWENTY-SEVEN

WEDNESDAY, JUNE 14

Delphine heard the shot but thought it was the old jeep backfiring. She put the dishes in the sink and was going to dust the furniture in the parlor when she glanced out the window and saw the Wagoneer still there. Funny, must have backfired and not started. She walked over to the window and saw Charlie lying still on the ground, a large red stain on his fresh white shirt.

Charlie lay very still. The side of his left chest hurt like a son of a gun. He had an almost uncontrollable urge to reach up and feel the damage. He was breathing, but he was trying to hold his breath, wanting whoever fired the shot to think he was dead. Maybe he was dead and this was heaven. Then he heard Delphine screaming, the door slamming behind her as she ran out, and he was convinced he was alive.

"Charlie," she screamed as she ran toward him. Kneeling down, she felt for a heartbeat. He had a good pulse. She turned him over and opened one of his eyes. He opened the other.

"Somebody just shot me and I want them to think I'm dead."

"You had me fooled. Don't know what I'm gonna do. You and Jake both getting shot. What's this town coming to?"

"Hope mine is worse than his," said Charlie, "else I'll never hear the end of it." He eased himself and Delphine closer to the car. He got his cell out of his pocket and called Jake. "Jake," he said when the sheriff answered, "almost lost a member of our team. Somebody just took a shot at me from the vacant house across the street."

"Damn," said Jake, "I was afraid of that. You okay?"

"I got shot in the chest. You just got it in the shoulder. I'd say my purple heart should be bigger than yours."

"You can have both of them as far as I'm concerned, smartass."

Jake arrived moments later in his police car. He and Delphine helped Charlie back in the house. They got his shirt off. The bullet never entered his chest cavity. It was a long wound where the bullet had grazed him, causing a lot of bleeding and probably a broken rib. To Charlie that's what it felt like. They washed the wound with alcohol and peroxide and applied a sterile dressing. Charlie was able to walk around. He listened to his chest with his stethoscope and heard good breath sounds, even though it hurt to take a deep breath. He was up to date on his tetanus and decided not to go to the hospital and set off a Chinese fire drill. If he got short of breath from a pneumothorax, he would go, but otherwise would treat this like a standard open wound. He hated to admit it, but maybe Jake's wound was worse.

Ruben dressed and went to his office earlier than usual, curious to see if Charlie Leveau had been brought to the hospital or had already been pronounced dead. He visited the emergency department and found it to be quiet as it usually was early in the morning. Nobody was talking about it and he didn't ask. Maybe Leveau hadn't been found or was taken directly to the funeral home. He went to his office and sat drumming his fingers on his desk. All he could do was wait.

Jake went to inspect the vacant house. He found the broken pane. The door was still unlocked. Afraid that he might find either dead bodies or encounter the shooter, he entered with his gun drawn, but the house was empty. He put the lone shell casing in a plastic bag to preserve for evidence, then called his deputy to report the crime scene and get some help going over it. By the time Jake got back to Doc's house, Charlie was ready to go.

"I don't think they'll try again soon; hopefully they think I'm dead. So, I should be safe today and I have a lot to do, with the funeral and all."

Jake wasn't so sure about that but just said, "Take your pistol with you in the car. You're still deputized so it's legal. Call me if you see anything suspicious. Don't try to do anything by yourself." He started back out the door and with an afterthought turned back to Charlie. "And if you do shoot anybody, get somebody else to operate on them."

Charlie picked up the sugar bowl to hurl at Jake, who performed an exaggerated evasive maneuver. Charlie agreed to be careful, then left through the front door for the third time that morning and went to Julius'.

The news of Doc Leveau's demise reached Julius' in the person of Billy Jack, who got there before Charlie. "We're all so sorry, Charlie," said old Tom Bradshaw when Charlie walked up, looking like he'd just been shot. "Can't believe it. We all thought Doc would pull through this thing. You know, he kept us straight. Without him we're just a bunch of old fools." Murmurs of agreement and one amen issued from the gathered coffee clique. "With Doc in our midst, we were village statesmen." Mr. Bradshaw, usually the quiet one, was doing the talking, but the others were nodding in agreement.

Billy Jack looked sheepish, worried that he had jumped the gun. Charlie was glad the news was out and he didn't have to be the one to spread it. He gave Billy Jack a reassuring look that said thank you.

Charlie thanked them for their words and said, "The funeral will be this Saturday. I'd appreciate it if all of you would be pallbearers. Dad would want that." Then looking at Mr. Charlet, he said, "They'll send his body up here. It's already in the casket and I see no reason to open it. Dad wanted it that way. It should arrive by this afternoon."

Pete said, "We'll take care of it, Charlie. Whatever you want." Then he called the funeral home to tell them to expect the body.

Mr. Julius seemed sadder than anyone. His eyes were red and he still had fresh tears in his eyes. "You know, Charlie," he said, "I know we're getting old, and I know things change. That's life. But I will miss Doc. He was a great man and I was proud to be his friend."

Charlie wanted to be certain that Ruben and the Vidrines got the news. The direct way always suited Charlie the best, so he went to the hospital. Not concerned about niceties, he bypassed the secretary and went directly to Ruben's office, opened the door, and walked in unannounced. Ruben, behind his desk, looked up and visibly paled.

"Ruben," said Charlie, "my dad died last night. Just thought you should know. His funeral service will be on Saturday. Since he meant a lot to this hospital and to this town before you came, it would be nice if someone, not you of course, but someone from the hospital could speak. This hospital was a major part of his life."

It was hard for Ruben to conceal his relief. Trying to act sympathetic and caring, he said, "Dr. Leveau, I didn't know your dad long enough to speak about him anyway, but I would suggest Beulah May, the nursing director. She worked with him for many years."

"That would be good," said Charlie. "I'll speak to Beulah May."

"And Dr. Leveau," said Ruben as Charlie was turning to leave, "please know that though your dad and I had our differences, he was a great man and will be missed by Bayou Belle and this hospital."

Charlie thanked him for those words, but he was afraid he might vomit before getting out of the room.

Charlie had barely left the room before Ruben called Vinnie. "Just thought you should know," said Ruben when Vinnie answered just as he was crossing into Texas, "a ghost just came in to see me."

"What're you talkin' about?" asked Vinnie, annoyed that he was having to talk to Ruben again.

"I mean, you shit, that Charlie Leveau just came in here to tell me his father had died and his funeral was Saturday. So just who in the hell did you shoot?"

"He was lying still on the ground with a bloody white shirt. I didn't go check his pulse, but he looked dead to me."

"The man who came in here didn't act like he'd been shot at all, ever, and for sure not this morning. Just who the hell did you shoot?"

"All I know is what I saw. You're not callin' me a liar, I hope." Vinnie was beginning to doubt himself.

Ruben didn't answer, just slammed the phone down. He called LSU to confirm that at least Doc was dead. The office there told him that Doc had died in the very early hours of the morning and that the body had left the hospital shortly after. They didn't know where it had been taken. Ruben, his hand shaking, still not sure, called Fuselier Funeral Home in Metairie. The woman there took several minutes on her computer but finally informed Ruben that Doc Leveau had not been taken to any of the New Orleans area funeral homes. He called Charlet's and was told they had just found out that the body was to arrive in the afternoon. Ruben sat at his desk again, drumming his fingers, then got up and paced the room. It didn't make sense. If Doc's body left LSU in the wee hours of the morning, it should have been there hours ago. Where was it in the meantime? Then it hit him like a bolt of lightning. Doc wasn't dead. They were hiding him for protection.

He called Vinnie. "I think they're hiding him. Get your ass back to New Orleans and find out where he was taken. And when you do find him and kill him, I expect proof if you want the rest of your money. You wouldn't get another chance, but I don't have anyone else. You fail this time, you're a dead man. Your heart and kidneys will be all that's left alive, but they'll be in somebody else's body."

Vinnie made a U-turn and headed back toward New Orleans. He began to wonder if he should try to disappear and not go to New Orleans at all. With both sides, the law and the mob, looking for him, he would be seeing his brother in hell sooner than he planned. On the way to New Orleans he stopped at a thrift store and bought the oldest, most tattered clothes he could find, trying to accomplish a disguise.

Charlie's side had begun to ache. He looked down and saw a spot of blood on his shirt, so he went home to change the dressing. He got a stethoscope and listened again to his left lung as he took a deep breath. He still had good breath sounds and was not short of breath. Delphine helped him change the dressing. Together they called the family. Charlie asked Page to write the obituary and email it to him as soon as possible. Chuck was to be on call at Parkland for the weekend, but since he was senior, he would get coverage and be home tomorrow. Charlie called Jan. She didn't pick up, so he left her a message suggesting that she might pick Page up in Riverton on the way to Bayou Belle if she planned to come to the funeral.

As Charlie was hanging up from leaving the message, Ellie came through the back door into the kitchen. Charlie liked that she would come in without knocking. "Hi," she said cheerfully.

"Hi, yourself," replied Charlie. Glancing at Delphine, he said, "She knows."

"Good," said Ellie.

"She is officially a Bayou Vigilante." Charlie grinned.

"I like that, I think." Delphine had a puzzled look on her face, and Charlie laughed so suddenly that he grabbed his left side and winced.

"What's wrong with you?" asked Ellie, a concerned look on her face.

Before he could answer Delphine piped in, "Not much, just got shot with a deer rifle this morning. You'd think it might slow him down some."

"What?" Ellie moved over to his side and insisted that he take off his shirt. She took off the bandage and looked at the wound, feeling along it. "I feel crackles," she said. "What is that?"

Charlie felt where she was and felt the same thing. "That is air under the skin. I don't think it came from the bullet holes, so it must mean I have some air leaking out of my lung." He got the stethoscope again and listened. He still heard good breath sounds and was not short of breath, but he obviously had a lung injury.

"Have you had it looked at?" asked Ellie.

"I'm a doctor," replied Charlie. "I looked at it."

Ellie turned her head to the side and looked at him incredulously. "Come with me. We're going to see Jim."

Seeing that there was little likelihood of convincing her otherwise and a little concerned about the crepitance he felt under the skin, he rode with her to the hospital. Bypassing registration, they cornered Jim when he came out of a patient's room and told him what had happened. Jim walked with them to radiology and got a chest film. It showed a cracked left fifth rib and a small pneumothorax, the lung collapsed less than 10%.

Jim said, "The pneumo could be from the broken rib, or you may have some blast injury from the high-powered rifle. Whichever, I think you used up one of your nine lives. A couple inches or less over and you'd be in somebody's morgue." Ellie looked like she might faint at those words. "What happened, Jan order a hit man?" Jim laughed but not like it was really funny.

"Somebody must have, but Jan would be down on my current list of possibilities. A week ago she might have been at the top, but others have taken her place." Charlie accepted some pain pills and antibiotics and a Heimlich valve that he could put in himself should he develop a tension pneumothorax.

CHAPTER TWENTY-EIGHT

WEDNESDAY, JUNE 14

Vinnie was paranoid. In a different car with a convincing disguise, he still thought everyone was looking at him. Every police car seemed to slow down when it passed, and he looked in his rearview mirror each time to be sure they weren't turning around and coming after him. And when they didn't, he was sure they were radioing ahead. He would be pulled over at any minute. New Orleans was the last place he wanted to be. With the mob after him though, he wouldn't feel safe in the deepest Amazon forest. As he drove closer to LSU hospital, his unease increased. Stopped by a red light at an intersection on Tulane Avenue, a police car, also stopped by the light, faced him on the other side. The officer was staring at him. Vinnie leaned over and tried not to look directly out the window. Then he was afraid that would look suspicious, so he straightened up. When the light changed he inched forward. The policeman looked at him long and hard as they passed, or so it seemed to Vinnie. His paranoia did not mean necessarily that he was wrong. So, he changed directions and drove over the Pontchartrain bridge to Mandeville, figuring to return to the city after dark.

Early that morning, when Doc's hearse left the hospital, it didn't stop until it reached the Airline Restaurant in LaPlace. There Doc was transferred to an ambulance for the rest of the trip to Ruston. He was accompanied by an FBI agent and a male nurse, each armed. The driver had directions to go through Baton Rouge, then north through St. Francisville, and cross the Mississippi River at Natchez. From there they would go farther north to Rayville, then head west on Interstate 20. The trip took almost five hours. No lights were flashing as they drove. Doc thought he was in good enough shape to ride in a car, but his doctors insisted on the ambulance. It was still morning when they arrived in Ruston.

The place chosen was a beautiful old home on the outskirts of downtown Ruston. The ambulance parked behind the house. Doc was taken in through the back door, into the kitchen area, and up an old staircase to a bedroom that faced the street. He was introduced to his new guard, one of two that would pull twelve-hour shifts. Morgan had the day shift. The kitchen was well stocked with enough food for several days. Doc requested some books to read. No telling how long he would have to be here. The room was old but elegant, beautifully furnished as was the rest of the mansion.

Morgan checked the place thoroughly, making sure every door and window was locked, and determined where the weak points were in the security. He hadn't been on the force long and wanted to make a good impression on the FBI and his chief. He understood they would be checking in sometime during the day.

Sure enough, a little after noon, Donnie walked into Doc's room.

"Donnie," exclaimed Doc, "what in the world are you doing here?"

Donnie laughed. "Hi Doc. You caught me. I'm FBI. I just clean floors because the government doesn't pay enough for a single man to support himself."

"I'm flabbergasted," said Doc. "Here, come sit down and tell me about it."

Donnie asked Morgan to leave the room while they talked. For the next two hours, they discussed everything from the meeting in New Orleans between Ruben and Hubert to their plan to catch the Vidrine group red-handed Sunday night. Doc told Donnie that the man who tried to kill him last night was the same one who was at the camp. Seeing his face again had brought the memory back. Donnie let him know that Charlie had already found the recorder. "They've been trying to kill you to keep you from talking. Now they think you're dead. By the way, your funeral is Saturday."

The only thing that Doc added to what Donnie already knew was his suspicion about Dr. Kaiser not being who he was supposed to be.

"At our meeting last night, Charlie intimated that he suspected something but wasn't quite prepared to say. It may have been about Kaiser."

"That may be," said Doc. "A surgeon knows other surgeons, how they say things and what they do. Something isn't right there, and Charlie would suspect it quickly."

"You just lie low here, don't get into any trouble, and let us take care of this so you can come home. And what a grand homecoming that will be." Donnie laughed, but something was making him uneasy. Too many people knew Doc was hiding. If the wrong people did find out and somehow learned where he was, Morgan would not stand up against trained killers, as good as he might be.

As Donnie was about to leave, Doc asked him, "How did you get the day off? Ruben is pretty ruthless with the help."

"I called in drunk." Donnie grinned, shaking his head. "If I'm lucky, he'll fire me. As it is I have to keep working this week so he won't be suspicious." He stuck his head back in the door after calling for Morgan to come back up. "Hope to see you next week in Bayou Belle at the after-funeral party. Maybe they'll let you reread your obituary to the crowd." He joked but he was still worried. Almost as an afterthought he walked back to Doc's bedside and stuck something under his pillow while Morgan was looking out the window. He winked at Doc and left. He was driving back to Bayou Belle when he got the call from Jake about Charlie being shot but that he was doing well. He was glad he hadn't known that in time to tell Doc.

Maria's shift started at eleven p.m. Vinnie got to the parking lot at ten and pulled in near her usual spot. A few employees were coming and going. He figured she would know where they had taken Doc Leveau. He saw her car when it came through the gate at ten thirty. She parked and opened her door to get out, but Vinnie was beside her with a gun in her side. She opened her mouth to scream, but Vinnie's hand was over it instantly. He forced her over to the passenger side and got behind the wheel.

"What do you want?" Maria cried. "Please let me go. You can have the car."

"Shut up," Vinnie said menacingly. "I gotta know what they did with Doc Leveau."

"They took him to the funeral home, for God's sake." Maria hoped she was very convincing.

He slapped her hard with a backhand across the face. "You're lying. He never got to the funeral home. Now, where did they take him? I'm in a hurry and I don't have time for bullshit. If you want to live, you'll tell me now."

"I really don't know," Maria whimpered, curled against the passenger door. "They just took him somewhere to get him out of danger."

"Where?" insisted Vinnie, raising the gun and putting it under her chin. "Where?"

Maria looked down as far as she could as if trying to see if it really was a gun, knowing full well that it was. Shaking, trying not to cry and hoping the tears would make him go away, she said, "I heard one of the men ask another the best way to get to Ruston, whether to go through Alexandria or through Natchez."

Vinnie lowered the gun for a moment. *Ruston*, he thought, *probably about four or five hours away*. Then he raised the gun again, this time pointing it between her eyes, and actually said, "I'm sorry, but I can't have you talking."

Her eyes widened, but she didn't make a sound. The silenced gun fired a bullet that entered her brain and exited her posterior skull before breaking the passenger side window as it exited the car. Vinnie, making sure he wasn't spotted, put Maria's still warm body into the trunk of his car. He then switched the license plates and drove away toward Ruston in Maria's car.

CHAPTER TWENTY-NINE

WEDNESDAY, JUNE 14

Preoccupied with the situation in Bayou Belle, Charlie had given little thought to his impending lawsuit. It was, however, foremost on Linda George's mind. She had an appointment to see Dr. Davis at two PM and arrived at his office at one thirty, not trusting Dallas traffic. Dr. Davis' nurse informed her that he had been held up at the hospital with an emergency and had cancelled his afternoon office hours. Linda let her know that she was not a patient but a malpractice defense attorney and that Dr. Davis had agreed to meet with her regarding a malpractice case.

"What time do you expect him to get through with the emergency?" asked Linda.

"He thought he would be through by three but couldn't be sure, and my experience is that he usually underestimates the time it will take." Knowing she was talking to a lawyer, the nurse was trying to be helpful.

"Would you mind if I wait in your waiting room in case he does come back?" asked Linda. "I have a lot of paperwork that I can do."

"You're welcome to wait if you'd like." She pointed to a table and said, "You can plug in your computer over there. Dr. Davis usually calls when he gets through, and I'll let him know you're here. But just so you know, there's a chance he won't be through until sometime tonight."

"I'll stay a while and take my chances," said Linda. "A quiet place and a change of scenery will be refreshing."

At four o'clock Linda was getting her things together to leave when the nurse called out that Dr. Davis was on his way. Fifteen minutes later, Dr. Davis stuck his head through the door and asked, "Ms. George?"

"Dr. Davis, thanks for seeing me. I know you've had a very long day, and I didn't mean to be a burden. My client is eager to hear what you have to say."

"That's quite all right," said Dr. Davis. "I hope I can be of some help." Dr. Ron Davis was a very distinguished-looking, tall, gray-haired man with thick eyebrows and a kind, gentlemanly manner. He led her back to his office and directed her to a comfortable chair. "So," he said, "what can I do for you?"

Linda expertly explained the details of the case to him and then showed him the x-ray of the line placement.

Dr. Davis looked at them for just a second, threw up his hands, and said, "There's nothing wrong with that placement. I have left them there many times, and under the circumstances you described, it was the only sensible thing to do." Linda was shocked at how easy that had been. "Who is the doctor and where did this happen?" Dr. Davis asked, putting the films back in the folder.

"It happened in Riverton, Texas, and the doctor's name is Charles Leveau."

Dr. Davis sat rubbing his chin. "I don't know anyone in Riverton, but that name sure is familiar."

Linda said she hadn't been there either. "I've gone to

Louisiana twice to meet with Dr. Leveau. He's there because his father was badly injured in an accident."

"Where in Louisiana?" asked Dr. Davis.

"We met both times in New Orleans, but he's been in a little town called Bayou Belle, where his dad also practices surgery."

Dr. Davis raised his left eyebrow and looked at Linda with a perplexed look on his face. "That is a strange coincidence," said Dr. Davis.

"Really?" asked Linda. "How is that?"

"I got an inquiry from a doctor in Bayou Belle a couple of weeks ago concerning one of our former surgery residents. If my memory serves me correctly, the doctor making the inquiry was a Dr. Leveau. That's an unusual name. I tried to get in touch with him to answer his inquiry, but his office has been closed."

"That makes sense," said Linda, "because he's at LSU in New Orleans with a head injury and may not live. He's Charlie's father."

"Sorry to hear that," said Dr. Davis. "I was going to give him a good report. He wanted to know about Robert Kaiser. Robert was a resident here and when he finished, he went to Africa to do medical missionary work." It hadn't taken Dr. Davis long to render an opinion, and now it seemed he wanted to visit. "He was very good, so good that I had hoped he would return here and join my practice." He hesitated a moment as if remembering Kaiser fondly, then continued. "I admit to being a little surprised that he had landed in a small Louisiana town. Oh well, you never know why folks make the decisions they do. I mean," he pointed at a residency class picture on the wall, "Kaiser was almost the perfect doctor. He was smart, hardworking, had a good rapport with staff and other doctors, and was technically advanced in his surgical skills. If he had a shortcoming at all, no pun intended, he was very short and sensitive about it." He walked over and pointed to a very short doctor in the front row of the picture. "That's him. He needed two standing stools to operate." Shaking his head, he said again, "He would have been a great addition to our staff."

Linda was packing away her papers and asked, "Dr. Davis, I hope that on the basis of your opinion that this lawsuit will be dropped, but if it isn't, would you agree to a more formal deposition?"

"Of course," said Dr. Davis. "I despise frivolous claims. They've ruined us."

"If that becomes necessary, I will contact your secretary and arrange a suitable time for the deposition to take place. And thank you so much for your time. Send your bill to our office, and you will be promptly paid for this consult."

"Thank you," said Dr. Davis, "it was a pleasure meeting you and glad to help. When you talk to Dr. Leveau, give him my best wishes for his father's recovery and ask him to contact me if they still want a recommendation for Dr. Kaiser."

It was Wednesday afternoon. She tried Charlie's cell phone but didn't get an answer. She left a message for him to call her back.

CHAPTER THIRTY

THURSDAY, JUNE 15

A warm, humid, early June day greeted Charlie when he went out to get the Thursday morning paper. Before going outside he looked up and down the street and noted the boarded-up windows of the vacant house, still decorated with yellow police tape. No cars were parked on the street. He even looked up at the trees to see if a gunman might be hiding. Surely the assailant had left, probably to return later, but Charlie thought he'd be damned if he'd let them change his life. He even refused the bulletproof vest Jake had offered. However, he did want to follow this matter with his father and Ruben Martin to its conclusion, and he did want Page's coming baby to know his grandfather. Then there was Ellie. So he was relieved when he was back inside with the paper, the door closed behind him, still alive with no additional bullet holes. His family would be arriving this afternoon.

Meanwhile, Vinnie was sleeping in at the Dollar Inn in Ruston. His plan for the day was to have a good breakfast, then make the rounds of the hospitals, nursing homes, and assisted living facilities looking for a new patient or resident brought in from New Orleans. The alarm sounded at four thirty, two hours after he had gone to sleep. He turned off the alarm, put the pillow over his head, and went back to sleep. *To hell with Ruben*, he thought. *A man needs his rest.* He'd find Leveau this afternoon.

Hubert was in his office reading the paper and waiting for his only appointment that morning, a real estate closing. He feared for his life, but felt much better about himself than he had in a long time.

Smoke was rising through the trees beside Billy Jack's house. He had risen early and his still was in full swing. Summer meant an increase in the demand for his recipe. A shipment of mason jars had been delivered by UPS the day before.

Ruben was in his office, looking at his phone, tapping his foot, thinking he should hear from Vinnie soon. If he hadn't heard by noon, he would call. He got some extra strength Tums out of his desk drawer and chewed six at one time.

Charlie was enjoying breakfast when his cell phone buzzed. The caller ID indicated a Texas number that looked familiar.

"Dr. Leveau?" asked the voice of Linda George when he picked up.

"Hi," answered Charlie. "How's everything going?" Charlie realized he had given no thought at all to his malpractice case or the deposition since he and Ellie had left New Orleans and met Jake at the camp house, and he really didn't have time for it now.

"I called yesterday and left a message to call me back." Linda George actually sounded excited.

Charlie wanted to scream into the phone that if she only knew what he had been doing, she wouldn't sound so damn cheerful, but he said, "I'm sorry. I didn't even know you called. Things have been pretty busy around here. What happened?"

"I met with Dr. Ron Davis yesterday. I told him the details of the case and showed him the x-rays. It took him only about five seconds to look at the x-ray and completely agree with what you did. He will gladly testify on your behalf if necessary, but he believes the case will be nonsuited, as do I."

Charlie was stunned. Something was actually going well. *Is this over?* He was speechless.

"Dr. Leveau? Are you there?" and a few seconds later, "Dr. Leveau? Dr. Leveau!" Linda worried that she had lost the connection, or that Charlie had fainted.

"No, I mean yes. I'm here." Charlie was regaining his composure. "Do you mean this may actually be over?"

"Yes," Linda continued, "I do." She hesitated for just a second. "I think there is an excellent chance the plaintiff will drop the case. With an expert like Dr. Davis testifying for us, there is hardly a chance of a jury verdict in their behalf. The plaintiff's lawyer probably won't be interested in incurring any more expenses to pursue the case in this circumstance. So, yes, I think it's over, not officially, but for all practical purposes."

Charlie took another moment to digest this new revelation, then said, "Thank you, Ms. George. I really can't thank you enough." He pumped his fist in celebration, momentarily forgetting his more pressing problems. "And how can I thank Dr. Davis? I'd love to shake his hand."

"I'm sure he'd be happy to hear from you," said Linda. "By the way, it's a remarkable coincidence, but he said your dad had contacted him by mail about the other surgeon in Bayou Belle, a Dr. Kaiser. Dr. Davis said he had tried to get back to him but hadn't gotten a response." She then continued. "I explained to him that he had been injured and was hospitalized in critical condition."

Charlie was confused. "How did that ever come up?"

"I told him you were in Bayou Belle and I had met with you in New Orleans. He recognized both the name of the town and your name as being the same as your father's."

Charlie was amazed. "Well, what did he say about Dr. Kaiser?" He couldn't wait to hear and was so glad his father had begun an investigation.

"Dr. Davis said he was one of the best surgical residents he ever helped train, and he had hoped Dr. Kaiser would come back and join his practice in Dallas when he completed his work in Africa."

Charlie was again truly and profoundly dumbfounded. "He said that?" He couldn't believe his ears. Emotional trauma can surely transform a person, especially someone in a stressful and demanding profession. He would have to give him more of a chance, knowing his potential.

"That's what he said," said Linda. "Thought you'd be glad that Bayou Belle had such a great young surgeon. Dr. Davis was surprised that he had chosen a small town."

"If I didn't know you talked to a man who trained him and

knew him well, I wouldn't believe it. Did he say anything else?"

"He did say that the only shortcoming was that he was just that."

"What?" Charlie waited.

"Short," Linda said. "He is so short that he needs two stools to stand on to operate." She went on. "He is sensitive about his height but usually handles it well."

Charlie leaned over, his elbows on the table. He looked at Delphine, started to get up, then sat back down. Picturing Dr. Kaiser, he thought, *He may not be tall, maybe five-foot-eight, but he certainly isn't short.* "Did he have a picture of the residency class?" Charlie pressed Linda George.

"Yes, as a matter of fact he showed it to me, with Kaiser in the front row." Linda was a bit taken aback. "Don't you believe him?"

"Oh, I believe him," said Charlie. "I believe him completely. It's just that we know a different Dr. Kaiser." He needed the good news. "I'll be out of touch the next few days. Family is coming in for Dad's funeral. But I want to hear the disposition of the case as soon as you know."

"Your dad died?" Linda was genuinely sorry. "I'm so sorry. I hope this legal matter didn't take you away from him more than it had to."

"No, no," said Charlie. "Not at all. Thank you for that thought. Like I said, a lot has happened here, and your call today was a welcome surprise in more ways than you know."

Delphine, washing breakfast dishes, looked around. "Good news?" she asked.

"Very." Charlie was still seated, trying to sort out what he had been told. "Looks like the malpractice suit will be resolved without a lot more trouble, and my lawyer may have helpful information concerning our current local problem."

"How's that?" Delphine asked, wondering how a lawyer in Texas would have any knowledge that might be helpful in Bayou Belle. Just then, Ellie came in the door.

"Good morning."

"Good morning to you too." Charlie stood and stared, a silly grin on his face.

"How 'bout some bacon and eggs," Delphine offered, "and the biscuits are still hot."

"No thanks, but a cup of coffee would be good." She looked at Charlie and asked, "How is your side?"

"A little sore when I take a deep breath, but not a problem."

Ellie looked at the wound, cleaned and redressed it. Charlie didn't really think the dressing needed changing, but he didn't mind.

The three drank coffee and visited, discussing music for the funeral and where they guessed Doc was hiding. Charlie told Ellie his good news about the case and what Linda George said about Dr. Kaiser.

"Maybe they have a picture of him and can fax it to us."

"Great idea. Why didn't I think of that?" Without waiting another minute, he called information, got Dr. Davis' office number, and called it. He explained who he was and asked the secretary to fax a picture of Dr. Kaiser's residency class to Bayou Belle. Ellie quickly looked up Hubert's office fax number and gave it to Charlie. Dr. Davis' secretary agreed to send it the first chance she had. They were closing the office for the day for a special occasion, and Charlie had called just as she was leaving. She asked if tomorrow would be okay. Charlie was disappointed, really eager to see the picture, but tomorrow would have to do.

A car drove up outside. Ellie went to the window to see who was coming. She didn't recognize either of the women getting out of the car.

Charlie walked over. Jan and Page were retrieving their suitcases and walking up the front walk. "That's my wife and daughter." Charlie looked at Ellie. "Don't go anywhere. I want you to meet them."

Ellie was not sure the timing was right, so she went back to the kitchen.

They didn't knock. Page opened the door, stuck her head in, and yelled, "Yoo-hoo, anybody home?"

"Right here," said Charlie as he walked over and greeted Page with a big hug. He looked over Page's shoulder. Jan was standing there with her suitcase, waiting to come in. Charlie opened the door wider and reached for Jan's suitcase, taking it and holding the door for her to come in.

"Hi, Charlie." Jan also gave him a hug. "I'm sorry about your dad. I know you've had a lot to deal with, and I'm sorry for what I've done to add to that." She looked around at the familiar living room, then back at Charlie and added, "Looking back, I know leaving like I did was bad timing, but it was necessary. I'm back for the funeral and for the kids, and I'm sorry for the way it all went, but I want to make it clear from the start, I meant what I said. This won't change anything." It sounded like she thought Charlie caused this to happen, like he had his dad killed to draw her back.

"Jan, I'm glad you came back for the funeral. I'm glad you are here for the kids. I understand you're not here for me. I never thought that. I get it. It's good we can clear the air now so we can get through this weekend." Charlie stared at Jan, waiting for a reply if one was coming. She just nodded. In an attempt at humor to lighten the mood, he added, "Just promise me you'll keep your shoes on the floor."

Jan took a step back and Charlie detected a slight smile. She liked being in control, but wasn't expecting this total capitulation by her husband. She had expected a fight and in her subconscious hoped for one. Charlie had disappointed. "I'm glad you understand. It'll make the weekend easier." Then she added, "I brought only one pair of high heels and will need them for the funeral. If I throw any, they'll be soft house shoes."

Delphine came in from the kitchen. "Hi, Miss Jan and Page. You all have a good trip over?"

"Hi, Delphine, good to see you." Jan and Page both met Delphine halfway across the room for welcome home hugs. "How are you?"

"Doing fine," said Delphine, "just missing Doc Leveau. Won't ever be the same around here without him. 'Bout got Charlie here convinced to come back here and take his place." She smiled a devilish smile directed at Charlie. The sound of the back door closing reached the living room. Ellie had apparently left and wanted Charlie to know it.

Delphine's pushing it, thought Charlie, but down deep he was glad she had broached the subject. "Come on, y'all. Let's get your things upstairs to the guest bedroom."

"Just a minute," said Jan. "You mean you're talking about moving here?" She laughed and looked at Delphine. "Don't get your hopes up." She laughed again, picked up her own suitcase, and carried it up the stairs, still chuckling to herself.

Charlie went back to the kitchen and rang Ellie's cell. "Where did you go? I was hoping to introduce you."

"I'll get a chance to meet them later. Just thought it would be easier for you not to have me in the way at first. But thanks for calling. Now you go and enjoy your family." Ellie sounded like her tongue was in her cheek.

Just then, Chuck and his fiancée, Michelle, came in the front door. Everyone was arriving.

CHAPTER THIRTY-ONE

FRIDAY, JUNE 16

By the time Vinnie finally got out of bed on Thursday and ate a big late lunch, not having eaten since early the evening before, he had just enough of the day left to learn his way around Ruston and do some preliminary detective work. Ruben would expect frequent updates, and Vinnie wanted something to report. He checked by the hospital, where a sweet volunteer told him she knew everyone who had been admitted the day before and there was no transfer from New Orleans. He got the same answer at the two largest nursing homes and assisted care facilities. He called Ruben to say he'd been looking since early morning with no luck and was told to keep looking. So he drove around for a while, ate dinner, and turned in early, having made up his mind to look for one more day, maybe at some outlying small towns.

Vinnie got up early on Friday, had a large breakfast in the lobby, and asked the concierge about surrounding towns and where there might be nursing homes. She mentioned a couple that Vinnie decided to check.

Back in Bayou Belle, Charlie was maneuvering among family, making arrangements for a sham funeral, and checking with Jake about strategy. His cell rang, the display showing a Texas number. It was Dr. Davis' secretary calling to say she had faxed the picture of Dr. Kaiser's residency class to the number Charlie had given her. Charlie thanked her and called Ellie. She agreed to pick the picture up at Hubert's office and bring it by Charlie's house in the afternoon.

By afternoon Vinnie had driven on every street in Ruston looking for any clue as to the whereabouts of Dr. Leveau. He looked for guards or medical equipment where one wouldn't expect them to be. A downtown restaurant called Ponchatoula's served large plates of boiled crayfish. No time now but this evening he would reward himself with all the boiled crayfish he could eat. Over dinner, he would figure out how to disappear so he wouldn't be permanently missing from this world. In the meantime he would look at some nursing homes farther out of town. He claimed to be a nephew trying to find his uncle who had been injured and was probably lost and couldn't tell anyone who he was. Vinnie got mixed reactions to his story, some sympathetic, while others doubted its veracity. Late in the afternoon, visiting his fifth nursing home, he thought he hit the jackpot. A nursing home in Dubach had admitted an old man from New Orleans at the time Doctor Leveau would have arrived. Vinnie went back to his car, attached the silencer to his pistol, and stuck it in his belt, pulling his shirttail out to hide it.

He inched down the hall, expecting a guard to exit Doc's room anytime. He was ready with his gun and would kill both the old man and the guard. When he reached Doc's room, he burst in with the gun ready. A little old lady in a wheelchair looked up at him, her eyes wide but unable to get a sound out of her mouth. She clutched her chest and fell back in her chair. The old man in the bed smiled with the right side of his face and waved at Vinnie, apparently happy to see him. Vinnie inexplicably waved back, then eased the door closed. There were two more assisted care facilities to check, but Vinnie had just lost interest.

Hubert couldn't contain his excitement when Ellie walked in his office. "I looked at the picture," he said, handing it to her, his hand slightly trembling.

Ellie studied the picture for a moment, then read the names at the bottom. She looked up at Hubert. Holding the picture and pointing to the short doctor on the front row, she asked, "Is that supposed to be our Dr. Kaiser?"

"I think so," replied Hubert. "You remember at your dad's house the other night, Charlie said he suspected something but wasn't ready to say what?"

"I bet you're right." Ellie placed the picture in a folder, thanked Hubert, and drove straight to Doc's house, this time knocking on the front door. Jan answered the door. "Hi," she said, "I'm Ellie Boudreaux. I have a photograph that Charlie wanted me to bring him."

"Thank you," said Jan, eyeing Ellie from the top of her head to her shapely ankles, "I'll see that he gets it."

Ellie hesitated. "If it's okay I'd like to give it to him. I have a question about someone in the picture." She really wasn't sure she trusted Jan to give Charlie the photo.

Jan eyed her more suspiciously, giving her the up and down look again, then relented. "Sure, come on in."

Charlie was coming down the stairs when Ellie entered the living room. Delphine came to the kitchen door, peeked in, raised her eyebrows, and returned to the kitchen. "Hi, Ellie," Charlie cheerfully called. "Come on in and have a seat."

"I got the picture at Hubert's." Ellie walked toward Charlie and handed him the folder. "I hope it was okay that Hubert and I both looked at it."

"Of course it's okay. What did you think?" Charlie took the picture out and began to study it.

Ellie looked at Jan and back at Charlie. "The name at the bottom says Robert Kaiser, but I don't see his picture in the group. It says the short guy up front is Kaiser, but it isn't the Kaiser I know. Could there be two Dr. Kaisers?"

"I suppose there could be, but our Dr. Kaiser's credentials indicate that he was in this residency class. Don't say anything about this for now. We may need the element of surprise."

Jan was standing there, taking all this in. "What is going on?" she asked, looking back and forth between Charlie and Ellie.

"What do you mean?" asked Charlie, somewhat guiltily.

"I mean, you two seem to be long-lost friends and in a short time are working on something together. I was just wondering what it was. That's all."

Charlie started to explain, then remembered he hadn't made a proper introduction, which he proceeded to do. Then he explained, "A lot has happened since I got back. Dad probably didn't have an accident. He was probably murdered."

Jan's mouth dropped open. "Go on," she said.

Charlie didn't want to go into detail, so he just said, "Jake suspects there is a connection to the trucking company outside of town." He drew a deep breath. He was not a good liar, and Jan knew him well enough to know when he wasn't being completely truthful. "There are also connections to the hospital and the new surgeon that we were looking into." He stopped there but was already sorry he said *we* instead of *I*. "I'm going to take this upstairs. Be right back." And he beat a swift retreat.

Coward, thought Ellie, *leaving me alone with those eyes burning into me*. She gave Jan a weak smile.

"So," said Jan, "how did you meet my husband?" She motioned for Ellie to sit down, and they both sat on the couch facing each other.

"I've known him most of my life," replied Ellie. "I was batboy for the American Legion baseball team when Charlie was in high school. I hadn't seen him at all until he took out my son's appendix the night he came to town to check on his dad." Ellie was relaxing. What did she have to be worried about? This woman had left Charlie, and she heard her say when she first arrived that nothing had changed. *Why is she giving me the third degree? Maybe it's my turn to ask a question.*

"Charlie said you were visiting your sister and that is why you haven't been here to help him with his dad. Is your sister okay?" Ellie couldn't help herself. This woman was beautiful, even at her age.

Jan laughed. "Is that what he said?" She looked across the room and thought a minute. "That is in a way the literal truth, but the underlying truth is that I left Charlie the night his dad was injured." She hesitated, then continued. "I'm not sure I did the right thing. It was a snap judgment that resulted from years of bad experiences. Never marry a surgeon." Then she stared at Ellie a minute before Ellie dropped her eyes.

Charlie came back down the stairs. Ellie looked up at him, thanking him with her eyes for coming back. "Ellie," he said, "Delphine has a great supper prepared. Chuck and Michelle are here along with Page and Jan. There's more than enough, and we'd love to have you stay and eat with us."

"Thanks, but Beau is home and hungry. One of Delphine's dinners sure is tempting, but I think Beau and I are going out for étouffée." She got up and moved toward the door.

Charlie walked quickly over and escorted her to the door. "I'll talk to you as soon as the next meeting is arranged. I'm thinking it'll be late tomorrow night at your dad's house again." He then watched a little too long as she walked down the sidewalk back to her car. When Charlie closed the door and turned back around, Jan's arms were folded across her chest and the look on her face was not happy.

With a hostile expression matching the one he had seen many times, most recently at his house in Riverton the night she left, Jan asked, "And what was that really all about?"

"Just what I said." Charlie wasn't doing such a good job of acting. His main concern was that Jan not figure out that his dad was not dead. She might throw a wrench in the whole thing.

"Charlie, you're having an affair with that woman, you son of a bitch."

"What in the world are you talking about?" Charlie tried to sound convincing. "She brought by a photo and I asked her to stay for dinner like any self-respecting Southern gentleman would do."

"I saw the way you looked at her. Jesus, Charlie, she's half your age. It sure didn't take you long."

"Jan, you for once listen to me." Charlie braced himself and continued. "You left. You didn't give me a chance to explain anything. You had to have been planning it for a while, and you were glad to have a good excuse to go ahead and leave. You have since made it clear on a couple of occasions that you made the right decision and have no plans for reconciliation. Well, I get it. You've made it crystal clear that we are through. I want this weekend to be as pleasant as possible out of respect for my dad, so I'm prepared to make it that way. But if you insist on behaving this way, I'll drive you to Baton Rouge tonight and pay for the first flight out to Houston. I'll pay for first class to get you out of here." Charlie took a breath, rubbing his forehead as a headache was forming behind his eyes.

"Are you through?" asked Jan.

"Yes," Charlie answered, then sat down in the easy chair, staring at the unlit fireplace.

"I'm sorry, Charlie. I know you can count on one hand the number of times you have heard that in twenty-some odd years, but I am sorry." Jan looked at him and continued. "I had not wanted to say anything to you until I was sure, but I was getting lonesome in Houston and thinking about coming home if you'd have me. I haven't made up my mind yet, but we had so much together. I know I lost my temper. But we have kids together and are going to be grandparents together. We should at least talk it over."

Delphine, sitting at the kitchen table, drinking coffee, and waiting for time to take the roast out of the oven, rolled her eyes again. *Oh Lord*, she prayed, *give Charlie the eyes to see what is happening here and the wisdom to handle it.*

"Are you saying now you want to come home?" asked Charlie.

"I'm saying I've been thinking about it, and I hope we can talk about it."

Delphine thought, *Yeah, you been thinking about it for about a half hour, since you saw Ellie at the front door. You were gone before that happened.* The timer rang and she got up to take the roast out. The dinner rolls had been rising on the counter. She put them in the oven. Mashed potatoes and string beans were cooking on the stovetop, ready any time. She went to the door and looked in at Charlie and Jan, who were sitting and staring at each other. "Y'all, supper is about ready. Better call everyone down. Be ready in about ten to fifteen minutes."

They all sat around the big round oak table for dinner. Chuck had had a good nap, tired from the trip and call the night before in Dallas. Charlie had met Michelle once when he had been in Dallas and had taken her and Chuck out to dinner. She was a nurse on the surgery floor at Parkland. Chuck met her shortly after arriving in Dallas for his residency in general surgery. He had gone to LSU Medical School in New Orleans and interned there also before accepting a residency at Parkland. Charlie broached the subject. "Michelle," he asked. "Did you happen to know a surgery resident by the name of Robert Kaiser in Dallas?"

"I did," she said. "He was a really good doctor and nicer than most of them. When he finished his training, he went to Africa on a mission trip. I remember hearing something about a tragedy there, but it was secondhand information and I never got the whole story. I didn't know him all that well, but everyone liked him. Why do you ask?"

Charlie went up and got the picture and brought it back. Pointing at the short doctor in front, he asked, "Is that him?"

"Yes, it is." She looked at the picture. "I know all the others in the picture also."

Charlie changed the subject to tomorrow's funeral. "We're supposed to meet at the church so they can tell us what to do. Beulah May from the hospital is going to give a eulogy, but if any of you want to say something, that would be good."

"What about you, Dad?" Page asked, obviously thinking that she wanted her dad to say something about her granddad.

"I'm not at all good at that sort of thing," said Charlie. "If y'all think I should, I will. I just want someone to do Dad justice, and I don't think I'm the one."

"Dad, for crying out loud, you're the only son. Anything you say would be right and well received. And if not, who cares. You have to give a eulogy. I'll help you write it tonight if you want."

When Charlie thought about it, he couldn't believe he had considered not giving a eulogy. What other son gets to tell his dad what he thinks of him in such a setting? "Sure, I'll do it."

"Good," said Page. "I knew you would. Everyone would expect you to."

Earlier in the day, Charlie had met with the preacher and music director and decided on "In the Garden" and "Amazing Grace" as the hymns. The preacher knew Doc well and didn't need any information to make his remarks personal.

Jan had been quiet for most of the meal. "Is Ellie going to sit with the family at the service?"

Charlie looked at her with what was to anyone's view contempt. "No," he said, "she's not part of the family."

Vinnie could taste the crayfish and was hungry again. If he were ever in a position to request a last meal, this would be it. The place was filling up. Two women were seated at the next table. One said to the other, "Mabel Turner was in the beauty parlor today, and she said there were lights on in the old Jones house last night and a police car was parked outside. She said an ambulance had been there earlier. Wonder what that could be about."

"I have no idea. That place has been empty for years." The woman stirred her iced tea. "Sometimes the family checks on it, but I can't imagine what an ambulance would be doing there."

Paying for his meal at the cash register, he asked the woman if she knew where the Jones house was.

"Everybody knows that," she said. "It's the big white mansion just on the north side of town on Vienna Street."

Vinnie knew the place. He'd driven by it several times. *Hiding in a very conspicuous place,* thought Vinnie. It was a possibility. After exiting the restaurant, he drove north on Vienna and passed the house. A car was parked in the driveway and lights were on upstairs. He parked across the street at a bank parking lot, then walked by the house. There was no way he could see to look in the upstairs window. They wouldn't be expecting visitors this time of night, so he decided to check it out in the morning before leaving town. He would take a direct approach and knock on the door.

Since the next day promised to be a long one, the Leveaus retired early. Charlie couldn't sleep, wondering what he would say at the funeral. It would have to be good because his dad would get to know what he said. After staring at the ceiling for a half hour, he wandered down to the kitchen for a glass of milk. He heard soft sobs before he got there. Jan was sitting at the kitchen table, dabbing her eyes with a Kleenex when Charlie walked in. "Can't sleep either?" he asked.

"Oh, Charlie," Jan sobbed, "I'm so messed up." She was wearing her sexiest nightgown, and her robe was open in front.

Charlie didn't reply; he just went to the fridge and poured a glass of milk.

"Aren't you going to say anything?"

"Jan, I've got a lot on my mind right now." Charlie went over and sat down opposite her. "On top of that I have a eulogy to prepare. We'll talk about it after the funeral."

"I do apologize for my reaction to Ellie." Jan looked up to see if he were listening. "I guess I went a little crazy, and jealousy was a big part of it. I may have left, but I'm not ready to let someone else have you." She got up, went around the table, and sat on Charlie's lap. "Can I sleep in your room the rest of the night?"

"Jan, I don't know if that's such a good…" but she was kissing him and he never finished the sentence.

The next morning, Charlie was looking at the ceiling as Jan was softly breathing beside him, her arm draped across his chest. Many thoughts were running through his mind, not the least of which was what he was going to do for the rest of his life and who he was going to do it with.

Jan stirred about then, looked up at Charlie, smiled, and said, "Can I assume we are reconciled?"

Charlie looked over at her, brushed some hair out of her eyes, and replied, "Is that what you call what we did?" He knew that Jan had always used sex when she wanted something. If she didn't want something from Charlie, she had never been the least bit interested. She always used it to reel him in, and he was pretty sure she had just done it again. However, she was his wife, and he had committed himself to the marriage long ago. They did have a family, which was about to grow. He couldn't help but wonder how committed she was to him, especially after the last couple of weeks. "We need to get down to breakfast before the kids come and jump in bed with us. There's a lot to do before the funeral, including having the house ready for the multitudes that will be coming by after the service."

CHAPTER THIRTY-TWO

SATURDAY, JUNE 17

Vinnie slept late and checked out of the hotel a little before eleven o'clock. Doc Leveau, if he were there, wasn't going anywhere. If Doc was at the Jones house, he would kill him and whatever incompetent guard was unlucky enough to be with him. He grabbed a sweet roll and some coffee on the way out, put his things in the backseat, and drove into town, where he parked across the street from the Jones house in a place that provided a good view of the back driveway. A different patrol car was in the driveway, parked farther to the side. The shifts had apparently changed. He attached the silencer to his gun and slipped it inside his coat pocket. He would need to act soon if he wanted to be far away by nightfall or the next shift change.

Inside the house, Doc was sitting at a table re-reading *Huckleberry Finn* under a lamp. It was dark because Morgan, having taken over the guard duties at seven AM, insisted on keeping the curtains closed. Doc was going stir crazy. Morgan kept going over to the window facing the street and peeking through the curtain opening. He didn't want to alarm Doc, but a man was sitting in a car looking at the house. He gave some thought to checking the man out.

"Say, Morgan, I'm awfully hungry. What do you say we get

an early lunch?"

"Sure, Doc." Morgan let the curtain close and looked back at Doc. "I'll go down to the kitchen and see what we have." He walked toward the bedroom door. "I'm pretty hungry myself."

"There's not anything worth eating in the kitchen. I looked down there this morning at breakfast and there's zilch."

"Maybe we could send out for a pizza." Talking about food made Morgan hungry.

"What I have in mind," said Doc, "is a big juicy hamburger and fries, maybe two orders. It's been so long since I've eaten anything but hospital food, I actually have a craving for a Big Mac. What do you think?"

"Sounds good to me too, but we have no way to get one. They don't deliver." Morgan was looking to Doc for his next choice.

"Tell you what," Doc asked, "what is the best burger in town?"

Morgan rubbed his stomach, above where it hung over his belt, and said, "Probably Chili's out on the interstate."

"How long would it take you to go there and get some burgers and bring them back here?"

"Ten or fifteen minutes, but I'd lose my job if somebody found out I left you here alone, especially, God forbid, if something happened to you."

"Listen. Not even my son knows where I am, and they won't let me tell him. And if it makes you feel better, leave me that gun you wear on your right ankle. I promise to shoot anybody who comes through that bedroom door, and I won't leave this room while you're gone. Scout's honor."

Morgan wondered how Doc knew about the gun. His

stomach was really growling and his resolve weakening. After all, he thought, the patient needed good food more than he did, and he was serving a dual purpose as guard and nurse. "Okay," he relented, "I'll be back in just a few minutes." Before he left, he called in the order so it would be ready.

"Wait." Doc held up his hand. "Weren't you going to leave me a gun?"

Morgan wasn't sure whether Doc was kidding or not. "I don't think so, Doc." He pictured Doc accidentally shooting himself. "I'll be back in a hurry." Morgan left the house, thinking he'd drive around and check out the man in the car on the way to Chili's.

Vinnie started his car and was pulling out of his parking place when he saw the guard leave the house. He stopped a minute and watched the guard drive off; then he drove down the one-way street and made the block to come around to the back where the guard had parked.

Morgan drove by the lot where he had seen the man and was relieved that he was no longer there. He thought about turning on the siren and driving faster but someone might be curious and follow him to Chili's.

Vinnie backed up to the back door, opened the trunk, and left it open. He was going to take Doc's body with him to show to Ruben. It was the only way he'd ever believe it. And he might have to make a quick getaway. The guard would probably not be gone long. Vinnie opened the old lock on the back door without much trouble and quietly entered the house. He couldn't hear a sound. Tiptoeing through the kitchen and into the hall, he came to the bottom of the grand staircase. The night before, the light had been on in the south bedroom, probably where Doc was. He slowly and quietly climbed the stairs. Suddenly, one of them creaked loudly. Momentarily stunned, he hesitated. Why should he worry? The old man was bedridden and alone. Besides, he wanted him to know he was coming. He had been too much trouble, and Vinnie was going to be sure Doc knew he wasn't surviving this time.

Doc heard the footsteps and then a loud creak. Old houses make lots of noises, but he was sure somebody was on the stairs. If the footsteps had continued, it would have been Morgan, back for something he had forgotten, but they'd stopped. Somebody was coming and was sneaking up on him. Doc went over to the bed, got under the cover, and watched the door through half-closed eyes.

After the hesitation, Vinnie crept up the rest of the stairs and eased himself into the room. He saw the old man in the bed for the third time in his life. Holding the gun down by his side, he walked to the foot of the bed. Doc opened his eyes all the way and was looking at the man who he had seen only twice before, each time leaving him for dead.

"You're not much of a hit man, are you?" Doc managed a chuckle.

"When I'm through with you, I'm going back and kill that worthless son of yours." If Vinnie's fate hadn't already been sealed, that would have done it for sure. "Enough talking," and he raised the pistol.

But Vinnie never got off a shot. Doc fired the 38-caliber revolver that Donnie had left with him through the bedspread, three times into Vinnie's chest. While Vinnie stared at Doc, stunned, Doc put the fourth bullet into his forehead. Vinnie didn't get blown across the room. He fell forward onto the bed, already dead so that the cushioned fall was of no benefit to him.

Doc checked his pockets and found a cell phone and a wallet with five thousand dollars in it. The bullets had barely missed the phone. Doc guessed that the money was what he had been prepaid for the hit, and he was using it instead of credit cards to keep from being traced. Doc acted quickly, dragging the man across the floor to the top of the stairs. There he pushed him and got a little help from gravity, getting him to the first floor, resulting in a trail of blood across the floor and down the stairs. He pulled him across the kitchen and out the back door. The man had left his trunk open, apparently planning to put Doc in there. Instead, Doc was able, with seeming Herculean effort, to cram him in and close the trunk. Keys were in the ignition.

Doc didn't hesitate. He started the car and left a few feet of tire marks in his haste to get away. He was tired of hospitals and guards and he was going straight home to Bayou Belle. According to what Donnie had told him, his funeral should be starting at one. He should arrive in Bayou Belle while it was still going on.

Morgan was waiting for the cheeseburgers at Chili's when his cell rang. *Oh no*, he thought. He didn't want the boss to know he had left Doc alone, but he had to answer the phone.

"Morgan," said the chief, "how are things there?"

"All fine," replied Morgan, sweat forming on his brow. "All fine," he said again unnecessarily.

"Thought I should alert you to something just so you know

to be extra alert."The chief sounded nervous.

"What's that?" asked Morgan.

"A nurse from the floor where the doctor was at LSU disappeared a couple days ago. They found her this morning in the trunk of a car in the parking lot with a bullet through her head. There may not be a connection, but somebody may have been looking for Doc. I'm just calling so you can be extra careful. I may even send Raymond over so two of you can be on guard."The chief signed off.

Morgan pocketed the phone and ran for the door. The waitress yelled behind him that his food was ready, but he didn't even look back. He turned the siren on and drove well over the speed limit to get back to the house, cursing all the way, banging the steering wheel.

He ran in the back door hollering for Doc, then looked down and saw the blood marks across the kitchen floor. Panic stricken, he followed them down the hall and up the stairs. With his heart in his throat and his gun in his hand, he ran into Doc's room. The room was empty of people, living or dead. He checked the rest of the house and couldn't put it off any longer. He called the chief, who didn't receive the news well. Morgan sat on the downstairs couch and began the process of figuring out what he might do next for a job. Flipping burgers at McDonald's seemed the best option.

CHAPTER THIRTY-THREE

SATURDAY, JUNE 17

The family gathered in a small room off the front of the sanctuary. Rev. Dudley led them in prayer, and the funeral director, Mr. Charlet, instructed them about where to sit and how to follow his lead. Page was inconsolable. It had suddenly hit her when they arrived at the church that her grandpa was gone. Chuck had his arm around her. Delphine was with the family, holding her head down, blowing her nose, and dabbing at her eyes. Jake was outside ready to lead the procession to the cemetery. Charlie chanced a glance at the crowd. Friends were standing in the aisles; all the folding chairs were in use. Many were standing in the foyer, unable to find standing room. Mr. Charlet gave the signal and the family filed in. Jan was holding on to Charlie's arm. She looked good in black. A veil covered her face. Maria Hebert sang "In the Garden," a little flat as always. Charlie remembered his mother cringing every time she sang a solo, trying with body language to coax the note a little higher. Mr. Julius read the Scripture, choosing the 15th chapter of 1st Corinthians, and proceeded to remind the congregation that Jesus had gone to prepare a place for us, and where He was, we would be also. If it were not so, He would have told us.

Beulah Mae was giving her eulogy. It was almost Charlie's

turn when his cell buzzed. The call was from New Orleans, so Charlie leaned over and took the call. It was from the FBI. "Charlie, I have bad news. Your dad is gone. The guard left him alone for a few minutes to get them lunch. When he got back, Doc was gone and blood was everywhere. So sorry, looks like this time they got him. I don't know what else to say, except that we screwed it up." He hesitated just a moment like he didn't want to tell the rest, then added, "They must have taken his body with them because it wasn't there."

Charlie couldn't talk, so he just hung up the phone. A terrific pain squeezed his chest.

Jan looked at him with concern. "What's wrong?" she whispered.

"They got him this time," Charlie whispered back. "Dad is dead. I couldn't protect him."

Jan looked at him as if he had lost his mind. Of course his dad was dead. *We're all sitting here in black, mourning his passing. I really must have put Charlie under a lot of stress. Now I've driven him crazy and may have caused a heart attack.*

Charlie looked back at the congregation to see if Ruben was there. Ellie was two rows back, looking at him. "Everything okay?" her eyes seemed to ask. He attempted a reassuring smile, then saw Ruben behind her, bent over, talking into his cell phone with his hand cupped over his mouth. Charlie, appalled but not surprised by his lack of manners, turned back around as the soloist was singing the last verse of "Amazing Grace," closer this time to being on pitch. He resolved to personally kill Ruben the first chance he got.

Charlie stood up to honor his dad and give his remembrance. "My dad," he said, his voice choking, "was a wonderful husband, father, and surgeon. He loved this town and he loved all of you. He didn't have patients. He had friends. He measured success not by how much he had in the bank, but by how much he loved and got that love back. He truly stored up treasures in heaven. Now he's gone." Charlie could now say that in church and not worry about it being a lie. "One of my biggest regrets in this life is that I didn't come back here to Bayou Belle and join my dad in practice. There is so much more I could have learned from him had I been here, things he tried to teach me growing up, but I wasn't always interested. I have too often measured my success by the size of my bank account, and that does not honor the great man who tried to raise me better."

Tears, genuine tears, were running down Charlie's cheeks. He took the handkerchief out of his coat pocket and blew his nose. Ellie knew something was really wrong. He couldn't be this good an actor. After a pause, Charlie continued. "The best way I can honor my dad now, though late, would be to move back home and take over his practice. I hope that will be possible." He then thanked them all for coming and invited everyone to the house after the graveside service.

Doc was about halfway to Bayou Belle when Vinnie's cell rang. He let it go to voice mail. After a few minutes he picked up the phone to listen to the message. Ruben's voice was on the line, whispering, "I'm inside the church at the funeral. Did you find him and have you taken care of it? Text me what's going on. I have to know and am tired of waiting."

Doc pulled the car over at the next opportunity and texted

Ruben a reply. "Dead in the trunk of my car. On way to Bayou Belle. Meet me at your office when funeral over. I want my money." Doc smiled as he put the phone back down on the seat.

The family all fit in the limousine for the trip to the cemetery. Delphine rode with them. Jake led the procession in his police car. They were barely seated when Jan asked, "Were you serious about moving back here to practice?" She looked at him with an incredulous look.

"Dead serious," said Charlie, looking straight at her and not smiling. "It won't be so busy. I'll have a lot more time for other things like travel. I'm not getting any younger. You'll just be a couple hours from New Orleans and closer to Lafayette. Just wish Dad was going to be here to practice with." His eyes dropped and he shook his head. A few deep sobs escaped him. Page scooted over next to him and put her arm around his shoulder.

Charlie's cell rang. He didn't recognize the number, started not to answer it, but looked at Jan, pushed the send button, and said, "Hello."

"Charlie, how are you? How did my funeral go? Lots of people said nice things about me, I hope." Doc laughed.

"Dad?" Charlie said without thinking. "Is that really you?" He looked across at his family. They all sat staring at him, mouths open, eyebrows up, some concerned, some astonished. Charlie couldn't pass up the chance, so he asked, "Dad, tell me, how are things in heaven? Is it as beautiful as they say?" He looked over at his family and continued. "He says it's great. All his dogs are there, but he hasn't seen Mom yet." He listened a minute, then corrected himself. "Oh, I'm sorry, I misunderstood, he did see Mom. She says Maria Hebert still can't carry a tune."

"Charlie, listen to me a minute." Doc could sense how much fun Charlie was having. "I have a dead body in the trunk of my car. I got him." Charlie just listened while looking at the unbelieving faces of his family. "I've got a little business to do, then I'm going to Billy Jack's house. Come see me there later, after my graveside service. And take notes. I may want to make some changes when one day this happens for real."

"Okay. I'll take good notes. And see you later." Charlie hung up the phone.

"Who was that?" demanded Jan. "I swear, I think you've gone absolutely nuts. I would think you would show more respect for your poor dead father, not even in the ground."

Charlie's phone rang again. It was the same number. "Yeah, Dad. Something else?" He looked at Jan and smiled.

"One thing I forgot. Give BJ some warning, I don't want him to die of fright. Are you to the cemetery yet?"

"We're just turning in now, so we'll be with you in just a minute." Charlie still couldn't resist.

Page, sitting closest to her dad, thought she actually heard her grandpa's voice on the phone, so the look on her face was puzzled, yet more believing than the others. Delphine was smiling. Chuck just looked out the window and didn't say anything, afraid of what might be going on with his dad. His dad was a joker, but this was a bit much.

The hearse pulled up to the gravesite. The family got out and sat in chairs facing the casket under a small tent. Many who had come from the church and others who chose to go only to the graveside service gathered around. The service was short and when it was over, mourners walked to their cars. Some came by to greet the family. Ellie came over. She shook everyone's hand and gave Page and Charlie hugs. While hugging her, Charlie said to be sure and come to the house and ask Hubert to come too. She nodded that she understood and would do it. Jan watched her walk away, then took Charlie's arm and walked with him to the hearse for the ride back to the church. Charlie looked around once more to see the expensive casket, in record time, holding only dust, being lowered into the ground. Maybe they were reusable. He wondered.

Doc drove the car to the hospital and parked behind Ruben's office. He entered through the anteroom as he had almost two weeks ago. When he entered the office, Ruben was looking the other way, going through his desk.

"You always show up on time when you want your money." Ruben talked into the desk. "I have it here." He reached in and came up with a thick envelope and turned around to see Doc facing him with a silenced pistol trained on his chest. "What the..." Ruben's eyes displayed pure fright and he was close to losing bowel control.

"Hi, Ruben," Doc said calmly. "You are no better at hiring hit men and killers than you are hiring surgeons. Matter of fact, I'd say you were an abject failure." Doc was smiling, enjoying the moment. "We can talk later, but for now I want you to come with me."

"I'm not going anywhere with you." Ruben was trying to

act brave, but he couldn't hide the dark spot on the front of his trousers, which was getting larger.

"I don't plan to kill you unless I have to. I am the one person in this room who is not a murderer. I have left many scars in my lifetime, usually with a scalpel, but I bet I could leave some doozies with a gun. Your choice. I'd hate to ruin that suit any more than you already have. So let's go."

Doc stood his distance and watched Ruben walk on wobbly legs out through the anteroom, across the lot to Vinnie's car. He opened the trunk, where Vinnie's body had continued to bleed. Blood was now congealed on his clothes. A neat red hole was in his forehead. His sightless eyes were still wide open, staring directly at Ruben. The look of surprise had not left his dead face.

"Get in." Doc motioned for Ruben to join the stiff in the trunk. "Now! Move it!" Doc put on his most menacing look, not too impressive but for the gun in his hand. He fired a round behind Ruben into the ground.

Whimpering like a two-year-old, Ruben started to get in the trunk, then stopped. "Please, Doc." In his most beseeching voice, he said, "Don't do this."

"Get in and I'm not going to say it again." Doc paused, looked away for a second as if considering, giving Ruben some false hope, then continued. "Or would you rather be fed to the alligators like you did my friend Ken." This time Doc pointed the gun at his head. Ruben almost jumped in and closed the trunk himself. Doc made sure it was completely shut, then got in the car and drove to Billy Jack's.

CHAPTER THIRTY-FOUR

SATURDAY EVENING, JUNE 17

The house was full of well-wishers. Stories were shared about things Doc had said or done, bringing on laughter and tears. There was food aplenty since so many folks had brought by casseroles and pound cakes. Charlie uncorked red and white wine, and Delphine made several pitchers of sweet tea. The evening was cool enough that doors and windows were left open, and the crowd spilled onto the wide veranda. Ceiling fans were running, helping the natural breeze that brought in the sweet smell of ligustrum and honeysuckle. A few local musicians who had brought a fiddle, a guitar, and a Cajun accordion were entertaining the crowd with old-fashioned Cajun music. A few guests were even dancing, unable to keep still with the infectious Cajun beat. There was the gaiety of a post-burial jazz funeral. Charlie looked out at the crowd and thought it a shame that Doc couldn't be here. This was right up his alley and the very thing he loved most to do, to be amongst good friends enjoying good food, drink, and merriment. Charlie was half tempted to go to Billy Jack's and get him. Then the party would really start.

Ellie donned an apron and was in the kitchen helping Delphine. Charlie saw Hubert come in the door and moved over to speak to him. "Hubert, thanks for coming by. Dad would appreciate your being here." He looked around. Page was the only person nearby. "Say, I need to go to Billy Jack's after this is over. Would you mind going with me?"

Hubert was visibly excited by the invitation. "Sure, Charlie. Anytime you say."

"I'll come by your house and pick you up when this is over. It shouldn't take long."

"It doesn't matter. I don't have to work tomorrow. And it wouldn't matter if I did."

Charlie thanked him and moved away. Many old friends came up and told Charlie how sad they were, but how glad that he was coming to Bayou Belle to practice. That was something Charlie had been thinking but had not planned to say at the service. But in a way he was glad he had said it before witnesses, because it would now be harder to back out.

Charlie looked across the room and saw Jan go into the kitchen. He sauntered over that way. The crowd was beginning to dwindle. Delphine was resupplying the hors d'oeuvres and Ellie was washing the dishes. Charlie looked in and saw that Jan had trapped Ellie at the sink and was talking a mile a minute. He wished he could hear what she was saying, but he didn't dare go over and interrupt. He turned back for a moment to say good-bye to the Bradshaws, then went back in the kitchen just as Ellie dropped a plate, breaking it on the floor. She bent to pick it up, then stood and ran out of the kitchen. Charlie hurried to follow her. By the time he reached the hall bathroom, the door was locked. With his ear to the door, he could hear soft sobs. "Ellie?" Charlie asked. "You okay?"

"I'm okay," she said. "Just give me a moment."

Charlie went back to the kitchen, where Jan was drying

dishes. Delphine cut her eyes toward Jan, then closed them and slowly shook her head in disgust. Jan turned around and saw Charlie. "Hi, hon," she said. "Is the crowd starting to go away? Hope they hurry. I'd like a repeat of last night if you're up to it. What do you say?"

"What did you say to Ellie?" Charlie walked over to where she was.

Jan continued to dry the plate in her hand, then put it down and turned toward Charlie. "Why are you worried about her? I am your wife. Why don't you care how I feel?"

"Jan, just settle down. I do care about your feelings, but I don't want guests in my home to leave crying."

"Did she leave? I thought she was going to find a Band-Aid."

"What did you say to her?"

"I told her that you were probably sorry that you had said you were moving to Bayou Belle to practice. That you said it when you were emotional and that you would be going home with me to Riverton because we are married."

Charlie backed up from Jan and leaned back against the counter and looked over at Delphine as if to confirm that Jan was telling the truth.

"That's not all you said," Delphine spoke up.

"Shut up, Delphine," screamed Jan. "Just you shut up. This is no business of yours."

"Nobody tells Delphine to shut up. And this family is my business. I been in it longer than you have, official papers or not. You gonna tell him or you want me to."

Jan turned her head and looked up toward a corner of the ceiling, shrugged her shoulders, and confessed, "I told her about the great night we spent last night, and that you would be returning to Riverton with me for sure." She looked at Delphine. "There now, how's that for truth?"

Delphine just nodded and looked down at the floor, hoping she hadn't messed up but glad she had done it. Charlie looked at Jan with a combination of disgust and pity. "Why?" he asked. "Why would you do that?" He thought a moment, then answered his own question. "As if I didn't know. Last night was all about getting to tell Ellie about it. You're just plain selfish." Then he continued. "You don't really want me; you just don't want anyone else to have me." Charlie turned and walked out of the kitchen. Just a few guests were left. Page was talking to them as they were leaving. Charlie added his thanks to Page's and they closed the front door as the last couple left.

"What's wrong, Dad? You don't look so good." She led him over to a chair and had him sit down.

Charlie's blood pressure was probably through the roof, and his head was starting to pound. "I'm okay," he said. "I have some business to take care of tonight, but I'll be back before long." He got up and went out the door.

Page went into the kitchen, where Jan was still sitting at the table, and heard her mother say, "I really botched it, didn't I?"

"I think you messed it up pretty good," agreed Delphine. "But was there much left to mess up? I mean, Miss Jan, I heard what you told him when you were barely in the door yesterday. The only thing that brought you round was Ellie."

"She really is beautiful, isn't she?" asked Jan.

"She sho is, and sweet as she can be on the inside," Delphine added, hoping Jan got the point.

Jan leaned forward with her face in her hands. "And now he has gone to her."

"I heard him talking to Hubert Polk earlier," said Page. "He was going to pick him up to take care of some kind of business. So I don't think he was going to Ellie's."

When Charlie got in the old jeep, he went straight to Ellie's. He left the car running in her driveway and ran to the door, ringing the doorbell three times. Beau opened the door.

"Hi, Beau, can I come in? I need to talk to your mom."

"Dr. Leveau," Beau was embarrassed to say, "my mom isn't feeling well. She's in her room and said not to let anyone in. I'm sorry."

"That's okay, Beau, I know you have to do what your mother says, but will you please just tell her that I really need to see her and that I'm going out to your granddad's? I hope she'll go with me."

Beau looked doubtful, but went to tell his mother what Charlie had said. He was back in just a few seconds. "She said she might see you tomorrow, maybe. She is already in bed and under the covers. Her eyes are red like she's sick, and she said she didn't feel well."

"Thanks for asking, Beau. Then I'll see her tomorrow." Charlie ached like a teenager who had just lost his first love. He'd have to get over it for now. There was work to be done.

Hubert was waiting by the door when Charlie drove up to his house. He hauled his bulk into the passenger side, and the two vigilantes drove to their hideout.

CHAPTER THIRTY-FIVE

SATURDAY NIGHT, JUNE 17

The Bayou Belle Vigilante committee arrived one at a time to Billy Jack's home. Billy Jack had arrived home from the funeral to find Doc sitting in his favorite chair. Thankfully, Charlie had warned him. He knew Doc was supposed to be alive and hiding, but Charlie had done such a convincing job of acting at the funeral service that Billy Jack thought that maybe he really was dead.

"It sure is good having you in my home, even if it is right after I went to your funeral," Billy Jack kidded. "Last time I saw you, you were lying in a pool of your own blood on the floor at your place."

"I know," said Doc. "You saved my life. I guess I'll have to be nice to you."

"Aw, don't do that," retorted Billy Jack. "It wouldn't feel right." Billy Jack sat across from Doc. "Charlie didn't have time to give me any details, but I can see you must be out of hiding."

"Not exactly. Only a few people know right now, and we should keep it that way until things get straightened out."

"That's what we're trying to make happen tomorrow night." Billy Jack didn't know how much Doc knew about that. "A group of people will be arriving here tonight. Most of them know you were hiding, so you won't look like a ghost to them."

"I didn't know that when I told Charlie I was coming here—just figured it'd be the best place to hide." Doc continued. "I do have a surprise, though, that we'll have to deal with one way or another."

"What's that?" asked Billy Jack. "Tell me."

"I'll do better than that," Doc said. "I'll show you." He got up and led BJ to the car. As they approached the trunk, he pulled the gun out of his inside jacket pocket.

"You carrying now?" asked Billy Jack. "What, you got an alligator in there?"

"Two bodies, one alive so far and one dead." Doc laughed at the unbelieving look on Billy Jack's face.

"You're pulling my leg."

"Here, Billy Jack, take this gun." Doc said it loudly so Ruben could hear. "When I open the trunk, shoot anything that tries to get out." Doc leaned over and opened the trunk wide while Billy Jack trained the gun on the open trunk.

Nothing moved. Doc wasn't sure whether Ruben was dead or too scared to move, and he couldn't say that he cared greatly which it was. Billy Jack stared back at the dead eyes of Vinnie, the third sightless eye between the other two. "Damn!" was all he could say.

"The one looking at you was in my house just before you were. He should have finished the job."

Ruben stirred. "You still alive?" asked Doc. "I thought you had scared yourself to death." Then with a little kindness he said, "I'll let you out in a little while, but not yet." Doc gave Ruben a bottled water, which he gulped down. Then Doc re-closed the trunk. "I don't want to let him out until the others get here. We're two old farts that he could get away from, and

I have a plan for him."

Soon the others arrived. Charlie and Hubert got there first. Doc took them to the car and showed them who was in the trunk. Hubert walked over to the side and threw up everything he had eaten at Charlie's, which turned out to be quite a lot. They all went inside and waited for Jake to arrive before getting Ruben out. Fifteen minutes later Jake drove up with Donnie. They didn't have to worry about Ruben running off. He could barely stand up. Donnie and Charlie assisted Ruben into the house. Hubert walked behind them, unnoticed by Ruben, but halfway to the house he went back and threw up again.

Jake was still in his car on a radio call. He got out as they were helping Ruben into the house. "What do we have here?" he asked, not really liking what he saw.

"He's my prisoner, Jake," said Doc. "I made a citizen's arrest."

"What was the charge?" Jake was trying not to grin.

"Whatever you want it to be. Anything from murder to hiring somebody to murder, to blackmail, whatever. I don't care what you charge him with, but I think he shot that man." Doc pointed to the open trunk.

Jake walked over and saw Vinnie looking exactly like he had most of the day. He didn't change much. "So you think Ruben here shot him?" Jake took off his hat and scratched his head as if enough weren't already happening.

"I found this gun in his pocket," he said, taking the silenced gun out to show to Jake.

Ruben was taking all this in, an incredulous look on his face but no longer looking down his nose. "Sheriff, I hope you know this man is lying." Ruben had gained some confidence with the sheriff there, thinking Doc wasn't as likely to kill him outright. Ruben also knew that James Vidrine had an agreement with the sheriff. The odds were evening out for Ruben. They all went into Billy Jack's great room. All, that is, except Vinnie. He remained in the trunk, the same look on his face.

"Where's Ellie?" asked Billy Jack.

"She wasn't feeling well and went to bed early. I'll catch her up tomorrow," said Charlie. His chest and abdomen ached again. Focus, he told himself.

Billy Jack accepted that but thought it wasn't much like his daughter.

Doc pulled Jake aside and told him his plan. "We're in it this far, and the son of a bitch deserves it," Doc convinced Jake, who thought he was probably going to lose his badge anyway.

Donnie also went along. He'd just deny he ever knew anything, and considering what Doc wanted to do, most people would probably believe that he didn't know. Nobody in his right mind would go along with this plan. He laughed to himself.

At Doc's direction, Billy Jack brought in a large mason jar filled with his best moonshine whiskey. Doc carried it over to Ruben and offered it to him. Ruben refused, waving it away with a nauseated look of disgust, almost knocking it out of Doc's hands. Doc then told him he really didn't have a choice. "You can take your medicine like a man or I'll pour it in through your nose."

Ruben accepted the jar and took a swig. His face contorted and he grabbed his chest as it went down. Some of the whiskey spilled.

"Careful," shouted Billy Jack, "careful with that whiskey. That's valuable stuff. And if you make that face again, I'll knock you out of that chair."

Ruben took another swallow, his face still contorted but less so, cutting his eyes toward Billy Jack as he did. "How much do you want me to drink?"

"That jar is all yours," said Doc. "When you finish that, I'll decide if I want you to have another." It was a quart jar full of 100 percent, 200-proof bootleg whiskey.

Ruben looked with despair at the large jar of booze. He decided he'd rather be drunk than put up with all the abuse. His attitude improved as he continued to drink. About halfway through the jar, Ruben got the giggles. "You assholes are in so m-much tr-tr-trouble. Y'all are g-g-going to j-jail for a l-long t-time, but I-I'll be s-sober t-tomorrow." Then he laughed at the joke, slapping at his knee but missing, almost falling out of his chair. With nothing in his stomach, he got very drunk very fast. He hadn't finished the first jar before he passed out. Doc watched him to be sure he was still breathing. He didn't want him to die from respiratory arrest from too much alcohol. When Ruben began to snore, Charlie and Jake carried him to the car and put him back in the trunk.

Charlie drove the car out to a small country road. Jake followed in the police car. They drove off the road and down into a shallow ditch. Jake helped Charlie get Ruben out of the trunk and positioned him in the driver's seat. They left Vinnie's gun in his lap.

Charlie rode with Jake back to Billy Jack's. When they were back, Billy Jack called the sheriff's office to report a car in a ditch he had seen when he was driving home from Doc's house, and he gave directions about where he had seen it.

Hubert was numb. He didn't know whether to laugh or cry.

Jake walked over to Hubert and assured him that this would all be straightened out. Hubert wasn't so sure, but he felt better. The next thing he did was walk over and pour himself a glass of Billy Jack's best. He had a designated driver, and he really needed a drink.

Donnie said, "We better start the meeting before Jake gets called about a murder." He continued. "It's really pretty simple. The troops will arrive in town about nine p.m. If they get here too early, we may give ourselves away."

Charlie piped in, "But we have to be sure no more innocents are killed. We have to stop them before they harvest the first live organs."

"From what I understand, they do the cadavers first, and then do the live donors last, usually starting about ten. I get that from what I have heard this last week listening to Ruben talk to Kaiser. I also think they're getting scared that someone is on to them, so tomorrow night may be their last for a while. We have to catch them red-handed. The tapes I recorded are probably not admissible as evidence.

"Charlie, we'll ask you to go up in your plane late in the afternoon and look at the place to see if anything is different than we expect. Hubert, you, Doc, and Billy Jack will stay here, wait for messages, and be troubleshooters. Hell, call the National Guard or governor if you have to. Jake and I will be with the state police. They're sending twenty officers. We've been over it with them. Some will keep the planes from leaving while everyone is rounded up. Any questions?" He looked around the room. "Okay, we're all set. And, Hubert, you all should be over here in place by five o'clock."

"Will do," said Hubert, his voice just a little slurred as he took another sip of the whiskey. "By the way," he asked, "what are y'all telling your families? My wife keeps asking me where I'm going. I don't think she believes I have this much work to do."

Jake laughed. "Somehow it got out at our house that there was some pornographic moviemaking going on out here with stars coming in from all over. We are investigating it on behalf of the town because we don't want the wonderful reputation of Bayou Belle besmirched."

"That's rich," said Hubert. He was about to comment further when Jake's radio call came. Jake put his phone on speaker.

The whole group heard Deputy Hancock say, "Sheriff, you just really aren't going to believe this, and I promise you I have not been drinking."

"What you got, Benny?"

"Honest, Sheriff, you sittin' down?" Benny paused just a second, apparently giving his boss a chance to sit down, then continued.

"I got a call about a car in a ditch. I might have left it 'til morning, but I wasn't busy and I thought somebody could be in the car. Well, when I got there and shined the light in, there was Mr. Ruben Martin, drunker than I've ever seen anybody still breathing, with a gun in his lap that had a silencer on it. There was a stiff in the trunk. It smelled like blood, vomit, and shit. Anyway, I blew my dinner right there on the side of the road just as that nosy old bitch Mrs. Poindexter drove by. I'm sure she could smell the alcohol and thought I had been drinking on duty, but I swear, Sheriff, I haven't."

He protesteth so much Jake wondered if he had been drinking. "Slow down, Benny." Jake was stifling a laugh, while Billy Jack was about to fall off his chair, holding his sides. Hubert had gone to the bathroom, missing most of the report. "So what did you do?" asked Jake.

"What did I do?" Benny asked like Jake should know the answer. "Hell, after I vomited my guts out, I called you. That's what I did." After another pause, Benny continued. "I can't wake Mr. Martin up, and I don't want to drag him out of the car. Maybe I'll call an ambulance. What do you think?"

"Where are you? I'll come help."

"Thanks, Sheriff. I was hoping you'd say that." He told Jake how to get there.

Jake bid farewell to the group, looking at them like Eisenhower must have looked at his troops the night before D-day.

CHAPTER THIRTY-SIX

EARLY SUNDAY MORNING, JUNE 18

The truck drove slowly down Conti. At three o'clock in the morning, this section of the Vieux Carré was relatively quiet. Even the Bourbon Street noise two blocks over was dissipating, as many partiers turned in for the night. A homeless man had been living in the alley halfway between Burgundy and Dauphine for the past three months. He had no friends and no known family. Two men from the truck slowly approached the man, who was eating part of a sandwich he had retrieved from a nearby garbage can. They looked around to be sure they weren't being observed, then grabbed the vagrant, pulled him to his feet, and placed duct tape over his mouth before he could protest. They marched him quickly to the back of the truck and tossed him in. The truck moved off.

Amy, seventeen, walking down Chartres after a long night plying her trade, was on the way to an apartment she shared with four other working girls. Abused by her family in New Jersey, she had run away to New Orleans. She looked for legitimate work but, unable to find it, turned to the oldest job of all. Nobody in her hometown would believe what she was doing, but she felt she had no choice. She was not going back home to an abusive situation, even if it meant hooking for room and board. The law might not understand, but she was not going back. She'd die first, though she hadn't expected to have to make that particular choice. The truck was waiting as she rounded the corner onto Esplanade for the last leg of her walk home. A man approached her from the truck.

"I'm off," she said. "I've been working for the past twenty-four hours and I'm going home." She kept walking, picking up her pace, an uneasy feeling in her belly.

The man grabbed her, clasped his hand over her mouth, lifted her kicking, and threw her in the truck with the home-less man. Both were cuffed to the inside of the panel truck. Duct tape was also placed over the girl's mouth. She stared at the homeless man. Each looked at the other with pure fright.

The next-to-last stop before Bayou Belle would be the funeral home. Before daybreak on Sunday morning, the pan-eled truck pulled up to the back of Fusilier Funeral Home. The driver got out of the truck and walked to the back of the mortuary and knocked three times on the door. An attendant at the funeral home cracked open the door, looked around outside, then opened the door just wide enough to let the man through.

The driver was carrying a heavy box that he was ready to put down. "I have three."

The funeral home attendant said, "I was expecting four."

"You'll have to divide these three four ways. They just gave me three. How many do you have?"

"I have four but I need them back by Wednesday." The at-tendant had a worried look. "What do I do if the families come early?" Even though this job was paying for his education at UNO, he wished he'd never gotten involved.

"I can't bring them until they give them to me." The truck

driver thought, *I don't care what you tell the families*, but he said, "All I can do is mention that you need them Wednesday. If you come up short, just use some sand. The weight is about the same, and nobody will know the difference. Now, where are the stiffs?"

"Back here." The attendant pointed to four body bags.

The driver called his assistant and together they carried them to the truck and drove off. The funeral attendant went to the break room and poured a cup of strong coffee. *I don't know how long I can get away with this. The money is good, but one day the boss is going to figure it out and there will be hell to pay.* After several months and some close calls, surely their luck would soon run out.

On the way out of town, the truck pulled into a truck stop, parked far away from everyone else, and the driver walked in to get coffee. A man sitting in one of the booths saw him come in and nodded. He reached into his coat pocket for his cell phone and made a quick call.

Ten minutes later a big black car pulled up behind the truck. The back of the truck was opened. Two men from the car roughly pulled a nattily dressed man, hands cuffed and mouth taped, out of the backseat and tossed him into the truck, slamming the door shut. The truck pulled away.

"Looks like we made another good haul," said the man riding shotgun. He took his cap off and wiped his forehead. "I don't know what happens when we get there, and I'm pretty sure I don't want to know." He looked over at the driver. "And I bet you that the old man doesn't have a clue either."

"Just shut up," said the driver, his eyes straight ahead. "They pay us well and all we do is deliver. The rest is none of our business." His face showed concern, and he was silent for about five miles, then turned to his partner and agreed. "I think you're right, though, about Mr. Martinelli. I don't think he knows. He is getting old and may be losing control."

"Sure hope they don't have recorders in this cab. We'd both be dead for thinking." They agreed not to discuss the matter further. Early Sunday morning the truck pulled into Vidrine Trucking Company, drove to the back of the property, and parked in a designated spot near the old house. They pulled the three captives out of the truck and herded them into the outbuilding containing the furnace, handcuffed them to a rail inside, made sure the window was sealed, and drew a dark shade. They found a place to sleep for a few hours. Their next job was to stand guard on the property during the weekly Sunday night activities.

CHAPTER THIRTY-SEVEN

SUNDAY MORNING, JUNE 18

Ruben woke up Sunday morning stretched out on a jail-house cot with a throbbing headache that announced loudly his every heartbeat. His mouth was dry, his vision blurred. The first things he saw and understood were the bars of his cell. He sat up so suddenly he almost passed out from the pain in his head. He got on his knees, leaning over the bed. Anyone not knowing Ruben might have thought he was praying. He crawled over to the corner commode and threw up everything in his stomach, then got the dry heaves. His head hurt so badly with each heave that he was sure he was dying. He crawled back to bed and managed to get in. Slowly the pain eased and his head began to clear. Yesterday had been a bad dream. It must have been. He had seen a ghost who forced him into a trunk with a dead man. He vaguely remembered Hubert Polk's name. It must have been a dream, but why was he in jail? He made the mistake of shaking his head to clear it, only to cause the headache to return.

Ellie had trouble going to sleep, then didn't wake up until after nine o'clock. She put on her robe and went into the kitchen. Beau had cooked his own breakfast and was still sitting there reading the sports page. "Hi, sweetheart," she said, "sorry I overslept. Do you need anything?"

"No, Mom, I just had some bacon and eggs." He looked at her, frowned, and asked, "You okay? You don't look so good."

"I'm okay," she said but obviously fighting back tears. "Just overslept." She went to the coffeemaker to brew a pot. "What are your plans for the day? Going to Sunday School?"

"I think I will. Then, this afternoon Jeremiah and I were going to do something, maybe go fishing or play some ball." During the funeral reception, he and Jeremiah talked about what to do on Sunday afternoon and decided it would be fun to visit Vidrine's and maybe see some porn stars. They were going to tell their folks they were going fishing.

"Tell you what, I don't feel much like cooking, so when Sunday School is over, come back home and we'll go have lunch at the Village Inn." She didn't really want to go out in public today looking tired and upset, but Beau had to eat and she was too strong a person to have a prolonged pity party. Charlie was, after all, still married to a very beautiful woman, and he had a nice family. She just couldn't forget what Jan had said or get the picture of it out of her mind.

Charlie was visibly depressed at breakfast. He was drinking his second cup of coffee and looking at but not seeing the newspaper. He had barely touched his food.

"You need to get your chin off your chest, Charlie Leveau." Delphine never circled a subject before landing. "You decide what you want to do, and do it. It's your life to live. I haven't seen you look this defeated since you and Jake lost in the state championship game y'all's junior year. Thought your life was over. Nothing would ever be right again. Then you came back the next year and won the whole thing. Life almost always gives you second chances. Just don't be feeling so sorry for yourself, or you'll miss it when it comes."

Jan came down for breakfast just as Delphine finished her soliloquy. "Good morning," she said. "You two in a deep discussion?" She had not heard the conversation but could guess what it was about. "You sure got in late last night, Charlie. It was after two o'clock when I heard the jeep drive up. Anything to tell me?" She asked it in a way that implied she really didn't care that much, but thought she should at least ask the question. Charlie and Delphine both shrugged their shoulders but said nothing except for wishing her a good morning. When they didn't respond to her question, Jan continued. "Charlie, I have an announcement to make. Page and I are leaving later today. I'm going to Houston to get my things at Ruth's and move back to Riverton. I've been very silly and want to make it up to you. We can continue our life in Riverton as before. You do your practice like you want, and I won't comment. I have my life there too. We'll soon have a grandchild to gloat over together. If you haven't changed the locks on me, I'll be there when you get home."

Charlie listened to all this with his mouth open and unbelieving eyes. All he could think to say was, "I'll be here for at least a few more days straightening out Dad's affairs, and I'm not sure how long it will take."

Delphine dropped a frying pan in the sink, making a loud noise that startled both Jan and Charlie.

Jan looked over at Delphine and said, although she had not been asked, "I'm not really hungry for breakfast. What do you say we all go to the Village for brunch. Delphine had a long day yesterday and could use some time off. What do you say?"

Charlie shrugged. "Okay with me. I have some things to do later, but if we go at noon it should be fine."

Delphine had a roast ready to put in the oven but it would wait until tomorrow. Maybe Doc would be home by then to enjoy it.

Billy Jack and Doc were up early. Old and big prostates make a long night's sleep almost impossible. Billy Jack, also an accomplished Cajun cook, had prepared shrimp and grits with tasso ham gravy that was as good as anything Doc had eaten since the last meal Delphine cooked for him. One more time Billy Jack said, "Did you see the look on Ruben's face when you gave him the first drink of moonshine?" Billy Jack leaned with both hands against the counter and tears came to his eyes as he laughed. Wiping the tears with his shirtsleeve he continued. "He didn't know whether to shit or go blind."

"And Hubert didn't look much better." Doc chuckled. "I guess we could all go to jail for a long time for what we did. The town would lose half its population." He paused, looked up at the ceiling, and added, "But it sure was fun and I wouldn't trade last night for anything, except for tonight if it all works out." An hour later both men were sitting in soft chairs in the big room asleep.

Hubert woke up with a headache almost matching Ruben's, but his head was clearer. He remembered everything, including the ride home and the greeting he had received from the missus.

"You should be ashamed of yourself," Helen Polk remarked when he came downstairs, looking a little the worse for wear. "You, a grown man, a pillar of the community, drinking and gambling 'til the wee hours of the morning, brought home by a man who just got kicked out of the hospital for drunkenness and is getting a divorce." She wouldn't stop. "Just what were you thinking? And right after a nice church service for a truly honorable man." She banged some dishes, then continued. "What do you have to say for yourself?"

Hubert tried to make the best of it and white lie about the night, all for a good cause. "Hon, we just got to playing cards and reminiscing about Doc Leveau. Billy Jack was passing around his concoction, and first thing you know it was after midnight. Didn't mean to make you worry." He looked her in the eye and held her massive shoulders and said sincerely, "I'm sorry. Please forgive me."

What could she say? He said he was sorry and obviously meant it. He was, after all, a good man, good to the point of boring. He never did anything out of the norm. Maybe she was secretly a little proud, even if she was a bit scared, that he had stepped out. Then she remembered the pearl necklace he had brought back from his New Orleans trip when everything seemed to change for them. She would let this go. To show him she forgave him, she got a couple of extra-strength Tylenols before he asked where they were, and put on the coffeepot. Then she hugged him and said, "I'm just glad you're home safe, and that you weren't driving in that condition."

Hubert, happy to be forgiven, thought, *I don't know what she would do if she knew about tonight, and there's no way I can tell her.*

CHAPTER THIRTY-EIGHT

SUNDAY MORNING, JUNE 18

Jake was sitting at his desk reading the morning paper when Ruben called out from the back. The sheriff's office had a couple of jail cells, located down a side hall and separated from Jake's office. "Sheriff!" Ruben called out again, louder this time, angry that his head throbbed again because he had to yell.

Jake got slowly out of his chair and walked back to the cell. "What can I do for you?" he asked.

"You can get me the hell out of here. That's what you can do. What kind of place are you running?" Ruben was trying to shake the bars, but they weren't moving, causing mounting frustration.

"I'm running a first-class jail," said Jake, "and in that jail right now is a man who is charged with, among other things, DUI, public drunkenness, and murder, not necessarily in that order."

Ruben looked around. He was the only one there. "Who are you talking about?" He was afraid of the answer.

"You're the only one I see here," replied Jake, pointing a long finger at Ruben.

"What are you talking about!?" Ruben backed up to sit on the cot, rubbing his forehead to make the pain go away again, then whispered so it wouldn't hurt more, "Please tell me what's going on."

"Last night you were discovered by my deputy behind the wheel of a car in a ditch with a flat tire. You were almost dead drunk. When the deputy opened the trunk to get the spare, he discovered a dead man. His blood was all over you. He had been shot several times, and a pistol was found in your lap." Jake was having fun watching the growing look of astonishment and disbelief on Ruben's face. "You'll be with us until tomorrow when the judge will decide if you get bail. You'll need a lawyer. I was letting you wake up on your own and get your head together. The lab at the hospital called to say you had the highest blood alcohol level they had ever seen in a living human being." That fact had given Jake the shivers. Maybe they had come a little too close to killing him.

"Sheriff, this is all a huge frame, and you are part of it. I saw you there."

"You saw me where?" Jake had thought about what he would say. "I was home last night until my deputy called me from the site. I have to say, you were drunker than anyone I have ever seen, and I have seen a lot in my particular line of work."

"Do I get to make one call?" Ruben was counting on something being true that he had seen in the movies.

"Sure," said Jake. "You can make a call. Maybe you should call your lawyer."

Ruben ignored him. "Just bring me a phone. I'll call who I want," he said as defiantly as he could manage under the circumstances.

Jake went back to his office and brought the portable

phone to Ruben. "Here, make your call, but murder suspects usually stay in jail at least until their hearing, and the earliest that will be is tomorrow when the court reopens. I'd suggest you make yourself as comfortable as possible."

"Just give me the goddamn phone," said Ruben, "and leave me alone while I make my call."

Jake went back to his office but stayed close enough to hear Ruben's end of the conversation.

"Jimmy, I need help. They got me in this two-bit jailhouse, and they're framing me for murder. You gotta get me out of here." Ruben almost sobbed.

"Wait a minute," said James Vidrine, "now say that again. Where the hell are you and what are you talking about?"

"I mean I'm in big downtown Bayou Belle in the godforsaken place they call a jail, and I am accused of murder, held right now by our soon-to-be reelected sheriff." Ruben was pacing in his cell, listening to the quiet on the other end of the phone. "Jimmy, I'm serious, you gotta help me. I'll go crazy in this place."

Vidrine was getting pure enjoyment out of Ruben's predicament, but he couldn't let it continue for many reasons. "Give the phone to Sheriff Sears and I'll see what I can do."

Ruben called out, "Sheriff, Jimmy, I mean Mr. Vidrine wants to talk to you."

Jake hesitated a few moments, then came around and took the phone, walking with it back to his office. "Hello, who is this?" he asked.

"Sheriff, this is James Vidrine. We have a problem."

"That right?" asked Jake.

"You have Ruben Martin in jail falsely accused. I want him

out of there."

"I'd love to help out, Mr. Vidrine, but there is a whole pile of evidence against him, and the judge won't be in until tomorrow morning." Jake was thinking on his feet. He didn't want to give in too easily, but it would be great to have Ruben out of his jail and out of his way.

"Sheriff, I don't think you're hearing me. Now listen up. I want Ruben Martin out of that country jailhouse of yours, and I want him out within the next hour. Otherwise, as you know, I'll have you in that same jail in about the same amount of time."

"I hear you, Mr. Vidrine. Would you mind giving me a little help?" Jake hesitated but Vidrine didn't respond. "I need a lawyer to come in here and sign for him and make a case for releasing him. That would help get me off the hook when somebody looks into the situation." Jake paused, hoping Vidrine would buy it. He didn't want to be too easy with a murder suspect and make Vidrine suspicious. "If you wouldn't mind calling Hubert Polk, he could come by here and make a case for getting Ruben out. That would provide me some cover, if you know what I mean."

"Dear God, I had a great day planned and now I'm calling all over southwest Louisiana for my goddamn brother-in-law. Maybe I should just let you keep him." Jake waited for him to finish. "I'll call Polk and send him over."

"Then I'll wait to hear from Mr. Polk."

Thirty minutes later Hubert came through the front door. "Got a call from James Vidrine that you are holding Ruben Martin for murder. Just how ridiculous is that?" Hubert winked at Jake and was talking loudly enough to allow Ruben to hear.

"The evidence against him is strong, Hubert, and I hesitate letting him go. What if he bolts and a murderer gets away, and I have to answer for it next month when I'm up for reelection?"

"I'll sign the papers and be responsible. I'll have him in court tomorrow at whatever time it happens to be. I'll watch him in the meantime." Jake thought Hubert would be a great Big Daddy in *Cat on a Hot Tin Roof*.

Jake walked with Hubert back to the cell and unlocked the door. Ruben, his hair disheveled, his wrinkled clothes covered with vomit and dried blood, tried to be as dignified as possible as he exited the cell, giving Jake an "I told you so. You should know better than to mess with me" look, and walked straight out the door and into Hubert's car, parked in the no-parking zone just outside.

Hubert drove toward Ruben's apartment but Ruben stopped him. "Take me to James Vidrine's home. I'm frightened that something else will happen to me, and I want to see my sister."

Hubert, not entirely surprised by the request, made a quick U-turn and pointed the car toward the Vidrine home, a couple of miles out of town. On the way Hubert's thoughts were occupied by how he'd ever get the awful stench out of his new car.

The Vidrine estate covered about twenty acres, with an ostentatious manor house in the center. A swimming pool, surrounded by a wall of thick bamboo, took up much of the backyard. The pool area was completely private.

Hubert walked with Ruben to the front door. The maid answered with a puzzled expression. "Can I help you?" she asked.

"I want to see my sister," said a very agitated Ruben. He

was looking over the maid's shoulder, trying to force his way into the house.

"Miss Adrienne, she's gone to New Orleans to see her dad. She left early this morning."

"Then I want to come in and see Jimmy Vee." He tried to push past her, but she held her ground. "Where is he?"

"He's out back by the pool, but I don't think he wants company. He mixes his own drinks and tells me to stay out. So I know he's not expecting anybody." She was trying to save her job and still give good advice.

Ruben finally got by her and, with Hubert right behind, marched straight to the back door. Approaching the pool, he found Jimmy in a reclining pool chair. A topless, large-breasted redhead was perched on his lap, running her fingers through his hair. Jimmy was enjoying it until he saw the approaching duo. Jimmy jumped up, propelling the redhead into the pool. "What the hell are you doing here?" He looked back and forth between the two men.

"Jimmy, I'm scared to go home." Ruben looked pathetic.

"My God, Ruben, What have you gotten into?"

With Hubert listening, Ruben tried to relate what had happened the night before. Vidrine looked like he was buying it until he came to the part about Doc Leveau being at the event.

"Go take a bath, Ruben. You smell and look disgusting. And burn those clothes." Vidrine looked over at Hubert. "You, get off my property. If my wife gets even a hint of what you all saw here, I'll kill you both with my bare hands, no questions asked. Is that clear?"

Hubert nodded, but couldn't take his eyes off the redhead

in the pool. She didn't seem to have any trouble staying afloat.

Hubert and Ruben walked toward the back door. Hubert chanced one more glance at the pool. He left and stopped at the sheriff's office to report what had happened. When he described the redhead, he stretched his hand out in front of him past his large belly in an effort to demonstrate her attributes. Jake took off his hat and marveled at the vision.

"Next time, I'll do my own deliveries," said Jake. Then he got serious. "Everything's a go. The reinforcements are en route. You be at Billy Jack's by five." Jake looked at Hubert with new respect. "I'm counting on everything going the way we planned. Otherwise we're hosed big time."

"I'll be there. Count on it."

Hubert left and Jake locked the office, heading home to eat and get some rest to ready himself for his second unwarranted raid on Vidrine Trucking.

CHAPTER THIRTY-NINE

SUNDAY NOON, JUNE 18

The Village Inn was doing a nice lunch business. Mr. Julius was closed on Sundays. The Methodists got there a little before noon, and the Baptists arrived between twelve thirty and one. Catholics, having been to Mass the night before, were eating either before or after their round of golf.

Beau and Ellie were seated at a table for two by the window. Bayou Belle flowed slowly in the distance. They ordered the buffet and were getting up to go through the line when Charlie walked in with his family. The five were seated at a table for six in the middle of the big room. Charlie saw Ellie and chanced a wave. Ellie pretended not to notice and made a beeline for the buffet line. Back at their table she felt every eye in the place watching her and felt she should be wearing a scarlet A on her dress.

"What's the matter, Mom? You're way too quiet and you haven't eaten anything." Beau was ready for seconds, and the dessert table loomed large in his mind.

"I guess I'm not very hungry," Ellie replied. "But you go ahead and get some more food."

The Leveau family was getting their food when Beau went back, having enjoyed a round of Bloody Marys first. "Hi, Beau," said Charlie. "How are you?"

"Hi, Dr. Leveau," Beau answered. "I'm fine, but Mom is acting funny, like she's sick or something. She's been that way since yesterday. I'm worried about her."

Charlie glanced her way, but her back was turned.

"I'll come over and see about her in a minute."

Jan heard him say that and shot him a look that could cripple a strong man. He deflected the look with a quiet smile.

When the family went back for seconds and Beau headed for the dessert table, Charlie walked over and took Beau's seat. Ellie looked up, surprised and not displeased. "You think it's a good idea talking to me?" Ellie seemed truly concerned, and not about herself. "I mean, I get the feeling everyone in town knows we had a thing going, and now your wife is here with a reconciliation in the works. Maybe you should just leave me alone, for your own good and mine."

Charlie wasn't sure what to say. "Maybe things moved a little too fast, but I enjoyed every second, and I wouldn't want to hurt you for anything in the world." Beau was coming back to the table, so Charlie got up and changed the subject before leaving. "You missed an interesting meeting last night. I don't know if you talked to your dad, but there were some surprises to say the least. I'll call you this afternoon and catch you up if that's okay."

"That'll be fine." Ellie didn't act like it would be fine, but she hoped he would call.

"What was that all about?" asked Jan when Charlie returned to the table with a new plate of food. "Is that where you were until two o'clock this morning?" She looked closely at him for his answer.

"I swear on my father's grave that I was not." Charlie was glad he could answer the question honestly. Jan could tell when he was lying and was pretty sure he was telling the truth. She let it go.

After lunch, Page and Jan packed up and left for Houston and Riverton. As they were driving away, Jan rolled down the window and said, "I'll be in Riverton by the time you get through here. Can't wait to take up where we left off."

Charlie smiled and waved but knew that where they left off was a shoe barely missing his head and his vintage Mercedes almost totaled in her haste to get away. If they were going to do this, they should start from somewhere besides where they left off, he thought.

Chuck and his fiancée left next. They had gone to look at the hospital after brunch and had driven around Bayou Belle. "She loves this place, Dad," Chuck had said before they said good-bye, "and you know, so do I." The house seemed very quiet. Delphine had gone to Jake's for a family lunch and would not be back until mid-afternoon.

As soon as Ellie and Beau got home, Ellie went to her room and Beau ran out the door to fish with Jeremiah. Jeremiah and Beau rode their bikes to Doc Leveau's camp and fished off the deck. They didn't think Doc would mind. He wasn't going to be using it anymore. The fish weren't biting and after a long, quiet spell, they looked at each other and decided it was time to do what they had discussed and head to Vidrine's. They laughed like the two young conspirators they were and hopped on their bicycles.

Ellie, after thinking it over, decided she had been too tough on Charlie. She had come on pretty strong, and she did have him to thank for taking care of Beau, but most of all, Charlie had made her feel things she hadn't since losing her husband. She went unannounced to the Leveau home and parked around back to encourage as little gossip as possible. She entered the kitchen, assuming Charlie was home because his jeep was outside. Hearing gentle snoring from the living room, she found Charlie asleep on the couch with his sock feet on the cushioned arm. Not wanting to startle him, she stood still and stared for a long while. It would hurt when he went home, but it was important to her that they depart friends. She tiptoed back to the back door, opened it, and closed it loudly, trying to wake him up. It worked. By the time she was back in the living room, Charlie was sitting up rubbing his eyes. He looked up, surprised to see Ellie standing there but extremely pleased, and his smile showed it.

"I'm sorry. Did I wake you up?"

"Not at all," lied Charlie. "I was just catching a few winks. Big night coming up."

"Tell me about it." Ellie was glad they had a reason to talk.

Charlie told her about the night before, about Ruben Martin and Vinnie dead in the trunk, about putting him in the car behind the wheel and about the murder charge. He laughed about Hubert's reaction and taking him home to Mrs. Helen Polk.

Ellie sat with her mouth agape and her hand occasionally raised over it.

"I'm glad you weren't there," said Charlie. "If this thing blows up in our faces, we could all spend a good long while inside the walls of Angola. Will you come see me if that happens?" Charlie smiled, trying to get back to where they were before Jan came to town. Her smile told him he was making progress.

"That would be one way to keep you in Louisiana," she said. "And if they send all of you, they may have to build a new Bayou Belle wing." She laughed, but with a worried look.

Charlie told her that his job was to reconnoiter Vidrine Trucking while there was still daylight to see if there had been changes, then to report to Jake and Donnie. "I wish we had considered catching Ruben red-handed with the others before we had him jailed for murder. If he gets out of that charge, as I am sure he will, especially since we all know he didn't do it, he may walk away from this whole thing."

"We still have Doc's tape, and Donnie has some stuff," said Ellie. "I don't think he gets away with all of it."

Charlie's cell rang. Jake was calling to tell him about Hubert taking Ruben to Vidrine's home and what they found.

"He's out," Charlie told Ellie. "Hubert is his lawyer and took him to Vidrine's home at Ruben's request." Charlie and Ellie looked at each other. "Then there is a chance he will be there too. Wish there was a way we could be sure."

"I need to get to the airport and make sure the plane is ready to go. Why don't you stay here with Delphine. We can keep you both posted with one call that way.'

"I like that idea. I don't relish enduring this night alone, wondering what is going on."

Charlie stood up to go and walked toward the door.

"Charlie," said Ellie, "take care of yourself. Don't take any more silly chances. I sincerely want you to get back to Riverton in one piece."

Charlie turned around and came back to where she was

standing. "I have no desire to go back to Texas. More and more every day I feel like my home is right here in Bayou Belle." He bent to kiss her, but she pulled back, putting her finger over his mouth, shaking her head and saying "No." He nodded understanding, touched her face, turned, and walked out the door.

CHAPTER FORTY

SUNDAY AFTERNOON, JUNE 18

It was mid-afternoon when the boys rode toward Vidrine's and a hopeful encounter with some naked movie stars. They rode fast, worried that they might be called home soon. The road followed the bayou part of the way, then veered off a half mile before the gate to the trucking company. They knew right where the old house was. Ditching their bikes in a small gulley, they squirmed under the fence and began making their way to the house. They used brush and a few cypress trees for cover, but most of the way was in the open. Dogs barked in the distance, but everybody had a dog and the boys weren't concerned. "What are we gonna tell them if we get caught?" Beau asked Jeremiah, looking over his shoulder, expecting at any minute to have someone come up behind them.

"We'll just tell them we were out hiking and got lost." Jeremiah seemed sure enough of himself that it somewhat eased Beau's mind, but Beau was beginning to wish they were still fishing. What had seemed like a grand idea now seemed a little shortsighted. Jeremiah was thinking the same thing, but neither said that to the other. So they slowly made their way toward the old house, which soon came into view through a clump of brush pines and honeysuckle vines.

"This looks like a good place to hide," said Jeremiah.

"Why do you say that?" asked Beau, standing on his tiptoes with his neck craned. "All we can see from here is one side of the house, and the windows are up high and it's too far away. If we can get behind that little house, it would be closer and we could most likely see something."

Jeremiah reluctantly agreed.

They looked in all directions and didn't see anyone, then ran at full tilt across an open lawn and dived behind the little outbuilding. Then sat there for a moment catching their breath, giggling nervously. This was a much better spot.

Five minutes later they heard voices. Chancing a high-five, they thought, *They're here.* Beau was on his knees peeking around the corner of the building. Jeremiah was standing behind Beau and leaning over him so that both were looking around the same corner for the movie stars.

"What you boys think you're doing?" The man's voice behind them was angry, and both boys jumped and fell backward on the ground, looking up at the man, who had a large double-barreled shotgun aimed at their chests.

They looked at each other. Beau was first to speak. Forgetting about the being-lost-hiking idea, Beau, in his honest way, said, "We heard a rumor they were making porno movies out here, so we thought we'd have a look."

"Ain't no porno movies or anything like that going on. I know that much. The other thing I know is that you was trespassin', and we shoot trespassers." He got the radio off his belt and called, "Hey, Joe, I got two boys here trespassin' and spyin' on the house. What do you want me to do with 'em?"

Another voice came over the radio. Not knowing the boys could hear, he said, "They made a big mistake—wrong place, wrong day." After a short pause, the voice continued. "Put 'em in the house with the others. We'll decide later what to do. Most likely the boss don't want no witnesses. Too bad you didn't just shoot 'em and then call me. That might still be the best thing. Naw, just lock them in the house. They ain't goin' nowheres."

Beau and Jeremiah looked at each other. "Shoot us?" asked Jeremiah incredulously. "You really going to shoot us?"

"Most likely," said the guard. "Like the man said, you are here on the wrong day at the wrong time. I just take orders."

"But my dad is the sheriff. No way you'll ever get away with it." Jeremiah tried to sound strong and brave, but was suddenly very homesick.

"It don't matter," said the man. "Nobody'll ever know what happened. We got a way of making people just disappear. We already picked up your bikes. Nobody'll ever know you were here." He motioned with his shotgun for them to stand up, then marched them around to the front door, unlocked it, and forced them in. He closed and locked the door from the outside.

The room was pitch black. The boys stood still for a while, waiting for their eyes to adjust, but there was no light for them to adjust to. Beau remembered seeing a window on the side and walked in that direction. Feeling his way slowly, his foot hit something and he fell forward, putting his arms out to break his fall. His hands, instead of encountering the hard floor, met what felt like lace-covered skin, and whatever it was moved. His body fell across several outstretched legs. "EIAHH," he screamed in sheer fright.

"What?!" was all Jeremiah could scream back.

Beau's voice was shaking, and he was scrambling to get off. He rolled and was soon free of legs and feet. On his hands and knees, he slowly crawled in the direction of the window, each time putting his hand out carefully, afraid of coming upon another stiff. Finally, his hand touched the wall and he felt his way along to the window. A heavy black curtain was blocking out all light. He pushed the curtain aside, letting in enough light to make out what was in the room.

"Beau!" Jeremiah yelled. "These people aren't dead!"

Beau looked back toward where he had fallen. He opened the curtain further for more light. To his astonishment, there were three people, bound and gagged. He and Jeremiah rushed to them, a young girl with bright red hair, dressed in a short skirt and black lace stockings, a man who looked like a hobo with dirty, ragged clothes and in need of a bath, and a man with slick hair, gold chains around his neck, and expensive-looking shoes. All were looking pleadingly at the boys to help free them, which they had already begun to do. The duct tape over their mouths came off first. The homeless man spoke. "I always knew there were angels." Beau got out his pocket knife and cut the rope off their feet. Their hands were more of a problem. They were in handcuffs that were also attached to the wall. The girl didn't look much older than the boys. She still seemed stunned by the whole ordeal and murmured a soft thank you.

The man with the gold chains was Mel. He knew the most. "They plan to take our organs, then put us in that oven" he said, pointing to the opposite corner. "There won't be any evidence that we were ever here."

Soft sobs escaped the young girl's lips. Nobody would ever

know what happened to her. The homeless man just looked resigned that this was happening to him. He hadn't really expected anything better.

Voices could be heard outside. One guard was loudly berating another. The voices were coming closer. "Get in there and tape their mouths and tie them up like the others. I can't believe you just threw them in there."

It was at that moment that Beau remembered the cell phone in his pocket. He struggled to get it out of his tight jeans pocket. As the guard was opening the door, he flipped open the phone and punched the speed dial number for his mother's phone. It rang so long he was afraid it would go to voice mail and afraid the man would see it and take it away. He put it beside him, concealing it as much as he could. As the man was walking toward them with a roll of duct tape and some rope in his hands, Beau said, "Don't tape our mouths, we won't yell. Why did you kidnap us and put us in this little house at Vidrine's? We didn't mean to trespass."

"Shut up," said the man. "I do what I'm told."

"Are you really going to kill us and ship our body parts all over the world?" Beau glanced at the man with the gold chains. "That's what he said."

"I just work here. I don't want to know what they do. Just shut up and hold your feet still." At that time the cell phone made a noise like it was turning off. "What was that?"

"My cell phone. I was trying to make a call when you came in," Beau replied honestly.

"Who did you call?" The guard was very nervous, grabbing for the phone.

"Tried to call my mother, but she didn't answer. That noise

meant that time for leaving a message was over."

"If I find out you're lying, I'll kill you myself. Understand?" Beau nodded.

Ellie was in the kitchen with Delphine when the call came. She heard several voices and got from it that Beau and Jeremiah were being held inside a little house at Vidrine's and that their lives had been threatened. She flew into a panicked rage. "They've got Beau and Jeremiah," she told Delphine, taking short, shallow breaths, hardly able to breathe or talk. "I'm going to get them."

"Then I'm going with you," replied Delphine. "They better not lay a hand on those boys or I'll hurt them."

"I don't have my gun with me, and I don't have time to go home and get one."

They ran to Ellie's car, peeled rubber taking off, and raced to Vidrine's. Ellie called Charlie on the way, but he was already taking off to canvass the site. She called Jake, but he didn't answer. She and Delphine raced down the small country lane at over eighty miles per hour all the way to Vidrine's, hit the brakes, and slid forward, turning sideways, then forward again, barely stopping before crashing through the gate. One guard was in the guardhouse. Ellie jumped out of the car and ran in, confronting the guard. "You kidnapped my boy and her grandson," she said, nodding toward Delphine, who stood with her hands behind her back. "I want them now."

"Lady, I don't know what you're talking about. Now you git back in your car and git out of here."

"Open that gate and let me go through or I'll bust it down.

I'm going in to get my son."

"I ain't opening no gate for no crazy woman. Now do like I say and git back in your car."

The guard's truck was parked inside the gate just outside the guardhouse door. *Maybe the keys are in it*, she thought. She started toward the door, but the guard roughly grabbed her arm and threw her against the wall, then backhanded her hard across her face. He then turned to get Delphine, but the only thing he saw was the barrel of a thirty-four-inch Louisville slugger just before it connected with his nose. He slowly crumpled to the floor, his eyes crossed, twisting as he went down. Ellie grabbed his gun and his truck keys. She then pulled the phone cord out of the wall and threw the guard's radio over in some bushes as she and Delphine got in the truck.

She didn't know the way to the old house. She took the road in the general direction of the bayou. On Sunday, nobody was working. She called Jake again—still no answer. Hearing an airplane, she looked up to see Charlie's Cessna. Somebody needed to know where they were. She called her dad, who picked up on the first ring. She told Billy Jack everything as fast as she could while speeding toward the old house and outbuildings.

Hubert, Doc, and Billy Jack were there when the call came. "Looks like things got moved up. We don't have time to wait for the troops. They have Beau and Jeremiah, and in a minute they'll have Ellie and Delphine."

As Ellie approached the old house, she noted a lot of activity. Dr. Kaiser's car was parked outside. An airplane was parked on the end of the runway. She skidded up close to the door of the outbuilding. A padlock was on the door. She looked in the

back of the truck and miraculously found a crowbar. As mad
as she was, and with the massive amount of adrenaline cours-
ing through her body, she busted the lock on her first tug and
threw open the door. With the light from the door she saw the
boys and three others bound and gagged. She and Delphine
made quick work of getting off the gags. Jake and Jeremiah
were talking so fast, trying to tell it all as quickly as possible.
Their feet and hands were tied with rope.

Ellie was untying Beau and Delphine untying Jeremiah
when they heard someone approaching the open door.
Delphine jumped up and ran to the side of the door. His shotgun poised, the man saw Ellie trying to get the rope off Beau's
wrist and said, "What the…" But before he could get out another word, Delphine connected again, this time to the back
of the man's head. He seemed to go down faster than the first
one, face first with nothing breaking his fall. "That's two for
two," said Ellie. "Now I know where Jeremiah gets his swing."

They closed the door so they wouldn't draw any more attention and opened the window for light. Beau went through
the guard's pockets and found keys. The captured mobster, Mel,
showed Beau which key was for the cuffs. Beau proceeded to
take the handcuffs off the others. The homeless man just stared
at Ellie and said, "Now they're starting to look like angels."

Armed now with two revolvers and a shotgun, they were
still outnumbered, but the odds were improving. They could
shoot anybody who came in the door, so right now it was probably better to wait for reinforcements than to try a getaway in
the truck. Ellie knew her dad would act quickly.

Billy Jack heard Charlie's plane make a low pass and ran out into the road in front of his house, frantically waving his hands to get his attention on the next pass.

Charlie noted that a jet plane was already on the runway and that there was activity at the house. Nothing else was different than what they had expected. They were probably dissecting the cadavers now and wouldn't get to the captives soon. On his next pass across the bayou, he saw Billy Jack waving his arms. Billy Jack put his hand to his ear, like he was talking on the phone; then he waved that hand at Charlie. It finally dawned on Charlie that Billy Jack was trying to get him to pick up his phone, which was in the copilot's seat. He saw that he had missed several calls from Ellie and from Billy Jack. He dialed Billy Jack's number and got as much of the story as Billy Jack knew. Billy Jack then told him to land on the road by his house. Charlie looked at the road. There was no traffic and a long enough straight stretch that would serve as a runway. Charlie landed.

From inside the small house, Ellie called Billy Jack. "Dad, we're all in the little outbuilding by the big house. Seven of us. We have two revolvers and a shotgun. And we have an unconscious guard lying here who may be playing possum just to keep Delphine from clubbing him again."

In spite of himself, Billy Jack chuckled. "Stay there. Don't do anything rash. I don't care if you kill anyone who tries to come in. Just don't go out." Billy Jack hoped she would follow that advice. "Charlie just landed here on the road, and he knows where you are. We're still trying to contact Jake."

Hubert came running out to the plane. "I have an idea." Both Charlie and Billy Jack looked at him, waiting for him to continue. "Billy Jack, that moonshine of yours would make one helluva bomb. Do you have any old rags?"

"Sure," Billy Jack said, seeing what Hubert was getting at. They pushed the plane off the road and ran back to the house. Billy Jack collected ten mason jars filled with his purest, precious liquid and watched Hubert take the lids off and put one end of an old rag down into each jar, then replace the lid. Billy Jack couldn't help himself. He cringed.

After Hubert had completed his work and asked Billy Jack for matches, he said, "Now Bayou Belle Vigilantes have an air force to be reckoned with. I'll go with you, Charlie, and be the bombardier. You can't possibly fly the plane, light these, and drop them too."

"Hubert, that's a great idea and should at least cause a great distraction. I don't want to hurt your feelings, but there's not enough room in the plane."

"I'll go," said Doc, who had been quiet to this point. "No reason I can't do something." It was settled. Charlie and Doc would man the airplane, leaving Billy Jack and Hubert to constitute the Bayou Belle Vigilante Navy.

Meanwhile, another guard reporting for work at the gate found his colleague, whose nose was more crooked than he remembered and groggy with some weird tale about two women. He tried to call to check it out, but the phone was dead. The safest thing for him to do was to report to Mr. Vidrine using his cell phone. "Mr. Vidrine," said the guard when Jimmy Vee answered, "sorry to bother you on a Sunday evening, but," and before he could continue, Vidrine said, "It better be good. This has not been a good day."

"Yessir," said the guard, "but I just got to work and the

guard who is here looks roughed up." Again, before the guard could finish his thought, Vidrine had slammed down his phone, leaving the guard staring at the phone in his hand, not sure what to do.

"Ruben!" screamed Vidrine. "Get your ass down here, now!" Vidrine was pulling on his pants and a polo shirt that stretched over his portly belly. He put on his shoes without bothering with socks and screamed again, "Ruben!"

Ruben stumbled, coming down the stairs, trying to put his shoes and pants on as he descended. "What is it?" he asked, looking over Jimmy's shoulder at the redhead who had just come out of the master bedroom tying her robe. A little disappointed, Ruben looked back at Vidrine and asked again, "What's going on?"

"There's trouble at the farm," he said, calling it by the familiar name he used when talking about their mutual business, probably a bigger harvest than most farms. "Two women broke in for God knows what reason. We need to get there and see what the hell is going on." They hopped in Vidrine's car and rushed toward the site. On the way, Vidrine phoned the old house.

Hubert and Billy Jack loaded a boat up with as many bottles of whiskey and old rags and matches it would hold and struck out for the old house, planning to approach it through the cypress copse.

Inside the house, the surgical team, as it were, had just completed harvesting the skin and bones and the other organs that would still be useful from the first cadaver, and were ready to send what remained to the oven in the little house. They had received instructions from Vidrine to move straight to the live donors. The assistant hauling the remains to the oven was told to bring the girl first. As he entered the little house, his head was the third to come in contact with Delphine's bat. Not knowing what was in the garbage bag, Jeremiah moved it to the side and handcuffed the man as he had already cuffed the guard. Mel took pleasure in placing duct tape over their mouths. Both were dragged toward the oven and out of the way.

Jake had walked down the street to handle a complaint called in from Corner Deli. A woman was refusing to pay for the giant poboy she ordered for her party because they had put tomatoes on it. She had specifically said to leave them off; taking them off now would leave a tomato taste, and some of her guests were allergic to tomatoes. Neither she nor Mr. Anderson would give an inch. Mrs. Anderson called Jake. After an hour, the woman's husband came, and he and Mr. Anderson were able to work out a compromise. Jake was almost back to his office when Donnie drove up.

"I've been calling your cell for the last hour and getting voice mail. Thought I'd better come down here and make sure you were alive and ready to go. The team should be here in about an hour."

Cell phone, thought Jake, feeling his pockets while looking on his desktop and in the drawer. "Oh shit," he said as he sprang from his chair and ran to his car. His cell was on the car seat. He had missed over ten calls.

He held up a finger to Donnie, asking him to wait while he listened to his messages. He became more and more agitated as he listened to each one. Donnie was concerned that something had gone wrong.

"Come on, let's go." Jake motioned for Donnie to hop in the passenger side. He advised Donnie of the situation as he understood it on the way to Vidrine's. All he really knew was that Jeremiah and Beau were being held, that Ellie and Delphine had gone out there for them, and that Billy Jack knew because he had sounded frantic, telling him the same thing. He turned on his siren. All secrecy and surprise be damned. Too late for that.

When Ruben and Vidrine reached the gate, the guard was outside flagging them down. "Just open the gate, asshole." Vidrine was furiously beating on the steering wheel.

The guard jumped back and, with hands shaking, was able to get the gate open for Vidrine's car to speed through. The car swerved side to side as it spun its wheels, searching for traction for a quicker trip to the old house.

From the air, Charlie and Doc saw the car carrying Vidrine and Ruben careening toward the old house. They had no idea who might be in the car. Billy Jack and Hubert were almost ashore and positioned in the bayou behind the old house. In the distance, the blue lights of a police car could be seen flashing and leaving downtown Bayou Belle in the direction of Vidrine Trucking.

Charlie called Jake. "The good guys are in the outbuilding with the oven. The bad guys, except for a few guards, are in the big house." Charlie paused, noticing the car racing toward the house. "And it looks like Vidrine's car hightailing it in that direction."

"Donnie and I are getting there as fast as we can. I wish there were a way to keep them all in the house. We're outnumbered and we need an advantage. If they're all in one place, we have a better chance."

"We may have a way," answered Charlie. Then he called Hubert and told him what they would try to do.

Vidrine and Ruben skidded to a stop in front of the big house, got out, and ran in. Charlie counted four guards about the property, all running toward the house. That seemed to be where everything was happening.

Jake stopped at the gate. When the guard came over, Jake pointed his .45 at his face as he got out of the car. He handcuffed him to the same radiator as his fellow guard, who was still there but didn't know it. He reached to pull the phone out of the wall but noted that it had already been done. Then they sped on toward the old house, stopping fifty yards or so away, not wanting to fall into a trap. Reinforcements were not scheduled to arrive for another hour. Donnie had called and told them to get there as fast as they could.

On their first pass over the battle site, Doc lit one of the Bayou Cocktails, so named by Hubert Polk, and dropped it out of the window of the Cessna. Charlie had wanted a sexy, low-winged airplane, but he had never been so thankful for the high-winged design that allowed a direct drop and a better view of the ground. The bomb hit twenty yards from the front door of the old house, causing an explosion that was heard on the far side of Bayou Belle. As the plane banked off, the people in the big house panicked and ran toward the back door, only to be met with a similar explosion thrown by the surprisingly strong arm of Hubert Polk, one of the two-man Bayou Belle Vigilante Navy. Billy Jack and Hubert had a high-five moment before settling back down to the serious matter at hand.

Charlie looked at his dad, smiling but still very concerned about Ellie and the rest. "I don't see any point in saving any of these." He looked back at the remaining nine homemade bombs.

The pilot of the large plane started a takeoff roll, leaving everyone he had brought. Every Sunday night several small jets flew in, bringing the harvesting team and flying back out with the team and the organs to be delivered to prearranged places. This night something had gone terribly wrong. The pilot was going to save himself.

Doc saw that the plane was lining up for takeoff. He pointed at it, and Charlie made a pass along the runway. When he was in front of the plane, Doc dropped a bomb that landed close to the front of the plane, causing it to veer off the runway and ditch in the tall grass, part of its nose missing. The pilot jumped out of the plane and ran in the opposite direction, toward the bayou. Obviously, he had decided that he would rather deal with alligators.

The occupants of the little house watched all this with growing glee and amazement.

Reinforcements hadn't arrived, and Charlie wanted to keep the bad guys in the big house, so he lined up for another pass.

The occupants of the big house saw the explosion in front of the jet and understood what was happening.

Charlie approached from over the cypress trees where Billy Jack and Hubert were holding their perimeter. This time the people in the house knew they were coming and were ready. As Charlie made his pass and Doc was dropping two more Bayou Cocktails out the open cockpit window, the guards in the house opened fire with pistols and one high-powered rifle. As Charlie started to pull out of his strafing run, a loud crashing sound announced a bullet entering through the roof of the cockpit, passing through the windshield, and entering the airplane motor. He had recovered from the shock and noted that his dad was not injured when oil splashed on the windshield and the plane lost power. He was not high enough to set up a landing approach. He had to put the plane down. Doc looked at him with an unconcerned, trusting look. He reached over and gave Charlie's shoulder a squeeze. Charlie realized that he had just enough time to land the plane on the runway with the wind. He was coming over the house again, and bullets were hitting the wing. If they struck an aileron or the elevator, he could lose control of the plane. A bullet struck the back of the cockpit, breaking a bottle of moonshine and starting a small fire that Doc was able to extinguish before it ignited the remaining bombs.

Charlie was over the house and confident he would make the runway when he saw the jet bringing the next team of organ snatchers coming from the opposite direction on final approach. It was shaping up to be a game of chicken. Charlie had no choice but to land the plane and hope the jet saw them in time. He would try to get off the runway soon enough to miss the jet, or maybe the jet could pull up in time. Neither happened. Charlie touched down, and the jet was coming toward him with no chance of landing without a collision. Charlie braked and stomped on the rudder, veering off the runway and causing his Cessna to turn so abruptly a wing touched the ground and broke off. The Cessna cartwheeled and came to a stop thirty yards off the runway, right-side up, both passengers only slightly shaken and without a scratch. The incoming jet saw the Cessna at the last minute but too late. The pilot tried to abort the landing and take back off. He didn't make it. Unable to gain sufficient altitude, the jet scraped the roof of the big house, taking off a part of the 200-year-old chimney. The pilot fought a losing battle. The plane crashed into the bayou between Billy Jack's and Doc's camp house. Nobody on that plane survived.

Inside the house, Vidrine saw that his only chance was to make a getaway. Otherwise he would go down with the rest. The plane dropping the bombs was down, so this was his chance. If there were any shooting, he would prefer that the opposition had two to shoot at instead of one, doubling his chances of a getaway. With his gun in hand, he and Ruben ran toward the car, got in, and started back toward the front gate. Jake's car blocked the road. He turned around and drove back toward a little known road that would get him out.

Ellie, Delphine, and the others, thinking things were under control, came out of the house. "Get in the back of the truck," commanded Ellie. "Let's get out of here while we can." With all her new and old friends, she started the truck and drove in the direction of the gate, only to be met head-on by the car driven by Vidrine, with Ruben riding shotgun. Jake, in his police car, was close behind.

Charlie confirmed that his dad was okay. He helped him out of the plane and walked him away from the plane to a place to sit. He looked up in time to see Ellie and the others get in the truck to make their escape. He ran as fast as his formerly good legs would carry him toward the coming confrontation of cars and people. He was unarmed. All his bombs had been dropped.

Vidrine, needing a hostage, headed for the oncoming truck. Ellie was trying to miss it and speed toward freedom, but the car veered her way, forcing her off the road. She got her gun and jumped out of the car, ordering the others to stay put.

Both Vidrine and Ruben, each armed, jumped out of their car. Charlie was running, screaming at the top of his lungs, toward the developing scene.

Mel, unable to contain himself, jumped out of the back of the truck and started to run.

Jake, after screeching to a stop, jumped out, screaming, "Vidrine, drop your gun. It's over."

Vidrine sighted him and got off a shot, barely missing. "Over my ass," he shouted back and turned and pointed his gun at Jake, who was running toward him.

Seeing this, Jake dropped to the ground and rolled to his left just as Vidrine's gun fired, missing Jake high and to the right. Jake rolled and came up with his gun pointed at Vidrine's chest and didn't hesitate as he fired three shots placed close together into the fat man's heart.

Charlie was still running full speed ahead trying to get to Ellie. Ruben, seeing him coming, fired at him. Charlie fell to the side, avoiding another bullet.

Ellie screamed at Ruben, "Drop your gun now!"

Ruben glanced in her direction and considered briefly firing at her, but he wanted more than anything else to kill Charlie Leveau. He continued to fire in his direction as Charlie made it closer and closer to Ellie and the others. "I said, drop your gun." Ellie sounded more menacing this time, so Ruben stood up and fired one shot her way before returning his fire toward Charlie.

Ellie fired two rounds at Ruben, both hitting him in the abdomen from the side. Dropping his gun and clutching his side, he went down.

Sirens were heard fast approaching the scene. When the full force got there, the battle was over except for the cleanup. Thinking the bombs had all come from the Cessna, Kaiser and his colleagues had decided to try an escape out of the back door. They were met with a Bayou Cocktail again thrown by Hubert, forcing them back in the house. Panicked, they all ran out the front door into the hands of the newly arrived Louisiana State Police.

CHAPTER FORTY-ONE

Vidrine was dead. Ruben was alive and screaming in pain, demanding attention as the ambulance pulled in to the emergency entrance. He needed emergency surgery in order to survive. Kaiser, or whoever he was, was under arrest and in custody of the FBI, and Doc was still too feeble to undertake a big operation. That left Charlie, who, because of Ruben, had no hospital privileges.

Charlie walked in to Ruben's stall in the emergency department after his IV was started and his antibiotics administered. Ruben was in a great deal of pain despite a large dose of Dilaudid. Unable to resist, Charlie carried a glass filled with cola diluted by half with water so that it resembled bourbon. "I'd be glad to help you, Ruben, but I don't have privileges, and so far I've had three of these." That was the actual truth in that Charlie had been very thirsty and had downed two glasses of water and a glass of Diet Coke on arriving at the emergency door. "Kaiser is under arrest, but I'm sure, under the circumstances, the sheriff would let him do your emergency surgery before hauling him off to jail. It might even help get his sentence reduced if the jury knows he helped out."

Ruben's wild eyes, raised brows, and sorrowful but alarmed face looked up at Charlie, and in a beseeching tone he pleaded, "Please, Dr. Leveau, you don't owe me anything, and you have every reason to want to see me dead, but if there is one bone with the milk of human kindness in your body, I'm begging you to help me, please, please, please, help me. I have seen the error of my ways."

Charlie believed everything except the last sentence. Harboring no misconceptions that Ruben really had seen the error of his ways, but understanding his calling as a surgeon, he agreed to operate to save his life.

Charlie wanted to be home celebrating the day with the Bayou Vigilantes.

Arrangements were made for the exploratory laparotomy within the hour. The OR team arrived within twenty minutes. The ER got Ruben ready for surgery. It was hard for Charlie to resist telling Ruben on the way to the OR that as far as Charlie was concerned, he would be better off with him dead. But he didn't.

During the laparotomy, Charlie found several holes through Ruben's small intestine and a large hole in his right colon. He was able to suture the holes in the small bowel, perform a right colectomy, irrigate the abdominal cavity, and close. The operation went well and there was no reason for Ruben not to recover, just as there had been no reason for Vinnie's brother not to do well.

Charlie accompanied the stretcher to the recovery room, dictated his operative note, wrote the post-op orders, and checked out the plan with the nurses before heading home.

Several cars were parked in front of Doc's home when Charlie arrived. He went in the front door and was greeted with cheers. Hubert was there with his wife, who was taking in the whole scene with unbelieving eyes. She kept staring at Doc, whose funeral she had attended yesterday. Delphine was in the kitchen, smiling. Where else would she be? The aluminum thirty-four-inch Louisville Slugger, however, was the centerpiece of the coffee table.

Beau and Jeremiah confessed to going to see some naked women. Everyone but Ellie and Jeremiah's mom laughed. After a little encouragement, they smiled. They had raised sons, after all.

When the laughter and jocularity subsided, and all was quiet for a moment, Doc raised his glass and proposed a toast. But first he called Delphine in from the kitchen and insisted that she take a glass and pour some spirit stronger than water into it before he again raised his glass and said, "To small towns, to good friends, old and new, to family, to right prevailing, to the end sometimes justifying the means, to a thankfully premature funeral, and to the hope of many more years of the same. And last but not least, to the assurance of a hereafter."

EPILOGUE

A year passed. Doc was hosting a party to celebrate living for a year after his funeral. He heard how much fun everyone had after his first service, and he figured he wouldn't be around for the next. The whole town turned out for it. Charlie and Ellie acted as host and hostess. They ate somewhere together most every evening. Several things had changed in Bayou Belle. Adrienne Vidrine had taken over running the trucking company. No jobs were lost. She gave the old home and the surrounding property to the town, and it was turned into a park. The house itself was made a historic landmark with a much more exciting story to tell.

Ruben and Kaiser were serving life without parole at Angola. Kaiser still maintained that he did not start the fire in Africa, but got the idea to take the identity after it happened.

Hubert gave the hundred grand to the hospital auxiliary. He was running unopposed for a seat in the Louisiana legislature.

Jake won reelection in a landslide. He got his gun back.

The malpractice suit was dropped shortly after the plaintiff's attorney heard Dr. Davis' testimony.

After the divorce was finalized, Jan started dating her lawyer. She and Charlie divided everything down the middle and remained friends.

Suzie, the seventeen-year-old hooker, was adopted by the

town. She worked as a waitress for Mr. Julius and was going to college to study nursing on a scholarship given by the auxiliary funded by Hubert's money. The homeless man went back to New Orleans to find another alley. Nobody had seen Mel since he ran away.

Page's husband returned home just before the baby was born. They called the baby Little Al, named Aloysius for his grandfather. They had come for the party.

For anyone brave enough to try, the special drink of the night was a concoction of one part BJ's whiskey and one part sugar water and mulled fruit, speared by a lighted sparkler, named the Bayou Cocktail.